GEO

12/03

D0458495

SHADOW OF DEATH

SHADOW OF DEATH

William G. Tapply

St. Martin's Minotaur
New York

www.minotaurbooks.com

Library of Congress Cataloging-in-Publication Data

Tapply, William G.
    Shadow of death : a Brady Coyne novel / William G. Tapply.—1st ed.
        p.   cm.
    ISBN 0-312-30377-7
    1. Coyne, Brady (Fictitious character)—Fiction.   2. Political cam-
paigns—
    Fiction.   3. Boston (Mass.)—Fiction.   I. Title.

    PS3570.A568S49 2003
    813'.54—dc21

                                                            2003046830

First Edition: November 2003

10   9   8   7   6   5   4   3   2   1

In memory of Jed Mattes

ACKNOWLEDGMENTS

Many people contributed to the making of this yarn, whether they know it or not.

Keith Kahla, my indispensable editor, and Vicki Stiefel, my best friend and best critic, made all the difference, as usual. They know what they did.

I'm also grateful to the good citizens of Hancock, New Hampshire, for their unwitting help in easing me into small town mode, especially Barbara at the real estate office, Mike at the post office, Robert at the inn, Jan at the cash market, Cathy at the dump, Tom at the garage, Tony and Peg, the young women at Fiddleheads, Bruce, and our neighbors on Antrim Road.

Live Free or Die

— NEW HAMPSHIRE STATE MOTTO

SHADOW OF DEATH

ONE

I found Jimmy D'Ambrosio where he said he'd be, slouched on the stone bench in the Public Garden beside the statue of George Washington astride his horse. In his rumpled beige trench coat and faded Red Sox cap, and with the silvery stubble on his cheeks and chin, it would've been easy to mistake Jimmy for just another bum who'd recently crawled out from under his newspaper blanket on what promised to be a pretty early-autumn morning in Boston.

In fact, Jimmy D., as he'd been called since he handled Kevin White's mayoral campaigns back in the sixties, was a kingmaker, one of the most powerful old-time Democratic pols in the Commonwealth, and presently the campaign manager for Ellen Stoddard, who hoped to become the first female United States senator ever chosen by the voters of the Commonwealth of Massachusetts.

Ellen also happened to be a friend of mine—I was her mother's attorney—which was why I'd agreed to meet with Jimmy D. on a park bench at seven A.M. on a Tuesday morning in the last week of September.

He was sipping from a large Dunkin' Donuts cup and eating a muffin, and when I sat beside him, he reached into his bag and handed a cup and a donut to me.

I broke off a hunk of donut and crumbled it in my hand. When I tossed the crumbs in the direction of Jimmy's shoes, half a dozen gray squirrels came scurrying over to fight for them.

"Very funny," said Jimmy, making a halfhearted kick at the squirrels, who ignored him. He made a show of sticking out his arm and frowning at his watch. "Six-fifty-five, it says." He tapped the face of his watch. "Hm. I don't get it. It's still running." He shook his wrist, squinted at his watch again. "Must be slow. I never heard of a lawyer who was early."

I pried the lid off the cup Jimmy had given me and took a sip. "Plain donut," I said. "Black coffee. You remembered."

"My job," he said, "remembering how people take their coffee."

"I know you," I said. "You've got it all on your computer."

He grinned. "I got more than that on my computer. What do you want to know about yourself?"

"You are a scary man, Jimmy D.," I said. "Somebody calls me at home at six-fifteen in the morning, wakes me out of a sound sleep, says he's gotta talk to me, insists on meeting on a park bench at daybreak, says he'll buy me coffee and a donut, I figure it's somewhere between important and urgent. So which is it?"

"If I knew which," he said, "I probably wouldn't need you. Maybe it's neither. Maybe it's nothing." He looked up at me from beneath his shaggy gray eyebrows. "It concerns our candidate."

2

"I guessed that much," I said. "So why am I talking to you, not her?"

"Actually," he said, "the problem isn't exactly our candidate. It's our candidate's husband."

"Albert?" I said. Albert Stoddard was a history professor at Tufts University. He and Ellen had been married for about twenty years.

"Albert's the only husband she's got," said Jimmy.

"I always thought Albert was a pretty good guy," I said. "He likes trout fishing."

"Everybody who likes trout fishing is a good guy?"

"Yes," I said. "Pretty much. So what's the problem with Albert?"

He flapped his hands. "If I knew, I wouldn't be talking to you, would I? He's acting . . . weird."

"Weird how?"

"He's pretty much dropped out of the campaign," Jimmy said. "He used to chip in. Go to events, stand at Ellen's side, participate in our meetings. Lately he seems evasive. Furtive. Like a man with a guilty conscience, something to hide. Can't be much more specific than that. Weird. Not himself. It's upsetting Ellen. Upsetting me, for that matter."

"You think Albert's fooling around or something?"

Jimmy shrugged. "First thing that comes to mind, isn't it?"

I shrugged. "A lot of people fool around."

"Me," said Jimmy, "I don't fool around. Do you?"

"Not anymore," I said. "Not since Evie. Anyway, my impression is that the voters nowadays are pretty tolerant of a candidate's spouse being involved in some extramarital dalliance. Hell, they're tolerant of candidates themselves."

Jimmy smiled. "Dalliance."

"So what's the big deal?"

"I never said he was . . . dallying," said Jimmy. "If that's what it is, okay, we deal with it. I just want to know." He turned to me and put his hand on my wrist. "Look, Brady. Ellen's really got a chance to win this thing. She's been an underdog from the get-go, but she's climbing in the polls. She's got the momentum. Any little thing could knock the pins out from under her."

"So why are you talking to me?"

"I want you to get the goods on Albert, if there are goods to be gotten, whatever those goods might be, before the newspapers do, and before her opponent does, and if there aren't any goods, well, terrific, I want you to find that out for me."

"Jimmy," I said, "I'm a lawyer, remember? Early for appointments, maybe. But still a lawyer."

"A lawyer who's made a career out of discretion," he said. "A lawyer who's bound by attorney-client confidentiality. A lawyer who is not associated with the Stoddard campaign." He touched my arm and leaned close to me. "A lawyer, however," he said, "who might have a cushy job waiting for him if the right people were grateful to him."

"I don't want a cushy job," I said. "I will refuse a cushy job if it's offered to me. My present job is plenty cushy enough."

"A federal judgeship, maybe?"

"Don't do that, Jimmy. I cannot be bribed."

"Hell," he said. "Everybody can be bribed."

I shrugged. "Anyway, I'm not a private investigator."

"But you know some."

"I know several."

4

"Any as discreet as you?"

I nodded. "A couple are, yes."

"Hire one for me, then."

"Why don't you hire one for yourself?" I said.

"Because it's got to be separate from the campaign, Brady. I'd've thought that was obvious. It gets into the papers we're hiring somebody to tail Albert, the faintest whiff of a scandal, you know how it goes. That's why we keep the distance. This cannot be connected to me or Ellen or the campaign. You're the man. The buck stops with you. Who you hire deals with you. You keep my name out of it. You pay them and I'll reimburse you."

"You are as Machiavellian as ever," I said. "I assume Ellen's okay with this."

"Of course," said Jimmy. "You don't think I'd do this behind her back, do you?"

I smiled. "Truthfully, Jimmy, it wouldn't surprise me."

He made a fist and punched his heart. "You wound me deeply." He put his hand on my arm. "I finally talked with Ellen about it last night. She agrees something's got to be done."

"Does she know you're talking to me?"

He nodded. "So whaddya say?"

"What if I say no?"

He shrugged. "I'll have to find somebody else."

"I'd sure hate to see Albert blow it for her," I said. "I think she'd make a terrific senator." I looked at him. "If I'm going to do this, I'll need—"

"Got it," he said. He reached into his trench coat and pulled out a big manila envelope. "Auto information. He drives a two-year-old light green Volkswagen Beetle, if you're curious. Home and business addresses, phone numbers, favorite hangouts, the names of friends and acquaintances. Basically, everything I could think of that might give a PI a start. You need something else, let me know."

I took the envelope and put it on the bench beside me.

Jimmy stood up and brushed crumbs off his lap. "You need to talk, use my cell phone." He turned to leave, then stopped and came back. "I just hired you to do something for me, right?"

"Hired?"

He rolled his eyes, then reached into his hip pocket, took out his wallet, and counted out some bills. He handed them to me. "Okay?"

I counted the bills. Five twenties. "This is about what I get for twenty minutes." I looked at my watch. "About right."

"So now I'm your client," he said, "and you're my lawyer."

I shoved the money into my pants pocket. "I'm not doing anything until I talk to Ellen."

Jimmy stared at me for a minute, then shrugged. "That's what she said you'd say." He took a notebook out of his pocket, scribbled on it, ripped out the page, and handed it to me. "Her cell phone. About five people in the whole world know this number. If she doesn't answer, leave a message, she'll get back to you." Then he turned and walked away.

I watched Jimmy D'Ambrosio shamble through the gate, cross Arlington Street, and disappear amid the early-morning sidewalk crowds on Commonwealth Avenue.

I finished my coffee and watched the rising sun brush the tops of the trees with golden light. Then I got up and headed back through the Garden, down Charles Street, across Beacon, and up Mt. Vernon to my new home on Beacon Hill, where Evie Banyon, my new housemate, and Henry, my new dog, waited for me.

A lot of things had changed in my life since August. After being divorced and living alone in a rented condo on the waterfront for eleven years, I moved to the townhouse on Beacon Hill, and Evie moved in with me. We'd bought it from Walt Duffy's son, Ethan, after Walt was killed. Henry David Thoreau, the Brittany spaniel who'd lived there with Walt and Ethan, came with the place.

So now I owned a home, shared it with a woman I loved, and had a dog who seemed to love both of us. Evie and I had junked all my old furniture, and most of hers, too, and bought new stuff. We had a housekeeper come in every week to vacuum up the dog hairs. I was learning to squeeze the toothpaste from the bottom and to unroll the toilet paper from the back and to pile yesterday's newspapers in the special box on the back porch. I was trying to remember to call when I was going to be late and not to make plans without consulting Evie.

Big changes, after eleven years. But so far it seemed to be working pretty well.

I went in the front door, poured myself some coffee, and looked out the kitchen window. Evie was in her bathrobe sipping coffee and reading the paper at the table in the little walled-in patio garden out back. Henry was lying beside her with his chin on his paws eyeing the gang of goldfinches that were pecking thistle seed from the feeders.

It was a tranquil domestic scene, and it made me smile.

When I stepped out the back door into the patio, the finches burst away in a flash of yellow.

Henry scrambled to his feet and came over to sniff my pant legs. I reached down and scratched his ears.

Evie looked up and smiled. "You frightened the finches," she said.

I went over, kissed her cheek, and sat across from her. "They'll be back."

"Where've you been?" Evie and Henry had been asleep when I'd slipped out of the house a little after six-thirty.

I shrugged.

"Ah," she said. "Lawyer business."

I nodded.

"And you can't talk about it."

"Nope."

"Not even to me?"

"Right."

She lifted her cup to her mouth and looked at me over the top of it. I couldn't tell if she was smiling.

"Client privilege," I said.

"Well," she said, "we've got some fascinating cases at the hospital. I can't talk about them, either."

"Medical privilege," I said.

"Aren't you curious?"

"Nope."

"One of the doctors is screwing two nurses," she said.

I smiled.

"Both of 'em at the same time."

"A neat trick," I said.

"He's married," she said. "So are the nurses. They use the custodian's room. The three of them together. You've heard of him. He's a world-famous surgeon."

8

"I can't talk about my clients, honey," I said. "Not even to you."

She stuck out her tongue at me. "You're no fun."

"I'm a lawyer," I said. "What'd you expect?"

Two

Back when I rented the condo on Lewis Wharf, I didn't have an office in my home. Another way to look at it would be: The whole place was my office. All four rooms were my space, and only mine, to occupy and use and mess up any way I wanted. I always tried to avoid doing office work at home, but when it was unavoidable, I used the kitchen table or the coffee table or the balcony that overlooked the harbor. I did most of my phone business sprawled on the bed.

When Evie and I moved into our place on Mt. Vernon Street, it was she who insisted I take the back bedroom off the kitchen for my office. When I told her I didn't need any office, that the very word "office" gave me the willies, she said, "Call it your cave, then. Every man needs his own cave."

I figured she just wanted to try to contain my mess someplace where she could close the door on it. But I quickly found that I liked my cave. Needed it, in fact, just as Evie said. I hadn't shared my life or my space with anybody for eleven years.

A week or so after we moved in, Evie gave me a carved wooden sign she'd had made. It said: "Brady's Cave." We screwed it onto the door.

I retreated to my cave often. I even found myself doing more work at home and less at my law office in Copley Square. I had a desk and a telephone and a computer and a little TV in there. There was a sofa bed for my naps and a dog bed for Henry's. I stacked my fly rods in the corner and my other fishing gear in the closet. One whole wall was a bookcase, and I had it stuffed with fishing books and novels and biographies. Not a damn law book in the whole place. My desk sat under a big window that looked out onto the patio garden so I could watch the birds while I talked on the phone.

Our deal was: I'd keep all my junk in my cave, and no woman would enter without permission, including the housekeeper.

So that morning after Evie left for work, I whistled up Henry, and he and I went into my little room. He curled up on his bed in the corner, sighed blissfully, and closed his eyes. I sat at my desk, found the scrap of paper Jimmy D'Ambrosio had given me, and dialed the number on it.

It rang only once before Ellen Stoddard answered. "Yes?" she said cautiously.

"It's Brady Coyne."

She laughed. She had a great, uninhibited, throaty laugh. From anybody other than the Democratic candidate for U.S. senator, I would've called it a sexy laugh. "Thank you very much," she said. "I just won five dollars."

"Huh?"

12

She laughed again, and I decided, candidate or no candidate, it *was* a sexy laugh. "I had a bet with Jimmy," she said. "I said you wouldn't agree to do it without checking with me. He said he could convince you. He has quite an inflated opinion of his persuasive powers."

"You're in favor of this, then?"

"Yes, Brady, I guess I am."

"You want me to hire a PI to tail Albert?"

"It's necessary."

"I'd like to talk with you about it."

"You mean, talk me out of it?"

"No," I said, "that's not what I meant."

"It's no big deal, Brady," said Ellen. "Women hire people to check up on their husbands all the time."

"It's always a big deal."

"Yes," she said. "I suppose you're right." She hesitated. "I can't talk now. I'm taping some TV spots in half an hour. How about lunch?"

"Can you break away?"

"Actually, I'd love to. Just you and me. No speechifying, no interviewing, no worrying about my makeup." She hesitated. "What about that place you always go to? Skeeter's?"

I laughed. "Skeeter's is a sports bar, Ellen."

"I like sports. Especially the Red Sox. Anyway, I hear Skeeter's has terrific cheeseburgers."

Cheeseburgers and baseball. My kind of senator. "Skeeter's it shall be," I said.

"Wonderful," she said. "I'll be there at noon."

I had no court appearances or client appointments scheduled for the day, so I called Julie, my secretary, and told her I'd be working at home. Julie wasn't happy about my increasingly slothful attitude to my law practice, billable hours, as she kept reminding me, being our lifeblood, but I assured her I'd keep track of all billable phone calls and work hard on the briefcase she's filled with paperwork and sent home with me the previous afternoon. She hemmed and hawed and then said, well, Megan, her daughter, did have a soccer game after school . . .

Quid pro quo. The lawyer's creed. I took the day off, my secretary got to leave the office a few hours early. A classic plea bargain.

I spent the morning dutifully catching up on my paperwork and making phone calls, and a little after eleven-thirty I walked over to Skeeter's, which was hidden at the end of an alley in the financial district. Ellen had made a shrewd choice. Skeeter's was always pretty quiet during lunchtime, and the State Street regulars who went there for cheeseburgers and beer cared more about sports than politics. They might recognize Ellen—Jimmy D'Ambrosio made sure her face was on the news most nights—but they wouldn't bother her.

If Nomar Garciaparra or Antoine Walker walked in, that might be another story.

I waited at the end of the alley, and on the dot of noon a black Ford Explorer stopped by the curb and Ellen got out. She was wearing big round sunglasses and a pale blue business suit. I was, as always, surprised by how small she was, even in heels. On TV she appeared to be a big, sturdy woman. She'd always had that solid presence about her. But in person, she was almost petite.

I stepped forward and stuck out my elbow. She smiled and hooked her arm through mine, and we went in.

14

Each of the four big-screen television sets behind the bar was tuned to a different channel. You had your choice of European soccer, women's golf, an old Sugar Ray Leonard boxing match, or the 1973 Super Bowl. All the sets were muted. There were a dozen or so patrons sitting at the bar with their backs to the door, about an equal mix of men and women, all in business suits. They were talking quietly among themselves, and they didn't even turn around when Ellen and I stepped inside.

When he saw us, Skeeter looked up from behind the bar and smiled. I arched my eyebrows and pointed at an empty booth toward the rear, and he waved his hand and nodded.

Ellen sat with her back to the room. I slid in across from her.

She pushed her sunglasses onto the top of her head, put her forearms on the table, and leaned toward me. "This is deliciously clandestine, Brady Coyne. I'm tempted to have a beer."

"The hopeful junior senator from the Commonwealth of Massachusetts, drinking beer in some dingy bar at noon-time?" I said. "What would the voters think?"

"Frankly, my dear," she said, "I don't give a damn."

"That wouldn't be cynicism I detect in your tone, would it?"

"I'm just tired." She blew out a breath. "I do want to be senator," she said. "But I've grown to loathe campaigning. There've been a hundred times I've been ready to bag the whole thing, just try to get my life back. If it wasn't for Jimmy—"

I held up my hand, and she stopped.

Skeeter had come over. "Mr. Coyne," he said. "How you doin'?" He nodded at Ellen. "Ma'am?"

"Ellen Stoddard," I said, "have you met Skeeter Cronin? He played a little second base for the old town team."

Ellen smiled up at him. "I watched you play. Your uniform was always dirty."

Skeeter shrugged. "That was a long time ago. You folks came here for privacy, I bet."

"Privacy and lunch," I said.

We ordered cheeseburgers and draft beer, and after Skeeter left, Ellen said, "Did Jimmy try to bribe you?"

"Offered me what he called a cushy job. Mentioned a federal judgeship."

She smiled. "I told him that wouldn't work."

"Jimmy seemed pretty intense this morning," I said.

"Jimmy's intense all the time," she said. "He wants to win. Claims this is his last campaign. 'It's me last hurrah,' he keeps saying."

I smiled at Ellen's effort to imitate Jimmy's imitation of an Irish brogue. "Hard to believe," I said. "It would be the end of an era. Jimmy D.'s been getting Massachusetts Democrats elected for close to forty years. I'd've thought the tumult and the shouting were in his blood."

"I've offered him a job," she said. "He says he's going to take it."

"If you win," I said.

"*When* we win, is how Jimmy puts it," she said.

We paused while Skeeter delivered our beers. Then I said, "You better tell me what's going on with Albert."

She combed her fingers through her hair. "I wish I knew. He's acting . . . weird."

"Weird how?"

"Like he's hiding something. Like he's done something

16

he's ashamed of." She waved her hand in the air. "Like . . ." She let her voice trail away.

"Like?" I said.

"I don't know. Like he's having an affair, I guess. That seems to be what Jimmy thinks. Jimmy doesn't have much of an imagination. I guess there are lots of things a man might want to hide from his wife."

"What do you think?" I said.

Ellen shook her head. "Truthfully, I don't know how Albert would act if he was having an affair, since as far as I know it's never happened. But I do know my husband, and I'm convinced there's something going on. Something's eating at him, and whatever it is, he won't talk about it. It's not like him to hide things from me. Makes me think it's something bad. It's got me very concerned."

"Jimmy's worried that Albert's going to lose the election for you." I arched my eyebrows at her.

"Well, if that's what happens, it wouldn't be fair to me or all the people who've worked so hard for us. Jimmy's got a point there." She shook her head. "But truthfully, it's Albert I'm worried about, more than the damn election. Albert and our marriage."

"Maybe he just doesn't like the idea of being married to a senator," I said.

"He was pretty supportive up until a few weeks ago," she said. "Attended most of the planning meetings, made some phone calls, helped raise money, even appeared in public with me a few times, as much as he hates that part of it. Anything I asked, really, he was happy to do. We even talked about my living in Washington and how his teaching obligations would mean he'd have to stay here, and he was all right with that. Then it all began to change."

17

"Changed how?"

"I hardly see him. He comes and goes at odd hours. He's avoiding me, Brady. It's like he's got some nasty secret and he's afraid if he so much as says good morning to me he's going to reveal it." Ellen shook her head. "I can't be any more specific than that."

"Sounds like a man with a guilty conscience."

Ellen shrugged.

"Is he working on a new book or scholarly monograph or something?"

"I don't think that's it. He's worked on books and monographs before and never acted like this."

"So maybe he *is* having an affair."

"Maybe he is," she said. "His world is full of pretty coeds. All I know is, the TV and the newspapers have started to notice."

"Notice what?"

She waved her hand. "Just that Albert's not around as much as he used to be. They're asking questions, and whatever is going on, I refuse to have them find it out before I do. It's none of their damn business. So will you do it?"

"You want me to hire a private investigator?"

"I can't think of anything else."

"I guess I can't, either," I said.

When I got back home, I dialed Gordon Cahill's number.

It rang four times, and then his sleepy voice mumbled, "Yeah, Cahill."

"Gordie," I said, "it's Brady Coyne."

"Christ," he muttered. "What time is it?"

"Two in the afternoon. Did I wake you up?"

18

"All-nighter." He yawned. "What's up?"

"I got a job for you."

"Tell me about it."

"I will when you get here."

"Oh-ho," he said. "One of your not-on-the-telephone jobs, huh?"

"That's right."

"So why me?"

"You're the best, Gordie. Everybody knows that."

"Yeah, bullshit." He sighed. "You at home?"

"Yes. Use the back door off the alley."

"Gimme an hour. Make sure there's coffee."

Henry and I went for a walk, and then I brewed some coffee and filled a carafe, and I was waiting at the table in the garden when there came a knock on the patio door. "It's me," called Gordon Cahill.

"It's not locked."

He unlatched the door, came in, and headed straight for the coffee. He poured himself a mugful, then sat down across from me. "So this vulture is getting on an airplane," he said. "He's got a big paper bag under his arm."

"Oh, jeez," I said. "Here it comes."

"The flight attendant says to him, 'May I see what you've got in that bag, sir?' The vulture opens the bag, and the stewardess looks in and sees that there are two dead raccoons in there. She looks at the vulture and shakes her head. 'I'm sorry, sir. We'll have to put one of these raccoons in with the cargo.' The vulture says, 'How come?' "

Cahill paused, sipped his coffee, and peered up at me.

I sighed. "Okay, Gordie. How come?"

19

"Airline policy," he said. "Only one carrion per passenger."

Aside from his unfortunate penchant for bad puns, Gordon Cahill was one of those utterly bland, forgettable guys who might sit beside you for nine innings at Fenway Park, and that same night, when he came into the bar where you were having a drink, you wouldn't make the connection. He was somewhere in his fifties, with brown hair going gray on the sides and thin on top. He was neither tall nor short, fat or skinny, handsome or ugly. He had a roundish face and bluish-gray eyes and a quick, shy smile when he chose to show it. He drove a sand-colored four-year-old Toyota Corolla, which was one of the most unnoticeable cars ever made.

I happened to know that Cahill had been there for the Saigon evacuation, ended up in a VA hospital, then put in twenty years with the Massachusetts state police, including several years undercover, before he took his retirement and opened his own shop on St. Botolph Street, just a few blocks from my office in Copley Square.

"How busy are you?" I said to him.

He shrugged. "I'm always busy."

"Too busy for another case?"

"You think I'm here because I heard there was coffee?" he said. "What've you got?"

I pushed the manila envelope Jimmy D'Ambrosio had given to me across the table toward him.

Cahill put his hand flat on top of it. "Tell me about it."

"Not much to tell," I said. "I want to know what this guy does with his spare time."

"Who's the client?"

"Me," I said.

"No," he said, "I mean, the fiancée, the wife, the employer, the insurance company, or what?"

"Just me, Gordie."

He shrugged, fumbled in his shirt pocket, and put on his reading glasses. Then he opened the envelope, took out the photos and papers, and studied them for several minutes while he sipped his coffee. When he was finished, he looked up at me over the tops of his glasses. "Albert Stoddard, huh?"

I nodded.

"Husband of the former cover girl for the Essex County D.A.'s office? The guy who's the future senator's husband?"

"Provided she wins the election."

"He's a college professor, huh?"

"Yes. At Tufts. History. Been there close to twenty years."

"And you suspect him of . . . ?"

I shrugged. "He's acting weird, quote unquote. Furtive. Evasive. Like a man with a guilty conscience. He might be fooling around."

Cahill nodded. "Okay," he said. "I get the picture."

"I knew you would," I said. "That's why I wanted you for the job. You'll do it?"

"Why not?"

"This has got to be superconfidential," I said.

He smiled. "I've been doing this work for a while, you know."

"I know, Gordie. I just—"

"Had some pretty high-profile clients. Never once . . ."

"I apologize," I said. "I trust you."

"You better," he said. He stood up and tucked the envelope into his jacket pocket. "You hear about the Buddhist monk, went in for a root canal?"

21

"Oh, jeez."

"Dentist wanted to give him a shot of Novocain," he said, "but the monk refused it." He arched his eyebrows at me.

"Gordie, I'm warning you—"

"Monk said he wanted to transcend dental medication."

THREE

Two nights after I hired Gordon Cahill to tail Albert Stoddard, Evie and I were sitting on our new living-room sofa watching the eleven o'clock news on our new big-screen TV with Henry, our new dog, wedged in between us.

And there was Ellen, delivering her evening sound bite at some fund-raising dinner in Springfield. Her theme was the overriding obligation of government to protect its citizens—women, children, ethnic and religious minorities, the elderly, the ill, the mentally incompetent, all the hopeless and helpless and downtrodden members of society—and her promise was to make sure that government fulfilled its obligation, should the voters of the Commonwealth see fit to elect her.

It was a smart strategy for a woman who'd built her reputation on prosecuting criminals, especially at a time when the threat of terrorism hung over the land like a distant grumbling thunderhead and greedy corporate CEOs were absconding with their employees' retirement money—and particularly when her Republican opponent, a conservative family-values African-American businessman named Lamarr

Oakley, kept pounding away at the importance of cutting taxes, reducing the size of government, requiring schoolchildren to pray and salute the flag, and keeping faith in good old American free enterprise.

I only half listened to what Ellen was saying. I'd heard it before. I was waiting for the camera to pan over the head table, and when it did, I looked for Albert.

He wasn't there.

I wondered where he was and what he was doing and if Gordon Cahill was sitting nearby in his sand-colored Toyota Corolla watching him.

Ellen finished her speech with her trademark refrain: "I will be the friend of those who have no friends and the enemy of those who make me their enemy." It was pure Jimmy D'Ambrosio, even if he'd stolen it from an old fifties television show called *Boston Blackie*.

"Oh, I like her," said Evie when the commercial came on.

"Me, too."

"You know her, right?"

"I've done some work for her mother," I said.

"Is she as attractive in person as she is on TV?"

"She's much shorter," I said.

When Ellen Gallatin Stoddard decided to run for senator, she invited me to join what she called her "brain trust." I declined, citing a mediocre and untrustworthy brain, not to mention a profound lack of interest in the hurly-burly of campaign politics.

I assured Ellen that it had nothing to do with my feelings for her, either as a candidate or a person. I told her I would talk her up with my friends, and I'd surely vote for her.

Anyway, the last thing she needed was some lawyer giving her advice. She already had Jimmy D'Ambrosio lined up to run her campaign. He was a brain trust all by himself.

Before she quit to run for the Senate, back when she was still putting away murderers and rapists for the Essex County D.A., Ellen and I occasionally bumped into each other in the lobby outside a courtroom. We never opposed each other, of course. She prosecuted high-profile criminal cases, while I did most of my low-profile work in the civil courts. But sometimes we both found ourselves free for lunch or for an after-court drink.

When her father, Clifford Gallatin, had his last heart attack in his duck blind on an Ipswich salt marsh, Ellen hired me to straighten out her mother's financial situation. Cliff had left chaos behind him—a thirty-year-old boilerplate will, stocks in his own name, scattered insurance policies, a few annuities, several real estate holdings, certificates of deposit in six different Massachusetts banks, and various checking and savings accounts in other banks in other states.

Doris Gallatin, Ellen's mother, a pleasant but severely scattered woman in her mid-seventies, had left the family's financial affairs up to her husband. She had no idea what she had coming to her, or even where Cliff had kept his records. When he died, she was totally flustered by the whole mess, to the point where she threw up her hands and refused to deal with it.

So I dealt with it. After the usual hassles with probate, we got everything into a tidy trust with Ellen as trustee, and everybody—especially Doris—was happy.

Ellen seemed to think I'd performed some kind of miracle. I protested that it was routine stuff that any lawyer with patience and perseverance could do with his eyes closed. But as far as she was concerned, I'd salvaged her mother's future and her own sanity.

Now and then Doris would call asking me to explain something or other, or to help her decide whether money should be moved around, or to consider whether the terms of the trust needed a tweak. I would've been happy to drive out to her house in Belmont, but the old lady used our meetings as an excuse to get dressed up, take a taxi into the city, and meet me for afternoon tea at the Ritz. I suspected that whenever Doris got it in her head that she thought she'd rather enjoy high tea at the Ritz, she dreamed up some issue that required a consultation with her lawyer.

I didn't mind. I never had tea, though. The Ritz made good martinis.

Ellen thought all this was pretty special. As far as I was concerned, it was business as usual, although I always got a kick out of how much fun Doris Gallatin seemed to have at our matinees at the Ritz.

And so, the way those things go, Ellen Stoddard and I became friends. She wasn't my client, and couldn't be. Her mother was my client. I could have played the conflict-of-interest card if Ellen had pressured me about joining her brain trust when she decided to run for senator, but she didn't. Maybe she was just being polite, asking me in the first place.

Albert was in his mid-forties, a few years older than Ellen. He was a gangly, sad-eyed, distracted sort of guy who always seemed preoccupied with thoughts that were too esoteric and obscure to share with laypeople such as me. He'd earned his tenure in the history department at Tufts when he published his only book many years before I met him. The book, Ellen once told me, explored the cultural roots of capitalism in

America, and there had been some chatter about a Pulitzer, although no nomination had been forthcoming. Ellen confessed that she found Albert's book turgid. I never tried to read it.

Albert and I had gone trout fishing a few times. He loved the outdoors and seemed to get as much of a kick out of spotting a cedar waxwing or a muskrat as he did from catching a trout on a dry fly.

I am a restless fisherman. I inevitably convince myself that there are more and bigger fish around the next bend, so I'm always on the move.

Albert, on the other hand, liked to find a good-looking spot and work it thoroughly. He could spend an entire afternoon happily—and optimistically—casting over the same water, even when he never got a strike.

That was pretty much the difference between Albert and me.

Albert and Ellen had been too busy with their careers to have children. From what I'd been able to observe, they were quite supportive of each other, but they had gone their separate professional ways from the beginning, and now they moved in worlds that couldn't have been farther apart—Ellen, always in the spotlight, first handling the pressure of life-or-death, headline-grabbing criminal trials, and now running for the United States Senate, with vague rumblings about the presidency down the road, and Albert, huddled up in a library carrel or cloistered in his office at Tufts, peering at a computer monitor or thumbing through musty old books and stuffing his laptop with footnotes and his head with theories.

Albert Stoddard just didn't strike me as the kind of guy who'd carry on some sneaky extramarital affair under any circumstance, but especially not when his wife was running for public office.

But I'd been wrong about a lot of people a lot of times.

On Saturday morning when Henry and I got back from our stroll on the Common, Evie said, "I thought I heard your phone ring while you were gone."

So I went into my room and checked my voice mail. The message was from Cahill. "Gimme a call," he said. "I'm on my cell."

I dialed his number.

"Yeah?" he said.

"It's Brady, returning your call," I said. "Where are you?"

"On the road," he said. "Got a pun for you."

"Don't you ever run out of them?"

"Nope. Some guys in my line of work, they do crosswords, listen to tapes, play solitaire. Me, I happen to enjoy wordplay. This job, I sometimes have a lot of time on my hands. Like now, driving the back roads. I could listen to the radio, play tapes. But what I do is, I make up puns. The trick is, you start with the punch line, and once you've got that, you work backward, make up the story that leads to it. It keeps my mind active and alert."

"Surely," I said, "there's got to be a more productive way to spend your time. Knitting pot holders, for example."

"Yeah," he said. "I knew a guy like you once. Told him some excellent puns, couldn't get him to crack a smile. It got to be a kind of challenge for me. Finally I made a bet with him. I bet him if I told him my ten best puns, one of 'em, at least, would make him laugh."

I figured I was being suckered, but I said, "And? Did it?"

28

"Naw," he said. "No pun in ten did."

I said nothing.

"You there, Brady?" said Cahill after a minute. "Did I lose you?"

"I'm here," I said. "You called me for that?"

"Sure. Well, I also wanted you to know I'm making good progress on your case."

"That didn't take long."

"This ain't brain surgery, you know."

"So what can you tell me?"

"Not quite sure what it adds up to yet," he said. "I'm working on it this weekend. Should have a handle on it in a day or two. Let's get together Monday morning. Sometime between seven and nine work for you?"

Cahill's office was in Copley Square, right around the corner from mine. I could leave for work a half hour early. "I'll be there around eight or eight-fifteen," I said.

His voice crackled and stuttered. I heard him say, "... bring me a muffin or something."

"You got the muffin. Can you hear me?"

"... losing you," he said.

"Where are you now?"

"Heading into the hills."

"What hills?"

"Hang on 'til Monday morning, okay? I don't..." His voice faded for a second. When he came back, he was saying, "... those boys ..."

"What?" I said. "What boys?"

But I'd lost him completely.

FOUR

Monday morning I left the house around quarter of eight—about half an hour earlier than normal—so I'd have time to talk with Gordon Cahill in his office and still get to mine by nine. Julie had a morning full of client meetings lined up for me, and being late would be a bad way to start the week. My clients could handle it, but Julie would make my life miserable.

It promised to be another fine Indian summer day in Boston. The maples and beeches on the Common and in the Public Gardens had started turning crimson and gold and bronze, and the low-angled morning sun glowed in the tops of the foliage. Squirrels scampered under their branches gathering acorns and beechnuts. Pigeons waddled around on the sidewalks looking for stale French fries and popcorn. Ah, Mother Nature.

It was the kind of early-autumn morning that gave me an itch to prowl through some real woods, spy on some wild animals, maybe even go trout fishing one more time before the snow flew.

I stopped at a coffee shop on Newbury Street and bought two large coffees and half a dozen bran muffins. As I recalled, Gordon Cahill liked bran.

St. Botolph Street runs between Huntington and Columbus Avenues behind Copley Place. Cahill's office was halfway down the street on the second floor above a Thai restaurant. The last time I was there he had the air-conditioning running high and was burning incense—a futile effort to neutralize the exotic aromas that wafted up from the kitchen below.

Gordie hated all Southeast Asian cuisine—a vestige, I assumed, of his time in Saigon thirty-odd years ago—but he wasn't thinking about moving. He said the rent was cheap and, anyway, he liked the fact that he wasn't too comfortable in an office. He liked being out on the streets where the action was.

When I climbed the stairway it was a little after eight-fifteen in the morning, and the restaurant was closed. Still, the mingled stale smell of curry and coconut milk and roasted peanuts and seared hot peppers lingered in the walls.

The door to Cahill's office was open a crack. With my briefcase in one hand and my bag of muffins and coffee in the other, I nudged it open with my toe and said, "Hey, Gordie. I come bearing muffins."

He didn't answer. I went in.

His cramped office was dominated by a big old oak desk with an Apple computer, two telephones, and a wire basket full of papers. A dirty window overlooked the back alley. A row of filing cabinets took up one wall. There was a mini-refrigerator and a microwave oven and a floor-to-ceiling bookcase that held mostly legal tomes, phone books, atlases, and other reference works.

To the left, the door to the conference room was ajar. I put the bag of muffins and coffee and my briefcase on Cahill's desk and stepped into the other room.

"Gordie, you here?" I said. "I'm in no mood for—"

That's when the gun barrel rammed into the back of my neck and the growly voice said, "Don't even blink."

"Hey," I said. "That hurts."

I recognized the growly voice. It belonged to my old friend—and occasional nemesis—Roger Horowitz. Horowitz was a homicide detective for the Massachusetts state police. Naturally, whenever I encountered him it meant that he was investigating a homicide, so naturally, as much as I liked him, I never wanted to encounter him. It usually meant somebody I knew had died under suspicious circumstances.

"Christ," Horowitz grumbled. "It's you."

"Please point that thing somewhere else," I said.

He hesitated, then shoved his gun into the holster under his armpit.

I poked my finger at his chest. "What are you doing here?"

"I'm the cop," he said. "I get to ask the questions. What are *you* doing here?"

"I brought coffee and bran muffins. I'm having breakfast with Cahill."

"Why?"

"Bran muffins are good for you," I said. "They keep you regular."

"Answer the fucking question, Coyne. I been up all night. I'm in no mood."

"He's doing some work for me," I said. "We were supposed to meet here and talk about it."

"What work?"

33

"Oh, no you don't," I said. "I came here to talk to Gordie, not you."

"Cahill ain't here."

"I see that."

"That's because he's dead," he said.

"Gordie?"

He nodded.

I sat heavily in one of the chairs at the conference table. "What happened?"

Horowitz blew out a breath and slumped in the chair across from me. "You said something about muffins. Got coffee, too?"

"Of course."

"Go get 'em."

"You want a muffin," I said, "you've got to tell me what happened to Gordie."

Horowitz narrowed his eyes, pretended to ponder the pros and cons of that proposition, then nodded. "I can tell you some things, I guess. That coffee better still be hot or the deal's off."

I fetched the paper bag from the other room, plunked it down on the conference table, and sat across from Horowitz.

He ripped the bag open, popped the top off one of the coffees, and took a sip.

"Hot enough?" I said.

He shrugged, picked up a muffin, and took a bite. "Car crash," he mumbled around his mouthful of muffin. "Around midnight last night."

"Where?" I said. "How? What the hell happened?"

He took another sip of coffee and wiped his mouth with the back of his wrist. "He was heading east on Route 119 between Ashby and Townsend. You know the Willard Brook State Forest?"

"I've driven through there, sure. It's a little ways past the Squannacook River, where I sometimes go trout fishing."

"Twisty road, all them big pine trees? No houses or gas stations or anything for maybe ten miles?"

I nodded.

"Cahill plowed into one of the trees."

"And he died?"

"Yep. He was going way too fast, and his front tire blew out." Horowitz made an exploding gesture with his hands. "There was a fire."

"Damn." I shook my head. "I can't believe it."

"Believe it," Horowitz said. "Your turn, Coyne."

"Wait a minute," I said. "I know about unattended deaths and all that, but why are you here?"

"Looking for clues. Why else?"

"You're investigating an automobile accident?"

"Who said anything about an accident?"

I looked at him. "You think he was murdered?"

He rubbed his bristly chin. "Officially, it looks like an accident, all right. No evidence to the contrary at this point. We got forensics and the accident-scene crew checking it out. How well did you know Cahill?"

I shrugged. "He's done some work for me over the years. He's very good. The best, actually. Thorough, absolutely discreet. Honest. Expensive. I knew him professionally more than personally, I guess you'd say. I liked him a lot."

"You know he used to be a state cop?"

I nodded. "Friend of yours, then?"

"I got to know him when he was undercover in Lawrence

and Haverhill. The man had balls, I'll give him that. Annoying habit of making up puns. You'd never know it to look at him, but he was absolutely fearless. He was undercover almost three years. Not a minute of it he wasn't at risk. But he got the goods on 'em. When he testified, of course, that was the end of undercover for Cahill. They put him behind a desk. He hated that. Finished out his twenty years, retired, and started doing this." Horowitz waved his hand around the office.

"So you're investigating this—this car crash—because he used to be a state cop?" I said.

He shook his head. "I told you too much already." He arched his eyebrows at me. "Quid pro quo, Coyne."

I shook my head.

"I'd really like to know what in hell Cahill was doing on Route 119 at midnight on a Sunday," persisted Horowitz. "Where he was coming from, where he was going."

"Of course you'd like to know," I said.

"Who he'd been talking to, what he was looking for."

"Key questions, for sure."

Suddenly Horowitz reached across the table and grabbed my wrist. "Dammit, Coyne. Gordie's dead. Don't you get it?"

"I can't tell you what he was working on for me, Roger. You know that. Not without my client's permission." I looked meaningfully at where his hand held my wrist.

He gave my wrist a squeeze, then let go of it. "Get it, then."

"You really think—?"

"I don't know." He leaned back in his chair, shook his head, and let out a long sigh. "For all I know, he had a heart attack. But you're a cop for twenty years, you accumulate a lot of enemies. You do PI work, you collect more of 'em. I owe it to Gordie to figure out what the hell happened, that's all. Help me out, okay?"

"I'll talk to my client, see what I can do." I stood up. "You want the rest of these muffins?"

He shook his head. "Bring 'em to Julie or give 'em to your dog or something. I prefer blueberry."

I went to the outer office and picked up my briefcase.

Horowitz followed behind me. "I'll be calling you," he said.

I swept my hand around Cahill's office. "You find anything useful?"

"You ask too many questions, Coyne."

I shrugged. "I notice that you're here alone."

"So?"

"I thought you guys always worked in pairs."

He flapped one hand and said nothing.

"So where's your partner?" I said.

"Home having breakfast with her husband, probably."

"You're alone on this?"

"What's it look like?"

"It looks to me," I said, "like you're working on your own hunches on your own time. I bet your boss doesn't even know you're here."

"None of his fucking business what I do on my own time."

I nodded. "I'm right, then. This is not an official investigation."

"None of *your* business, either."

"Well," I said, "your interest in my client suggests maybe

it is. You want my help, you've got to convince me there could be a connection. So what makes you so sure this wasn't an accident?"

He blew out a breath. "I just knew the man, that's all," he said. "Gordon Cahill was very careful, precise, unexcitable. Plodding, almost. You don't survive undercover for three years if you're not. It would be entirely out of character for him to drive recklessly, exceed the speed limit. He'd never drink or do drugs if he was driving. He wouldn't fall asleep at the wheel. Nothing could make him panic. He just wouldn't have an accident. Not Gordie."

"Unless?"

Horowitz shrugged. "Think about it."

"Unless someone was chasing him? Is that what you're thinking? Somebody forced him off the road or something?"

He waved his hand. "We'll see what the crime-scene people, forensics, M.E.'s office come up with. You talk to your client. Then we'll put our heads together."

"No promises," I said. I opened the door and stepped out of Gordon Cahill's office.

"Hey, Coyne," said Horowitz.

I stopped. "What?"

"There's nothing left of him but a cinder," he said.

I looked at him.

He made an exploding motion with his hands. "It was a fireball. As bad as anything I've ever seen."

"I'll see what I can do," I said.

I left Horowitz pawing through the papers in the wire basket on Gordon Cahill's desk. I knew he wouldn't find anything.

38

Gordie was way too careful to leave anything useful on top of his desk.

It was barely a five-minute walk to my own office, and I used the time pondering the possibility that Albert Stoddard had figured out that Gordon Cahill was tailing him and had run him off the road in the Willard Brook State Forest.

That struck me as even more out of character for Albert than speeding was for Cahill. But I was a notoriously poor judge of character. I generally assumed the best in people. That, I'd learned over the years, was a surefire formula for disappointment.

Still, I rather liked that about myself. I knew a lot of lawyers, especially, who instinctively assumed everybody lied, cheated, and beat their wives. Mistrust was probably a useful trait for a lawyer, but it was a piss-poor trait for a human being . . . which shows how much interest I had in being a successful lawyer.

But then I remembered the last words Cahill had spoken to me on the telephone before we lost our connection. "Those boys," he had said.

Boys? Albert?

If Albert Stoddard was fooling around with boys, if that's why he was acting weird and furtive, and if Gordon Cahill found out about it, and if Albert knew that Cahill knew . . .

Sometimes it was hard to think the best of people.

Julie didn't look up from her computer when I walked into the office. The arch of her neck was decidely hostile.

I glanced at my watch. "Hey, I'm only twenty minutes late."

"Mrs. Brubaker arrived thirty minutes ago," she said without lifting her head.

"Well," I said, "you're the one who always likes to keep the clients waiting."

"We would like to promote the patently absurd illusion that you are busy and that your services are in high demand," said Julie, "as ridiculous as we both know that is. I can carry it off when you're holed up in your office reading fishing catalogs and the client arrives in the waiting room. It's more difficult when I'm forced to usher the client into your office and serve her coffee and make small talk because you have yet to arrive and we don't want her to see you straggle in."

"I don't really care whether Mrs. Brubaker thinks I'm busy or not," I said. "I don't think she cares, either. Hell, I'm not that late." I plunked the bag of muffins on her desk. "For you. Bran. Good for your bowels."

"Since when are you worried about my bowels?"

"I worry about everybody's bowels."

She glanced at the bag. "It's torn. Where'd you get it?"

"I confess there were originally six muffins in there," I said. "I ate one and Roger Horowitz ate two."

She cocked her head and looked at me. "Detective Horowitz? Now what?"

"Gordon Cahill," I said. "He died in a car crash last night."

Julie shook her head. "Oh, dear." She hesitated, then said, "Detective Horowitz is with homicide." She arched her eyebrows, making it a question.

"Don't ask," I said, "because I can't talk about it."

Julie nodded. "So you *have* been busy."

"A veritable whirlwind of thoroughly depressing activity," I said.

"I'm sorry about Mr. Cahill," she said. "He was a nice man."

"Yes," I said. "He was. I liked him a lot and I'm very upset by this."

She hesitated. "You think he was murdered?"

"I don't know."

"But you and Detective Horowitz are going to find out, huh?"

"Not me," I said. "I've got a law practice to run."

Julie laughed quickly. "Sure you do. So why don't you go accrue some billable hours for a change? Mrs. Brubaker seems quite distraught this morning."

I snapped her a salute, then went over to the coffee machine, poured myself a mugful, and headed for my inner office, where Harriet Brubaker was waiting for me, twisting her handkerchief around in her hands.

FIVE

Harriet Brubaker's husband, Charlie, had recently been diagnosed with Alzheimer's. The doctors told Harriet that within a year—two at the most—Charlie would be past the point where she could take care of him, and she should begin making arrangements immediately. "Making arrangements" meant moving Charlie into an assisted-living facility. It also meant working out the financing so that Harriet wouldn't be left destitute.

So she came to me. Helping elderly people make arrangements for their last years of life is one of my specialties. I also do wills and divorces and adoptions, with a smattering of tax, small business, and real estate law. When my clients have other kinds of legal problems, I refer them to friends of mine who specialize in those fields.

I know what I can do, and more important, I know what I can't do, and most important of all, I never hesitate to admit it. My clients seem to appreciate that.

When I was in law school, I aspired to argue First Amendment cases before the Supreme Court. But I was also determined to be my own boss. I vowed to join no firm and take on no partner. So I set up my own lone-wolf practice in downtown Boston and accepted the cases that came to me. I built my practice around a relatively small number of clients who liked and trusted me, and I acquired new clients now and then through the referrals of old clients.

It was unexciting work that rarely required me to argue anything before a judge or jury, never mind a groundbreaking issue involving free speech. Most of my work got done on the telephone or with a fax machine or at a conference table.

As routine—boring, even—as it usually was, I liked the nonadversarial kind of legal work I did. I helped people with their problems, and I slept well at night.

I also happened to make quite a bit of money at it.

When I hired Julie, of course, I ended up with a boss anyway. I wasn't much of a businessman. I needed a boss.

When I walked into my office, Harriet Brubaker looked up and dabbed at her eyes with her ever-present lace handkerchief.

When she and I walked out of my office an hour later, she was smiling.

You can't beat that.

I refilled my coffee mug and told Julie to hold my calls for a few minutes. Then I went back into my office and rang Jimmy D'Ambrosio's cell phone.

"Yeah, Jimmy D.," he answered.

"It's Brady Coyne." I heard the muffled sound of voices in the background. I figured Jimmy was in a crowd.

"Hang on," he said.

I waited.

A minute later he said, "Okay. I'm in the men's room. What's up?"

"When can you break away?"

"You got something for me, huh?"

"Not on the phone, Jimmy," I said.

"Why the hell not?"

"Well, if I told you that, it would be on the phone, wouldn't it?"

"Guess it would," he said. "How about a hint?"

"You're the one who's insisting on discretion."

"Yeah, fine," he grumbled. "Lemme check my schedule." He paused. "Between three and four this afternoon looks okay. Same place?"

"Under the watchful eye of General Washington, three o'clock."

"This better be good," he said.

"It's not," I said. "It's bad."

I made it a point to be ten minutes late this time. I had a responsibility to my profession. I didn't want Jimmy D. to get the wrong idea about lawyers.

He was talking on his cell phone and sipping from a tall foam cup with a Dunkin' Donuts logo on it. When he saw me approaching, he quickly snapped his phone shut and slid it into his jacket pocket.

I sat beside him, and he handed another cup to me. "Iced coffee," he said. "Black. You're the only man I know who drinks black iced coffee."

"I suppose you know which leg goes in first when I pull my boxer shorts on, too," I said.

He smiled. "Trust me," he said. "You don't want to know what I know." He sipped from his cup. "So what's up? Your man get something on Albert?"

I shook my head. "I can't tell the state police that you're my client without your permission," I said. "I want it."

"You ain't serious, Coyne."

"They want to talk to Albert," I said, "although they don't know it's Albert yet. It's pretty important."

"Now I know you're kidding."

"I'm dead serious, Jimmy. The PI I hired for you was killed last night, and it weighs heavily on my heart."

"Get another PI on the job, then," he said.

I lit a cigarette and glared at him.

He tried to glare back at me. Then he shrugged. "How'd he get killed?"

"His automobile crashed into a tree and caught fire."

"Well, that's a shame. But I don't see—"

"The cops don't think it was an accident."

"All the more reason why you can't involve me," said Jimmy.

"Listen," I said. "The man who died was on the job for me. For us. You and me. We're responsible."

"We are? How do you know he was working on our case?"

"Okay," I said. "I don't know. I want to know. I want the police to figure it out. So I want to give them your name, and when they talk to you, I want you to give them Albert Stoddard's name."

"Abso-fuckin'-lutely not," said Jimmy. "You keep me and Albert out of this, or I promise you, I'll see that you're disbarred."

"You leave me no choice," I said. "I guess I'll have to talk to Ellen."

He shrugged. "You can talk to Ellen if you want. But it doesn't matter what she says. I'm the one who hired you, remember? I'm your client."

"Seems to me she's the one who hired you," I said.

"Well, Ellen can fire my ass and it won't change anything. I'll still be your client, and I'll still say no."

I stood up. "I'm disappointed in you, Jimmy."

He shrugged. "You're certainly not the first one."

"A man was killed last night."

"Damn shame," he said. "But we got an election coming up."

"Think about it," I said. "If you change your mind, let me know."

"Don't hold your breath." He stood up and started to walk away.

"Hey, Jimmy," I said. "I got a question for you."

He stopped and looked at me. "What?"

"Does Albert fool around with boys?"

He came over and sat down again. "Boys?" he said. "Albert?"

I shrugged.

"Jesus," he said. "What makes you think that?"

"Something our PI told me before he died."

Jimmy was quiet for a minute. Then he said, "Boys, girls, barnyard animals, it doesn't change a damn thing. You can't give the cops my name."

I got back to the office a little before four, and on the assumption that if Jimmy was free between three and four,

47

Ellen would be, too, I called her secret cell phone number.

When she answered, I said, "It's Brady."

"Oh, hi," she said. "I've got about three minutes. What's up?"

"I just talked with Jimmy," I said. "I asked him to release me from my confidentiality commitment."

"He refused, I assume."

"Yes."

"And you want me to say it's okay?"

"Yes, I do. It's important."

"I'm listening."

"The PI I hired to tail Albert was killed last night," I said. "It's not clear whether it was an accident or a homicide or even whether he was on our case at the time. The state police are investigating."

"And you think Albert might've had something to do with it?"

"I have no idea. I just want to assist the police. I thought you—"

"Yes, I get the picture." She paused, then said, "I've got to go along with Jimmy on this one, Brady. I'm sure you understand."

"I'm not sure *you* understand," I said. "A man died last night, Ellen. A man I hired to do some work for you. A man I liked very much. It makes me sad and angry when people I like die."

"And you don't like feeling that you might somehow be responsible," she said.

"I don't like feeling that I might be standing in the way of justice being done," I said.

"Or that I might be standing in your way," she said.

"Well, yes."

48

"Even if I agreed with you," said Ellen, "you can't do anything about it without Jimmy's permission."

"I'm sorely tempted," I said.

"It's a slippery slope, Brady Coyne," she said. "Be careful. Jimmy's your client on this one, and even if I'm his boss, I'm not going to second-guess him. If he says no, no it is."

"Is getting elected that important to you, Ellen?"

She said nothing.

"I apologize," I said after a minute. "That was completely uncalled for."

"Apology required," she said. "And accepted."

I heard somebody speak to her. She said, "Yes, okay." Then to me she said, "I've got to go now, Brady."

"Think about it please?"

"If you come up with something you think will change my mind," she said, "do let me know."

"You can count on it."

Six

On a Friday afternoon the previous May, Albert called me in my office. "I just turned in my grades," he said. "I want to go fishing."

I rarely turn down a chance to go fishing.

We met in front of Papa Razzi, the Italian restaurant near the Route 2 rotary in Concord. Albert transferred his gear from his Volkswagen to my BMW, and we headed for the Nissitissit River in Pepperell.

As we drove, I asked Albert what he thought about Ellen's decision to run for the Senate.

He turned to me and smiled. "I suppose I'll vote for her," he said.

"It's going to change your lives," I said.

"Oh, yes," he said. "That's what I'm afraid of."

Then he changed the subject.

Before we moved in together, back when Evie and I saw each other mostly on weekends, we took turns cooking. Both of us liked to put together meals for each other. Although neither of us was a particularly gifted chef, we were tolerant of each other's efforts and encouraged experimentation. So when we decided to buy the place on Mt. Vernon Street and share our lives, we figured we'd continue to have fun taking turns in the kitchen.

But Evie worked long hours running the business end of things at Beth Israel Hospital, and Julie kept me pretty busy, too, so usually by the time we got home, all we wanted to do was sit outside in our little walled-in garden, have a gin-and-tonic or a Bloody Mary, watch the birds flit at the feeders, scratch Henry's belly, and talk about baseball or the movies or the sex lives of famous surgeons.

Except on weekends, neither of us had much energy or enthusiasm for cooking.

So we either ate out—there were dozens of good restaurants within a fifteen-minute walk of Mt. Vernon Street—or one of us brought home takeout.

It was my turn, so perhaps subconsciously inspired by the aromas that had seeped into the walls in the stairwell leading up to Gordon Cahill's office, I stopped at the Thai restaurant on Charles Street and picked up two helpings of Pad Thai and some salad that featured oriental cabbage, shiitake mushrooms, bean sprouts, and lemon grass.

By the time we sat down it was dark outside, so we ate in the kitchen. Henry lay under the table with his chin on my instep, alert for falling noodles.

After a while, Evie dabbed at her mouth with her napkin and said, "What's up, Brady? You haven't said five words since you got home. I've been doing all the talking."

I smiled. "I enjoy listening. You tell good stories, and you've got a very sexy voice."

52

"Oh, sure," she said. "You can't fool me that easy. Something's eating at you."

I nodded. "A friend of mine died last night."

She reached across the table and touched my hand. "I'm sorry, honey. Anybody I know?"

I shook my head.

"Do you want to talk about it?"

"Not really. He was a PI working on a case for me."

Evie's eyebrows arched. "Working on a case? What happened?"

"Car crash."

"So it wasn't . . ."

"It was an accident, babe. Nothing to worry about."

She smiled. "I do worry, you know. You always seem to get yourself into—"

At that moment the telephone rang. Evie got up and answered it. She listened for a moment, then looked at me and frowned. "Yes," she said into the phone. "He's here. Hold on, please." She held up the phone for me. "For you."

I got up and took the phone from her.

It was Horowitz.

"I told you to call on my other line," I said to him. I glanced at Evie. She was peering at me out of narrow, suspicious eyes.

"No you didn't," he said. "You didn't say anything about any other line. When you lived by yourself, there was only one line. Why'd you have to go make things complicated?"

"You're interrupting my dinner, you know."

"Yeah, really sorry. So whaddya got for me?"

"I talked to my client," I said. "The answer is no."

"You know I can handle it for you, Coyne."

"Forget it, Roger. It's not going to happen."

53

"You interested in what I found out?"

"Yes," I said. "But not now. Now I want to finish my Pad Thai and bask in Evie's beauty. I'll call you later."

"When you hear what I got to tell you," he said, "you'll change your mind."

"My mind isn't the relevant one," I said. "I'll get back to you."

When I hung up, I saw that Evie was still looking at me. "Basking in my beauty? Did you really say that?"

I smiled.

"Accident, huh?" she said. "Nothing to worry about, huh?"

I shrugged.

"That was Lieutenant Horowitz," she said. "I know what he does."

"Honey—"

"Your friend got murdered, didn't he?"

"Maybe," I said. "I don't know."

"And you're going to end up playing cops and robbers and getting shot at and ..." Her voice trailed off.

I went around the table, lifted Evie's auburn hair away from her neck, and nuzzled her. "I'm just a family lawyer," I said. "Don't worry about me. Horowitz wants to know the name of my client, and I can't tell him, and once I convince him of that, it'll be the end of it."

"Oh, right," she said. "Fat chance. Dammit anyway, Brady Coyne. I know you."

I kissed the magic place just under her ear.

"Cut that out," she said.

I did not cut it out, and after a minute she sighed and arched her neck to give me easier access to her magic place. "Mmm," she mumbled. "That's really not fair."

54

After supper Evie and I took Henry for a walk on the Common, where we let him off his leash so he could trot around and sniff the benches and trash barrels and give chase to some squirrels. Henry was a little overweight, and he needed his exercise.

I figured by the time we got back home Evie would've forgotten Horowitz, but when I told her I was going to make a few phone calls and catch up on my e-mail, she said, "If Roger Horowitz tries to drag you into some murder case, you tell him that our divorce will be on his conscience."

Henry followed me into my room and curled up on his dog bed. I pried off my shoes, propped my feet on my desk, and called Horowitz.

"Cahill was murdered," he said.

"You're sure?"

"What else would a bullet hole in the left front tire of his vehicle mean?"

"Bullet?" I said. "What kind of bullet?"

"Who gives a shit." Horowitz let out an exasperated breath. "For your information, it wasn't technically a bullet. It was a load of buckshot. Point is—"

"I get the point," I said.

"Ballistics can't do anything with buckshot."

"I understand that."

"But you've got a client," he said, "and that client asked you to hire a detective to investigate somebody. It's that somebody I'm interested in."

"What else did they find?" I said.

"Who?"

"Your experts."

"Why should I tell you?"

"Same reason you told me the tire got shot."

"To convince you to do your duty," he said. "Right. Well, so far, nothing. They haven't dug into it yet. The M.E. hasn't had a chance to look at what's left of Gordie's body. He always procrastinates with charred corpses, for some inexplicable reason. The tire was obvious, though, and all by itself it tells us this was murder. And that, by God, should be enough for you."

"Roger," I said, "that is plenty for me. But I'm not the one who counts here. I will talk to my client again, given this new information. I don't want you to get your hopes up, though. My client has very good reasons for wanting to preserve our confidentiality. Anyway, Cahill had lots of clients, plus I imagine he accumulated a goodly number of enemies over the years, probably going back to his undercover days with the state cops. Those mob families have long memories."

"Yeah," he said. "I'm looking into that angle. There's too damn many suspects, actually. I just want to make sure I don't overlook anybody."

"Whatever you come up with on your own is fair game, I guess," I said. "But you can't expect me to help you."

"I haven't ever helped you?"

I sighed. "Sure you have."

"Well?"

"What did you find in his office?"

Horowitz laughed sarcastically. "You kidding? Cahill was worse than you when it came to protecting his clients' damn privacy. You'd think, an ex cop . . ."

"I'll talk to my client again," I said. "That's all I can do."

After we hung up, I tried Jimmy D'Ambrosio's cell phone. His voice mail invited me to leave a message. I declined. I

56

figured he'd know what I wanted and take his time returning my call, if he ever bothered to. I'd keep trying.

I swiveled around and turned on my computer. Having my own home computer was Evie's idea, and I was still trying to get used to it.

I checked my e-mail. A dozen or so new messages had come in since last time I looked. Charlie McDevitt, J. W. Jackson, Doc Adams. Fishing reports, probably, or maybe, even better, fishing invitations. I'd read them later.

There were a couple of commercial solicitations, which I deleted without opening, and a short note from Joey, my younger son, reporting from Stanford, where he was a sophomore.

Joey was a dutiful e-mailer, though his notes rarely amounted to more than Hi-I'm-fine-how-are-you.

Billy, my older son, was a fishing guide and ski instructor in Idaho. He didn't own a computer and, as far as I could tell, rarely even had access to a telephone.

I read Joey's letter. He was still fine. He liked his classes. He was writing for the school paper.

I didn't recognize the e-mail handle of the last message. When I opened it and saw who it was from, I got a shiver.

Gordon Cahill. A message from a dead man. He'd written it at one o'clock Sunday afternoon. Less than twelve hours before he died.

"These two boll weevils, they're brothers, they grow up in the cotton fields of Alabama," his note began, without so much as a Dear Brady. "One of the boll brothers decides to head off to Hollywood and seek his fortune. The other one stays behind, eating cotton and making life miserable for the farmers. The first weevil becomes a famous movie star. The

57

second one doesn't amount to a damn thing, and he's known among his acquaintances as . . . Well, I'll tell you what he's known as when I see you tomorrow. I'm attaching some documents here for you. Look them over, and we can talk about them Monday morning. Don't forget to bring coffee and muffins. And give some thought to those weevils." He signed it "Gordie."

Damn you, I thought. *The last thing you say to me in your life has to be a pun? And a pun minus the punch line, at that?*

I smiled. It actually wasn't a bad way to remember him.

I downloaded all the documents he'd sent me, then skimmed through them. There were about two dozen pages that he'd apparently scanned into his computer. The four most recent months of Albert's MasterCard statements. Four months of phone bills—his office phone at Tufts, his cellular phone, and the home phone he shared with Ellen. Four months of bank statements for his personal checking account. The quarterly statement from his stockbroker. The previous two years' joint tax returns. A statement from a national credit bureau. A year's worth of statements from his HMO.

There were also two photographs. Both showed a small, single-story wood-shingled house set in a grove of pine trees. The first shot was taken from about a hundred yards away, looking down a sloping dirt roadway. In this one you could see the glint of a woodland pond through the pine trees beyond the house and the rise of a round mountain in the distance.

The second shot was taken through a long lens. In this photo, the house nearly filled the frame, though the glimmer of the pond behind it still showed. In this shot it was apparent that the structure had fallen into disrepair. A screened porch ran the full length of one side of the house, and the screen was torn and the corners had peeled down in a couple of places. The old white paint on the shingles was dirty and flaked. Behind the little house loomed the corner of another structure. It looked like a weather-beaten barn.

Cahill had included no explanation for this little place in the woods. No doubt he'd intended to tell me its significance when I brought him muffins.

What was the point?

I looked at the close-up photo again, and then something caught my eye. It was a shape and a color—a swatch of shiny green showing in a cluster of pine trees on the far side of the house. It was a color that didn't match the greens of the surrounding foliage.

I enlarged the photo on my computer screen, and then I knew what I was looking at.

It was a section of the rounded roofline and rear end of a Volkswagen Beetle.

Albert Stoddard drove a green Volkswagen.

Not to jump to unwarranted conclusions, but it did appear that Gordon Cahill had tracked down Albert Stoddard.

I popped up the documents on my monitor one at a time and skimmed through them again. Nothing as obvious as a green Volkswagen jumped out at me from the various collections of numbers—not surprising, since I didn't know what to look for.

At this point I didn't much care where Albert was or whether he was fooling around with boys. I cared about the fact that Gordon Cahill had been murdered.

I had no idea whether these documents that Gordie had collected in his investigation of Albert had any bearing on what had happened to him around midnight on Sunday night on Route 119 in the Willard Brook State Forest somewhere between Ashby and Townsend.

I was briefly tempted to print out the whole batch of documents and give them all to Roger Horowitz. The hell with client privilege. Gordon Cahill had been murdered.

Nope. Gordie wouldn't do it. Neither would I.

I saved everything in my hard drive, shut down my computer, leaned back in my chair, and stared up at the ceiling.

After a minute or two, I found myself smiling.

That second boll weevil, the one who didn't go to Hollywood?

The lesser of two weevils.

Bad, Gordie.

SEVEN

I slept poorly, and when I finally decided I was awake for good, it was still dark outside. I lay there for a while, staring up at the ceiling. Evie was sleeping on her belly with her leg hooked over mine. I liked the feeling of her warm smooth skin against mine and the way she sometimes hummed in the back of her throat when she slept.

After a while I slipped away from her, went downstairs, and started the coffee. Henry, who'd been snoozing on the floor beside the bed, followed me. He went over to the back door, prodded it with his nose, and whined. I let him out into the backyard.

After my shower I slipped into a pair of jeans and a sweat-shirt, poured a mug of coffee, fetched my portable telephone, pulled on a fleece jacket, and went outside to join Henry.

The sky was just beginning to turn from purple to pewter, and already some early birds were at the feeders. The nip of autumn was in the air. Pretty soon all the summer birds would be gone, and we'd be left with the year-rounders, the finches and chickadees and titmice, the juncos and nuthatches and woodpeckers, who would depend on us for their meals during the frozen months.

I sipped my coffee and thought about what I had to do. It was a little after six in the morning.

The hell with it. I dialed Ellen Stoddard's unlisted home phone number.

After four rings she answered with a throaty, "Yes?"

"Ellen," I said, "it's Brady."

"You woke me up."

"I'm sorry."

"I don't get much sleep these days, you know."

"It's kind of important."

She sighed. "I suppose it is."

"That detective I hired to follow Albert?"

She said nothing.

"He was murdered," I said.

"Oh, dear," she said.

"He was a friend of mine."

"I'm so sorry."

"I want to talk to Albert."

"You can't do that, Brady."

"Ellen, for God's sake, you're a prosecutor. You, of all people, know what needs to be done. Somebody killed a man. Albert probably has no connection to it, but—"

"Albert's not here," she said.

"What do you mean?"

"You can't talk to Albert because he's not here. I haven't seen him since Friday morning."

"Where is he?"

She sighed. "I have no idea."

"I mean," I said, "would you expect him to be there?"

"Of course I would," she said. "He's my husband. We live

together. We sleep together most nights, have breakfast most mornings and drinks before dinner and everything, just like regular married people."

"So—"

"It's not like Albert," she said. "Not like him at all." She hesitated. "Brady, why don't you come over. I think we better talk about this."

"Now?"

"Yes. Now. Before Jimmy arrives. Before I have to wiggle into my panty hose and fix my face and go read a Winnie-the-Pooh story to the third-graders at the Baker Elementary School in Dorchester and remind the reporters about my commitment to public education."

"I'll be there in less than an hour," I said.

I went into my room, fired up my computer, and printed out the two photos of the ramshackle little house in the woods that Gordon Cahill had e-mailed to me the afternoon before he died. That took ten minutes.

I wrote Evie a note and headed out. It took me another ten minutes to walk to the T station at the end of Charles Street, about fifteen minutes to ride the Red Line outbound to the Harvard Square stop, and ten more minutes to walk from the T stop to the old Federal-period hip-roofed house behind the wrought-iron fence on the quiet side street off Garden Street in Cambridge where Albert and Ellen Stoddard had lived for as long as I'd known them.

As predicted, it took me less than an hour. I was one lawyer who didn't like to be late.

As I mounted the front steps, the door opened and Ellen stepped out onto the porch. She was wearing blue sweatpants and a red Mt. Holyoke sweatshirt and white socks. No shoes, no makeup. Her hair was pulled back in a loose ponytail.

63

One curly wisp fell over her forehead. She looked about ten years younger than she did on TV.

She gave me a quick hug, then pulled me inside. "Let's go to the kitchen," she said. "I toasted some English muffins."

I followed her through the house to the kitchen in back and sat at the table.

Ellen poured us coffee, put a plate of muffins and a jar of marmalade on the table, and sat across from me.

"Ellen," I said, "about Albert—"

"First," she said, "tell me about the detective."

So I told her how Gordon Cahill's front tire had been blown out by a load of buckshot, how he'd died in a fiery crash, and how, the afternoon before that happened, he'd sent me a collection of stuff about Albert via e-mail.

Ellen was shaking her head as I talked. When I finished, she said, "You can't think Albert had anything to do with that."

"I don't know whether he did or not," I said. "But I definitely think he should talk to the police. Roger Horowitz is on the case."

"Yes," she murmured. "I know Detective Horowitz. He's dogged."

"Horowitz will make the connection to Albert sooner or later," I said. "Our best chance for keeping it, um, discreet is if Albert goes to Horowitz rather than waiting for Horowitz to catch up with Albert."

"That would mean telling Albert . . ."

"That you hired a detective to follow him. Yes, I guess it would."

"If any of this got out, Jimmy would blow a gasket."

I shrugged. "A man was murdered."

"I'm sure Albert had nothing to do with that."

64

"He's got a motive," I said.

"He's got something to hide, you think?" she said. "So he kills the private investigator who's spying on him?" She let out a short laugh. "That's absurd."

I thought about asking Ellen whether she had any suspicion that Albert was fooling around with boys, but it seemed pointless and unnecessarily hurtful.

"It's you and Jimmy who seem to think Albert might have something to hide," I said. "Many murders have been committed to protect secrets."

She shook her head. "Not Albert. He couldn't hurt anybody."

"How many gentle, mild-mannered folks have you prosecuted for murder?" I said.

She looked down at the table and shrugged. "Point taken."

"Ellen," I said, "what the hell is going on? Where's Albert?"

"I don't know."

"He's disappeared?"

"Sort of, I guess."

"Has he ever—?"

"What, disappeared?" She shrugged. "Albert goes off by himself sometimes, if that's what you mean. More often lately. Since the campaign. But you know him. He's in his own head most of the time. He goes off hunting and fishing, or looking for collections of old documents, or he gets involved in his writing, and sometimes he loses track of the time. If he doesn't come home some night, I don't think much about it. I don't necessarily expect him to call, and more often than not he doesn't. Both of us, we've always been independent like that. He's got his life, I've got mine, and they're different lives, different worlds. We've always felt that we enrich each other. We laugh sometimes about how it would be if I were an academic like him, or if he were a prosecutor like me. We figure we'd've been divorced years ago." She smiled. "Our lives intersect in a lot of places, too. It's a good marriage, Brady. Different from most. Good, though." She looked at me and smiled. "Very good."

"But . . ."

She nodded. "Recently he's been different, like I told you the other day. Maybe it's just the campaign. Hiring the detective was Jimmy's idea."

"You haven't seen him since when?"

"Friday morning. We sat right here and had breakfast together."

"Did he say anything?"

"We talked about the Middle East, as I recall."

"Nothing about his plans for the weekend?"

She shook her head. "He teaches Tuesdays and Thursdays. His weekends start on Friday and go through Monday. Lately, with my schedule, we might not see each other for a day or two over the weekend."

"So maybe that's all it is," I said. "He took a long weekend, went fishing or something."

"Maybe," she said.

I looked at her. "You don't sound convinced."

"Today's Tuesday," she said. "He's got a nine o'clock class this morning. He should've been home last night."

"So you *are* worried."

She nodded. "I suppose I am. What happened to that detective, that makes me worry more."

"Do you have any reason to believe . . . ?"

"What?" she said. "That Albert could be in some kind of trouble?"

66

"If not in trouble," I said, "in danger."

"He's an historian, for God's sake. An absentminded college professor."

I took a bite of English muffin and said nothing.

"I don't know what to think, Brady," she said after a minute. "He's never been away for four days and nights without telling me."

"Do you have any idea where he might've gone?"

"No."

"Might he have slept in his office at Tufts?"

She rolled her eyes. "He doesn't even have a sofa in his office."

I reached into my shirt picket, took out the pictures of the house in the woods that Gordon Cahill had e-mailed to me, and unfolded them on the table.

She glanced at the pictures, then looked up. "Where'd you get these?"

"Our detective e-mailed them to me the day before he was killed."

"Why?"

It's where Albert brings his boys, I was thinking. But I kept that thought to myself.

"Do you recognize this place?" I said.

She peered at the pictures for a moment, then looked up at me. "Yes and no," she said.

"Huh?"

"No, I don't actually recognize the place," she said. "I've never been there. But yes, I know about it, assuming it's the place I think it is."

"And what place is that?"

"Albert's retreat. His hunting camp, he calls it."

"His cave," I said.

She smiled. "Exactly. His grandfather built it, and then it was his father's, and now it's Albert's. It was a place where the men in his family went to get away from the women." She smiled. "An old Stoddard family tradition, according to Albert. Makes perfectly good sense to me."

"So Albert's a hunter?"

"Birds," she said. "Grouse, pheasants, ducks. He and my father used to hunt together."

"Where's this place located?"

"I'm not exactly sure. Somewhere near where Albert grew up, I assume."

"Where was that?"

"Southwick, New Hampshire."

"Never heard of it."

"No reason you should. It's your typical old New England mill town off some back roads in southwestern New Hampshire near Mount Monadnock, and you probably wouldn't go there unless you got lost. Southwick has a general store and an old inn and a couple of antique shops, and not much else. Albert took me there once before we got married and showed me around. Said he needed for me to understand his roots. As I remember, it was mostly hills and ponds and dirt roads and pine woods and stone walls and a few dairy farms and apple orchards. In some surprising places you'd suddenly come upon a beautiful eighteenth-century brick colonial or a rambling old farmhouse that some rich people had fixed up. I liked it around there. It's a pretty area. Reminded me of the way New England used to be a hundred years ago." She shrugged. "It's probably changed since then. Albert's family is all gone, and we never went back." She looked up at me. "I haven't gone back, anyway. Maybe Albert has.

Maybe that's where he goes on weekends when he . . . when he goes away."

"I'm pretty sure it is," I said. I placed my forefinger under the tiny blob of greenish yellow. "See this?"

She bent close to the print. "What is it?"

"I enlarged it on my computer. It looks like the roof of a Volkswagen Beetle."

"It looks like Albert's car," said Ellen. "When was this photo taken?"

"Friday or Saturday."

"So that's where he is," she said.

"It's where he was on Friday or Saturday, apparently."

In my head, I popped up a mental map of New England and tried to figure how I might drive from Boston to Mount Monadnock in southwestern New Hampshire. There were a lot of ways to get there. One fairly direct route would take me through the Willard Brook State Forest between Townsend and Ashby, Massachusetts.

"Does Albert own shotguns?" I said.

Ellen looked at me. "You're not thinking . . ."

I didn't say anything.

She nodded. "Yes, as a matter of fact. He has quite a collection of shotguns. He considers them works of art. Shotguns are very expensive. They're Albert's only extravagance." She paused, then added, "As far as I know."

"He's a hunter, you said."

"Birds. He doesn't hunt animals."

"You hunt birds with shotguns."

"Well, sure. He uses some of his guns for hunting, I guess. I never paid much attention. Doesn't seem to me he's done much hunting in recent years. Albert and my father used to

69

go hunting together. Once in a while he came home with a couple of ducks or something, and when he did, he cooked them himself. He always made a production out of it. Said that preparing the birds he'd shot elegantly and eating them ceremoniously was a way of honoring them. He cooked wild rice and found some fresh asparagus and bought an expensive wine, and I must say, they were unfailingly delicious." Ellen narrowed her eyes at me. "I know what you're thinking, Brady Coyne. It's crazy."

"One of us has to be objective," I said.

"Albert keeps his shotguns locked up in a steel cabinet in the basement. He's got the key."

"Maybe he keeps one at his camp," I said.

"Maybe he does. I don't know. But even if he does . . ."

"I need to talk to him," I said. "The sooner the better."

"Well," she said, "I wish you would. You might be thinking about who blew out that poor man's tire with a shotgun, but that's not what I'm thinking about."

"I know."

"Brady," said Ellen, "will you find Albert for me?"

"I don't know if I will," I said. "But I'll try."

EIGHT

By the time I got home from my visit with Ellen, Evie had already left for work. On the bottom of the note I'd written for her she'd scribbled: "Tonight's my turn," followed by several X's and O's.

That meant she loved me and would take care of dinner.

I put on a fresh pot of coffee, and while it was brewing I opened my big Rand McNally Road Atlas. I flipped to the index for New Hampshire and ran my finger down the list of New Hampshire towns. Southwick wasn't listed. It puzzled me until I deduced that towns with populations under five hundred didn't qualify for mention in the Rand McNally index. I guess you've got to draw the line somewhere.

I turned to the state map and finally located Southwick about halfway between Keene and Peterborough in the southwestern quadrant of the state. Just one road—it didn't even have a route number—passed through the town. There appeared to be no straightforward way to get to Southwick from Boston. A series of state highways and secondary roads that included Route 119 through the Willard Brook State

Forest in north-central Massachusetts looked as direct as any.

I figured it would take a little over two hours to drive from Boston to Southwick no matter what route I took, although in late September on those winding two-lane country roadways if you found yourself behind a caravan of station wagons full of out-of-state foliage worshipers—we New Englanders called them "leaf peepers"—it could add an hour to the journey.

By now it was a few minutes after nine, so I called Julie at the office. My only appointment for the day, she said, was the Randolph St. George divorce, and he wasn't due until eleven-thirty. I told her that's when I'd be there, and when I was done with St. George I'd probably leave for the afternoon.

She didn't even argue with me. Since Evie and I started living together, my formerly slave-driving secretary had become somewhat more tolerant of my halfhearted commitment to hanging around the office, hustling for new clients, and accruing billable hours. Julie valued romantic love and domestic bliss above billable hours, even, and I guess she figured that since I'd "settled down," as she put it, working at home was a respectable alternative to going to the office, as long as I could convince her that I actually worked.

Well, I was grateful for her new attitude. It made no sense to me, of course. But I never pretended to understand how women think.

After I hung up, I poured a mug of coffee, fired up my computer, and printed out all the documents Gordon Cahill had e-mailed to me. When I finished I had a stack of papers half an inch thick.

Then I went looking for the Southwick, New Hampshire, connection.

I started with Albert's phone bills. From his office at Tufts he'd made several calls to Durham, New Hampshire, and a couple of others to Hanover, in the previous three months. The University of New Hampshire was in Durham, which was over toward the seacoast on the opposite side of the state from Southwick. Dartmouth College was in Hanover on the Vermont border, more than seventy miles north and west of Southwick.

I discounted those calls. I figured Albert talked with colleagues in the history departments of many universities in many states, and calls he'd made to Ithaca, Ann Arbor, South Bend, Austin, Berkeley, and a dozen or so other college towns confirmed it.

He'd made no other phone calls to anywhere in New Hampshire from either his home or his office. The phone bills didn't list calls he might have received, of course.

Four months' worth of credit-card receipts showed not a single purchase charged in the state of New Hampshire. As well as I could determine, Albert paid cash for the gas he put into his car, so I couldn't tell where he'd been.

His bank statements included photocopies of every check Albert had written in the previous four months. Not one check had been made out to a New Hampshire business or deposited in a New Hampshire bank. Nor had he made any unusually large deposits into or withdrawals from his accounts.

By now I had a stiff neck and eyestrain. Poring over documents and interpreting the significance in them was an important part of the private investigator's job. Gordon Cahill and other gumshoes I knew constantly complained about the tedium of their work. I didn't envy them. We lawyers spent a lot of time squinting at musty old lawbooks and agonizing over the difference between a semicolon and a comma, but I wouldn't think of swapping jobs with any PI.

I wondered if Cahill had intended to point out something in these documents that explained Albert's "weird" behavior recently. If so, I couldn't see it.

I certainly saw nothing to suggest that Albert was hiding something worth committing murder to keep secret.

I ended up with two possible conclusions: One, Albert's visits to his New Hampshire hunting camp were no more than what they appeared to be—innocent weekend getaways; or, two, Albert had been scrupulous about covering his tracks. He could've made phone calls from a pay phone or cell phone. He could've paid for everything in cash.

I hoped it was the former. I knew I'd feel a lot better if I was positive that Gordon Cahill hadn't died doing the job I'd hired him for.

So would Ellen Stoddard.

I glanced at my watch. Ten-thirty. I went back to the phone records and dialed the number for Albert's office at Tufts.

It rang five or six times before his voice mail answered. I didn't leave a message.

The phone book gave me the central number for Tufts University in Medford. I rang it and asked to be connected to the history department.

A woman answered, said I'd reached the history department and her name was Terri. She sounded downright cheerful.

I asked to speak to Professor Stoddard.

"He's not here right now," Terri said. "Do you want his voice mail?"

"I tried his office," I said. "He wasn't there. I need to speak to him directly. It's important."

"I can leave a message in his box, if you want."

"Have you seen him today?"

"Um, no. But I think he has a class this morning. Hold on a minute . . . yes. Colonial History, nine to ten-fifteen. He's supposed to be having his office hours now. You tried his office, you say?"

"I did, yes. Do you know if he was in class?"

"Well," she said, "he didn't call to say he wouldn't be. Wait a minute. Nellie?" It sounded as if she'd lowered the phone, but I could hear her say, "You had Colonial with Dr. Stoddard today, right?"

I heard another voice, too muffled to understand, and a moment later Terri said to me, "Hm. He didn't show up for class. That's not like him, not to call in."

"It's not?"

"No. Professor Stoddard is very conscientious. Well, did you want to leave a message?"

"Tell him to call his wife," I said.

I took Henry for a leg-stretcher on the Common, and when we got back home, I changed into my office pinstripe, stuffed my jeans and sneakers into an athletic bag, and started for the door.

Henry was sitting there looking at me.

"Not today," I said to him.

He stood up and prodded the door with his nose. His little stubby tail was a whir.

"It's the athletic bag, isn't it?" I said to him.

He sat down, cocked his head, and perked up his ears.

"Oh, okay," I said. "I could use the company."

So Henry heeled along beside me while I retrieved my car from the garage on Charles Street, where I rented a space by the month, and he rode in the backseat while I drove to my parking garage in Copley Square, and he heeled again from the garage to my office.

We got there in time for Henry to curl up on my old sweatshirt in the corner, and for me to be sitting at my desk pretending to study legal documents, the very model of a busy Boston barrister, when Randolph St. George, my day's only appointment, arrived at eleven-thirty.

Randy and Susan, his wife of twenty-nine years, were divorcing. Massachsetts is a no-fault state, so the reasons for the St. Georges' split were legally irrelevant. Still, they were emotionally critical to Randy. A week after the wedding of their youngest daughter, Susan told him that she'd put up with him without complaint for all those years, and now she wasn't going to do it anymore. She'd already talked to an attorney. The papers were being drawn up.

Randy claimed he never saw it coming. The first time he came to me, he was steaming with fire and brimstone. He wanted to fight it.

I reminded him that it didn't work that way. In Massachusetts, if one party wants a divorce from the other, it happens. All that's left is working out the details of the settlement.

Randy said okay, fine. She wanted a settlement? He'd give her nothing. How's that for a damn settlement?

I told him it didn't work that way, either.

So over the past couple of months there had been a lot of back-and-forthing between me and Barbara Cooper, Susan's lawyer, working out the details, and what it finally came down to was the collection of watercolors by various semi-well-known Cape Cod artists that Randy had given to Susan over the years as birthday, anniversary, and Christmas presents.

Randy claimed that since he'd bought them, by God, they were rightfully his and he intended to have them.

Susan, of course, claimed that inasmuch as Randy had given them to her, they were hers, and she had no intention of relinquishing them.

Well, divorce always has that effect on people.

When Julie ushered Randy St. George into my office, he was, as usual, huffing and puffing in wounded indignation. The issue for Randy wasn't really a collection of watercolors. It was the inconceivable absurdity of the notion that any woman would not want to be married to him.

I let him vent for about five minutes. Then I said, "She's not going to change her mind, you know."

"It's ridiculous," he grumbled.

"Doesn't matter. We've got a date at Concord District Court, and on that day, which is a little over a month from now, November 3, a Thursday, at ten A.M., regardless of how ridiculous it is or what you want, you're going to get divorced. All that's left is the division of assets."

"I want those damn watercolors," he said.

"So does Susan," I said. "We got two choices. You and Susan can agree on what to do with them before November 3, or we can have a trial and let Judge Kolb decide."

"Fuck it," said Randy. "Let's have a trial."

"Knowing Judge Kolb," I said, "he'll just send us out to the lobby to work it out, and if we can't, he'll bring us back into court and make us argue about it for a long time in excruciating detail, and when we're done, he'll give all the paintings to Susan. Judge Kolb gets irritated whenever these things aren't ironed out ahead of time, and he's a notorious wife's judge, so he'll probably give Susan a lot of other stuff you thought you were going to keep, too. Meanwhile, Attorney Cooper and I will pile up a lot of billable hours arguing our old arguments that won't get us anywhere."

Randy ran the palm of his hand over his bald head. "So I get screwed no matter what. I'm losing my wife, and I'm losing my possessions, and it's costing me a shitload of money."

I nodded. "It's the way of the world, I'm afraid." I leaned across the conference table and tapped his arm. "Look," I said, "it's time to put aside all the hurt feelings and the self-righteous indignation and the vindictiveness. Let's settle this thing, huh?"

Randy frowned. "You're my lawyer. You're supposed to stand up for my rights."

"Well," I said, "as I've been trying to tell you for two months now, your legal claim to those paintings is questionable at best. An old friend of mine used to say, 'When you're right, go for the kill. When you're wrong, go for the compromise.' You're pretty much wrong here. But I bet we can convince Susan to compromise on the watercolors."

"Hm," he said. "Compromise. Goes against my grain."

"Then let's just give her the damn paintings and be done with it."

He waved that idea away with the back of his hand. "I spent a lot of money on those things."

I shrugged.

After a minute Randy said, "Compromise how?"

"Pretty obvious," I said. "You take half the collection, she takes the other half."

"That's not compromising," he said. "That's admitting defeat."

"Well, then," I said, "we could cut each painting up the middle, give each of you half. Judge Kolb would love that."

"Be serious," he said.

"I am serious."

"That's ridiculous."

"Think about it." I sat back, folded my arms, and looked at him.

Randy glowered back at me for a minute. Then he shook his head and smiled. "Damn you, you're plagiarizing from the Old Testament."

I shrugged. "I happen to know that Judge Kolb is a big fan of the Old Testament. So what do you think Susan would say?"

Randy let out a long breath and nodded. "She loves those damn paintings. She'd rather I had them than they got ruined."

"Let her have them, then," I said.

"I hate to lose," he growled.

"If it's your idea," I said, "it's not losing."

He looked up at the ceiling for a minute. Then he leaned back in his chair and sighed. "Okay. Fuck it. She can have the damn watercolors. I wouldn't know what to do with them anyway. I don't even like them. Seagulls and sand dunes and old rowboats and shit."

"You want to think about it for a couple days?"

He hesitated. "You think Susan's going to change her mind?"

"About the divorce, you mean?"

He nodded.

"No," I said. "Susan's got her mind made up."

Randy waved the back of his hand. "I don't want to think about any of this crap anymore. Let's just get it over with."

"I'll give Attorney Cooper a call, then," I said. "We'll work out some language for it."

"I hope she appreciates it," said Randy.

"Attorney Cooper?"

"Susan," he said.

"I'm sure she will," I said. "But it's not going to change her mind about divorcing you."

After I walked Randy to the door, I went back into my office and changed into my jeans and sneakers. Henry roused himself from his midday snooze, took a few laps at the water dish Julie kept full for him, and looked at me with big hopeful eyes. He always assumed that jeans and sneakers for me meant an adventure for him.

I told him to be patient. If he behaved, we'd go somewhere in the car.

With that, he promptly lay down in front of the door and plopped his chin on his paws.

The word "car" was one of those magic dog words that bore deep and complex meaning for Henry. "Dinner" and "run" and "outside" were others. These magic words, I imagined, conjured up in his mind entire sagas. They contained the collective unconscious of his species. They were imbedded deep in his DNA and had been passed down through countless generations of Brittany spaniels.

Well, maybe not. Brittanies, after all, originated in the

province of Brittany where French had always been the primary language.

Pavlovian conditioning, more likely.

I called Evie's office, and when her secretary gave me her voice mail, I told her that I had Henry with me, that I wasn't sure what time I'd be home, but that I hoped she wouldn't eat supper without me, and especially that I loved her.

When Henry and I went out to the reception area, Julie looked me up and down. "You're really leaving, huh?"

I nodded.

"Going fishing, are we?"

"Sort of."

She narrowed her eyes at me. "You're off sleuthing again, aren't you?"

"Yes," I said, "I guess I am."

"And which client is this for?"

"It's not really for a client," I said. "It's—"

Julie held up her hand. "You going to be gone for a week, like you were that time when Evie ran off, or that other time you went to Maine, almost got yourself killed? Or is this one of those adventures where you're going to keep calling me every day telling me to cancel your appointments? I just need to know."

"I'll be in the office tomorrow, bright and early."

She nodded skeptically. "Or else you'll call, right?"

"Right," I said. "I'll keep you posted. Definitely."

She rolled her eyes. "Did you talk to Evie?"

"I left her a message. Told her I loved her, might be a few minutes late for supper."

"Well," said Julie, "I suppose that's progress."

And on that relatively positive note, Henry and I got the hell out of there.

NINE

I opened the sunroof so Henry could stretch his neck and snuffle the breeze, loaded the CD player with Beethoven piano concerti, and aimed my BMW at Southwick, New Hampshire.

This promised to be one more in a long series of Brady Coyne wild-goose chases, windmill jousts, and white-whale hunts. But Gordon Cahill's death—make that murder—was a leaden weight in my heart. I needed to know if it was connected to the job I'd given him, and the only way I could think of to learn that was to talk to Albert Stoddard.

If I was going to talk to Albert, I had to find him. The only way I knew to find him was to find his hunting camp in or near Southwick and hope he was there, hiding out from the turmoil of his wife's campaign, fishing in his pond, maybe, or reading an old history book, or writing a new one. If I knew Albert, he'd be amused when I told him that Jimmy D'Ambrosio had asked me to hire a PI to tail him, and he'd surely be saddened to learn that Gordon Cahill had been killed.

In the back of my mind, of course, I acknowledged the possibility that Albert knew all about it.

Okay, the possibility, even, that Cahill had caught Albert doing something scandalous and unforgiveable in his hunting camp, and that Albert had murdered him.

The fact that he had skipped class troubled me.

From Charles Street I curled onto Storrow Drive, which took me along the Charles River and past Fresh Pond and the Alewife T station to Route 2, where the afternoon rush-hour traffic had not yet thickened, and from there I had clear sailing.

At the rotary in Concord I turned onto 2A, and a little over an hour after I'd pulled out of my parking garage, I found myself entering the Willard Brook State Forest on Route 119 west of Townsend. Here the woods were dark and cool. The roadway was lined with tall pines and maples and oaks that arched overhead, forming a narrow, shaded tunnel. The road twisted and turned back on itself as it followed the random meanderings of the rocky little brook that gave the forest its name.

By now Henry was pacing in the backseat, so I pulled into a picnic area and let him out. He headed straight for the brook and flopped on his belly in the shallow water. I sat at a picnic table and waited for him. Henry drank lying down, then stood up, shook a shower of water out of his fur, and peed on several tree trunks.

When we headed back to the car, Henry was soaked. I always kept my old army blanket spread over the back seat for him. He knew that the front seats were off-limits. We had a territorial understanding about the car, Henry and I. He'd probably growl at me if I tried to sit in back. A couple growls from me early in our relationship had established the front as mine.

I pulled back onto the road and continued on. I drove slowly. I was looking for the place where a load of buckshot had blown out Gordon Cahill's left front tire and he'd swerved off the pavement and slammed into the tree. I was heading west. According to Roger Horowitz, Gordie had been traveling east—heading home to Boston, I assumed, from wherever he'd been—the night he died, so I expected to see a ring of yellow crime-scene tape somewhere alongside the eastbound lane on my left.

I'd've missed it entirely if it hadn't been for the pair of black rubber skid tracks that were burned into the pavement in front of me. They began to my left in the eastbound lane and veered acutely across my side of the road, and it was easy to visualize the little tan Corolla traveling at high speed suddenly losing control, and Gordie standing on his brakes and fighting the wheel as he skidded and squealed across the incoming lane.

There was no crime-scene tape. Either the state police experts had finished their investigation here, or else Roger Horowitz had been unable to convince them that the scene was worth securing and investigating. By the time they'd figured out that a load of buckshot had blown out Gordie's front tire, it would've been too late.

I pulled over a hundred feet past the place where the burnt rubber angled across the pavement, told Henry to wait in the car, got out, and walked back.

I wasn't the first one who'd tromped around there. The soft sandy shoulder was trampled with footprints. EMTs working to get Cahill out, tow-truck operators hooking up the blackened corpse of the Corolla, cops poking around for evidence, passersby sating their morbid curiosities.

Even with all the footprints, you couldn't miss the pair of deep troughs in the sand where Cahill's little car had slewed off the pavement. They ended abruptly at a white scar about bumper-high on a pine tree that was as thick as a telephone pole.

There were shards of glass and flakes of chrome scattered on the ground at the base of the tree. But what struck me was the rectangular patch of black on the sand. It was roughly the shape of a small car—a small car that had spilled its gasoline and burned with enough heat to sear the sandy soil.

As I interpreted it, Cahill's Corolla had hit the tree so hard that it actually bounced back two or three feet—with enough force, I guessed, to rupture the gas tank. The gasoline spilled onto the sand, and some spark from the engine ignited it, and it exploded in a great, sudden, black-and-orange ball of flame—with Gordie behind the wheel, cocooned and imprisoned by his air bag and his seat belt.

I wondered if he was still alive then, if it was the flames and the heat that killed him.

I hoped to hell he was unconscious, at least, when he gasped fire into his lungs.

Well, maybe it hadn't happened that way. But that's how I imagined it, and it made me shudder.

The medical examiner would know, and I intended to convince Roger Horowitz to tell me, even if it meant promising him information I couldn't—or wouldn't—give him. I could always renege.

I scooched there beside the road thinking about Gordon

Cahill and imagining the horror of what had happened to him. If I'd had any reluctance to do whatever was necessary to find Albert Stoddard and learn what I could about where Gordie had been and what he'd been doing on the Sunday night he went up in flames, seeing this place dispelled it.

I just needed to know if Gordie had been on Albert's case the night he died.

I went back to my car and slid behind the wheel. Henry licked the back of my neck. He was happy to see me. I was happy to see him, too. I reached behind me and patted his muzzle. It felt good to be loved unconditionally. It felt very good to be alive.

I started up the car, pulled back onto the road, and resumed my trek to Southwick, New Hampshire, backtracking Gordie's route, I assumed. Route 119 emerged from the western end of the Willard Brook State Forest at Route 31, which went south to north. I turned right, heading north, and entered New Hampshire a few minutes later. When I got to Route 101, an east-west highway that paralleled the Massachusetts border about twenty miles into New Hampshire, I went left—westerly.

A few minutes later, as I approached Mount Monadnock and the range of lesser mountains around it, the highway began climbing and then descending through some foothills. I remembered that on Saturday when I talked to Cahill on his cell phone, he said he was driving in some hills, and we'd eventually lost our connection.

I figured these were those hills.

Assuming I was tracing his route, assuming Gordie knew what he was doing, and assuming he'd been looking for Albert Stoddard that day, it was a good bet he'd been heading to Southwick, most likely to Albert's hunting lodge on the pond, where he took some photos and later e-mailed them to me.

When I found myself approaching the outskirts of Peterborough I pulled over and conferred with Rand McNally. According to Mr. McNally, the way to Southwick involved several secondary roads and many turns. I studied the route until I had it memorized.

A woman would have asked directions. Not me. We guys pride ourselves on our map-reading skills and our uncanny sense of direction. We never get lost.

Sometimes we discover creative ways to get there. But we always know where we're going.

The countryside approaching Southwick was pastoral as hell, especially now, in late September, with the peak of the foliage season only a week or two away. The serpentine two-lane roads were lined with ancient stone walls and clumps of white birches and giant sugar maples aglow in scarlet and gold. In places the rolling wooded landscape opened to a sloping green pasture where a few cows or horses or sheep grazed under the watchful eyes of a two-hundred-year-old farmhouse and a weathered, tin-roofed barn.

The winding road into Southwick followed alongside a rocky stream. I found it hard to keep my eyes off the water. The stream was running low, but even so, I spotted some delicious little runs and pools that had to harbor trout. Brookies, maybe, New England's only native trout. The male fish would be in their spawning colors, more beautiful even than the New England autumn foliage that reflected on the water.

I drove slowly. The stream passed under narrow bridges in a few places where dirt roads cut away from the paved road I was driving on, and it was hard to resist the temptation to turn onto one of those dirt roads and stop, get out of my car, and peer over the bridge railing. Surely I'd spot a trout or two.

I always kept an old fiberglass fly rod and a box of trout flies and a pair of hip boots in my trunk for unexpected trout streams. You should never spit in the face of serendipity.

Well, maybe on my way home . . .

The village of Southwick appeared without warning. One minute I was driving alongside trout streams and past meadows and through forests, and the next minute I found myself in what I guessed was the heart of the village, such as it was.

Southwick was as Ellen remembered it—tiny and quiet and postcard-pretty—and once again I was struck by the many different worlds that lay within a two-hour drive of my townhouse on Beacon Hill in the heart of the city.

Like many New England villages, Southwick was an old mill town that had grown up on the banks of running water. Sometime back in the early nineteenth century, the little stream that paralleled the road I'd followed into town had been dammed to provide water power for a factory. The old red-brick building that had housed the town's industry was still there, rising straight up from the banks of a pretty millpond. Now the margins of the pond were a little manicured park, with fieldstone paths and well-mulched flower gardens and mowed grass.

According to a sign, the old factory building that overlooked the millpond had been converted into an independent-living facility. During the Civil War they had manufactured gunpowder there.

I crept through the town, taking its measure. The window in the general store promised beer and wine, night crawlers and shiners, newspapers and rental videos, along with its very own ATM machine. The carved sign hanging in front of the Southwick Inn across the street announced that it had been accommodating wayfarers since 1789. There was a real estate office, a two-bay auto-repair shop, a Congregational church, a garden store, a library. I counted two antique shops and one art gallery. On a little round hill overlooking a cemetery studded with weathered headstones stood a big square white building that had once probably been a grange hall and now, according to the sign, housed both the town offices and the police station.

Beyond the cemetery, the town's main drag sloped down the hill and curved back into the forest.

And that, apparently, was the entire village of Southwick.

I wondered what the kids did for excitement.

TEN

I parked in front of the general store, opened all the windows a crack for Henry, and got out. A middle-aged couple were sitting on the bench in front with their heads together, drinking bottled water and studying a road map. Out-of-staters, I guessed, trying to figure out how they'd ended up at this place, or how to find their way out of it.

I looked around, and my eyes settled on the real estate office across the street. If anybody knew where an old house on a local pond was located, it should be a real estate person. How many houses and ponds could there be in a town the size of Southwick?

The office was located in a lovely old brick colonial. A bell dinged when I went through the front door and stepped into the empty reception area.

A minute later a slim fiftyish woman wearing tailored slacks and a red sweater appeared from around a corner. A pair of glasses was perched on top of her head. "Hi, there," she said. "I'm Carol. Can I do something for you?" She was pretty and blond and had what I guessed was a New Jersey accent. New York, maybe. Certainly not New Hampshire.

I told her my name, and we shook hands. "I'm afraid I'm not in the market for real estate," I said.

"You're not the only one," she said. "You lost?"

"Well," I said, "I wouldn't have said so. But I'm looking for a place, and I don't know where it is, so maybe I'm lost at that."

She smiled. "Try me."

I pulled out the two pictures of Albert's hunting camp and spread them on top of the unoccupied receptionist's desk. "Does this look familiar?"

She put her glasses on and peered at the pictures. Then she looked up at me and shrugged. "I don't recognize it. You think it's in Southwick?"

"It might be. I'm pretty sure it's somewhere around here."

She touched the pond on one of the pictures. "Doesn't look like any of our ponds."

"You have many ponds in Southwick?"

"Four," she said, "not counting the millpond. One's the town pond with the swimming beach out past the cemetery. This isn't that one. Two of our ponds you can't get to except by hiking through the woods. No buildings on any of them." She smiled up at me. "My husband's big on portaging canoes. He drags me to these places."

"What about the fourth pond?" I said.

"Oh, a road goes all the way around that one. It's lined solid with cottages. I've sold a bunch of them, actually, mostly to folks from Connecticut and New York. Not recently, though." She smiled. "You want motorboats, water skis, Finn Pond's your place. You can see"—she pointed again at the picture—"this one is nothing like Finn Pond."

"I guess it's not in Southwick, then," I said.

92

"I'm sure it's not," she said.

Well, that would've been too easy. "The place I'm looking for belongs to a man named Albert Stoddard," I said. "Does that name ring a bell?"

"Does he live here in town?"

"No. His family's from here, though. This camp, it was in his family."

Carol frowned. "Stoddard," she mumbled. "Same name as that woman who's running for election in Massachusetts?"

"Yes," I said. "Same name. She's running for the Senate."

"I've seen her on TV," said Carol. "A Democrat, right?"

"Yes. So what about Albert?"

"Nope." She shook her head. "I don't recall any Stoddard family in town. But, hey. I don't know everybody. Let's try the phone book."

"That's inspired," I said.

She pulled out a rather thin phone book, flipped through it, and ran her finger down a page. Then she looked up at me and shrugged. "No Stoddards in Southwick or any of our adjoining towns."

"I know my friend grew up here in Southwick," I said. "I assume this camp is somewhere around here."

"You should talk to Harris and Dub," she said. "The Goff brothers. They run the auto shop down the street. Local characters. They know everybody and everything. There've been Goffs living in Southwick since the Pilgrims, practically." She smiled. "Me, I've only been here twelve years. As far as the local folks are concerned, I'm still that brassy broad from Pennsylvania, and I guess I always will be."

Pennsylvania. I would've sworn New Jersey. Northeastern Pennsylvania, no doubt.

I folded the pictures, stuffed them in my shirt pocket, and

started to thank Carol when the front door opened and the bell dinged and a young couple came in, followed by a lanky sixtyish woman wearing a flowered dress and sandals. They were all laughing about something.

"Helen," said Carol, "got a minute?"

"Just about one," said the woman. She had sharp blue eyes and a long iron-gray braid and a tanned, weathered face. "We need to make a phone call, check a couple things on the computer. What's up?"

"This is Mr. Coyne from Boston," said Carol. "He's got a question." To me she said, "Helen's lived in this neck of the woods all her life."

Helen smiled and held out her hand. I shook it. She had a manly grip and a no-nonsense manner. "What's your question, Mr. Coyne?"

Her clients hovered behind her. I sensed she was hot on the track of a sale.

I took out the picture of Albert's camp with the pond in the background and spread it on the desk for Helen. "I'm looking for this place. I think it's around here somewhere. Carol says it's not in Southwick. Maybe in some nearby town?"

She put her hands flat on the desk and bent to look at it. She frowned, then looked up at me. "I don't recognize it. There are lots of ponds around here."

"The camp belongs to a friend of mine named Albert Stoddard," I said. "It was in his family. Albert grew up here in Southwick."

Helen glanced back at her clients, then smiled quickly at me. "There was a Stoddard family in Southwick, oh, twenty-five, thirty years ago, as I recall. They moved away."

I started to ask Helen if she'd heard anything about Albert

since then, or if she realized that it was his wife who was running for U.S. senator from Massachusetts, or if she had any suggestions for how I might locate his camp, but she had already turned to her clients and was ushering them into an office. At the doorway, she glanced back over her shoulder, gave me a quick shrug, went in, and closed the door behind her.

"Well, hm," said Carol, "that was kind of rude."

"No, that's all right," I said. "She's busy."

"Still . . ." She shook her head. "Business has been awfully slow lately," she said. "Me, I try to take the long view, but Helen worries. The fall's normally our best season, but that couple are the first hot clients either of us has had in about three weeks. I apologize for her. She's usually friendlier."

"No problem," I said. "You've been very nice."

"Not very helpful, though."

"I'll try the Goff brothers. Harry and Bub, was it?"

She smiled. "Harris. Harris and Dub. You'll find them, um, amusing. Don't be fooled. They both went to college."

"I'll keep it in mind." I lifted my hand. "Thanks for every-thing."

I went back to the car and got in. Henry was snoozing on the backseat. He opened his eyes, yawned at me, then closed them again. Henry liked the car and didn't mind being left alone in it. He knew I'd always be back.

I could have walked to the Goff brothers' garage, but I liked to keep my car in sight when Henry was with me. It was a two-minute drive.

I parked out front by a pair of old gas pumps that were no longer in operation. Environmental laws have made the old-fashioned gas pumps obsolete, and only the wealthy mul-tinational companies can afford to update them, so many

95

small family-owned gas stations have either shut down or been bought out.

Good for the environment, bad for small business. It's the way of the modern world. Somehow, environmental laws never seem to cause big multinational corporations too much suffering.

The Goff brothers apparently had managed to stay in business without selling gas. The side lot was littered with vehicles. Many were quite old, and a large percentage of them were pickup trucks, although there was an interesting mixture of Ford Escorts, Volvos, several species of SUVs, and at least one Jaguar.

The garage itself was a peeling old white two-story clapboard structure, with an office area on the left side and two bays on the right. There were curtains in the upstairs windows. A Coke machine stood against the outside wall next to the office door. A sign over the bays said GOFF'S GARAGE. The doors to the bays were up, and from inside came loud rock music. A Dell Shannon song, if I wasn't mistaken.

I opened the office door. No one was there, so I went around to the bays. There were two lifts with cars on them, and under each car was a man digging and poking at the undersides of the engines. Both men had black beards streaked with gray and wore workboots and greasy overalls with raggedy T-shirts underneath. One had thinning gray hair. The other wore a backward Red Sox cap and rimless glasses. I guessed they were both in their early fifties.

I stood there for a minute, but neither of the men seemed to notice me.

"Excuse me?" I said.

The music was very loud, so I stepped inside, and in a louder voice I repeated, "Hello?"

96

The man with the cap and glasses craned his neck around and peered at me. Then he returned his attention to the engine he was working on.

"Sir?" I said. "You got a minute?"

"Hold your horses," he mumbled without looking at me.

The man under the other car, the one with the thinning hair, turned to look at me. Then he went back to what he was doing.

A minute later the one with the glasses came over. He wiped his hands on the seat of his overalls. "You got a problem?" he said.

"Not with my car," I said. "Carol over at the real estate office said you might be able to help me."

He leaned around me and looked at my car. "Beemer, huh? How do you like it?"

"I like it a lot."

"Folks think Beemers're yuppie cars," he said. "You a yuppie?"

"I'm too old to be a yuppie."

"They're good cars," he said. "Don't listen to 'em."

"I try not to." I smiled. "My name's Brady Coyne," I said. "From Boston."

He looked at his greasy hand, shrugged, and held it out. A test, maybe.

I shook it without hesitation.

"Dub Goff," he said. "That"—he jerked his head toward the other man—"that's my kid brother Harris. He's the one give me this name. Dub. Short for Dubber. How he said 'brother' when he was little, and I got stuck with it. Name's actually Lyndon. You had a name like Lyndon, you wouldn't mind so much being called Dub. So Carol sent you over, huh?"

97

I nodded. "She said you and your brother have lived around here for a long time."

"Too long," he said.

I took out the picture of Albert's camp. "Recognize this place?"

Dub Goff glanced at the picture, then turned his head and yelled, "Hey, Harris. Turn off that goddamn radio and come over here."

A minute later the radio went off and Harris Goff was standing beside Dub wiping his fingers on a rag that looked dirtier than his hands. "Take a look at this," said Dub.

Harris looked at the picture, then looked at Dub. "That's Stoddard's old camp, ain't it?"

"You're right," I said. "Can you tell me how I can find it?"

"You a friend of Albert's?" said Harris.

I nodded.

"So how come you don't know where his camp is?"

"I'm actually more a friend of his wife," I said.

"His wife, huh?" Harris looked at Dub. They exchanged grins.

"That's right," I said.

"So you're not Albert's friend."

"Sure," I said. "I'm Albert's friend, too."

"But you never been to his camp?" said Harris.

"No," I said. "You guys know him, though, huh?"

"Albert?" said Dub. "He grew up here, we grew up here. Hard not to know him, whether you wanted to or not."

"You saying you didn't want to know him?"

"Saying nothing like that," said Dub. "Albert Stoddard didn't matter one way or another. He was younger than us. We didn't hang out together."

98

"Have you seen him lately?"

"You lookin' for him, or for his camp?" said Harris.

"Both," I said. "Either."

"Well," said Harris, "couldn't tell you where Albert might be, but I s'pose we know where Albert's camp is, don't we, Dubber?"

"Yep," said Dub. "S'pose we do."

"Not sure Albert would like us tellin' some friend of his wife's where it is, though. Whaddya think?"

"I think you got a point, brother." Dub poked my arm. "What do you think, Boston?"

"I think," I said, "that you guys are having some fun for yourselves. Me, I just want to find this place. You going to tell me where it is or not?"

They looked at each other, pretending to ponder the question. Then Harris nodded, and Dub said, "Well, I guess any friend of Albert Stoddard's wife oughta be considered a friend of ours. You want to get to this place, you gotta head up to Limerick. Next town to the north. Fifteen, twenty minutes from here." He hesitated. "Shit, Harris, fetch that DeLorme from the office, willya? We don't want Boston, here, driving that pretty Beemer down some dead-end road where he can't turn around."

Harris went into the office, and a minute later he returned with a tattered book of topographic maps. He and Dub spread it on the hood of my car, and Dub used a ballpoint pen to trace the route from the village of Southwick to a little round pond buried deep in the woods in the northwest corner of Limerick. They showed me where the long driveway led off the dirt road to the camp. I'd spot it about fifty yards after I crossed a wooden bridge where a brook passed under the road.

"Long ways in," said Dub, tracing with his finger the distance from the road to the pond.

"Close to a mile, I'd guess," added Harris. "Long ways in a Beemer."

I studied the map, then looked up and nodded. "Got it," I said. "Thanks."

"You ain't gonna get lost, are you?" said Harris.

"No," I said. "I've got it here." I tapped my head.

Harris looked at Dub. "He must've went to college."

"I did," I said.

"You got one of them cell phones with you?"

I shook my head.

"What're you gonna do if you get stuck?"

"I guess I'll have to walk," I said. "You think I'll get stuck?"

"Not unless you get lost."

"I won't get lost," I said. "Thanks for your help. I better get going before it gets dark."

Harris nodded. "Gets dark early this time of year. That's when the bears come out."

"Lotta bears around here," said Dub.

I smiled. "I'll keep an eye out for bears." I climbed into my car and pulled away from the garage. Harris and Dub stood there side by side, watching me go. I lifted my hand, and they both lifted theirs.

I decided to get Henry some water and something to drink for myself before I headed to Limerick and went looking for Albert's camp, so I stopped at the general store.

When I went in, Helen, Carol's partner at the real estate office, was standing by the counter talking with the elderly man at the cash register. She was leaning over the counter patting his cheek, and they were laughing about something. When they saw me, they stopped laughing.

I said hello to Helen, and she nodded to me. I found the cooler at the back of the store. I got a bottle of orange juice for me and a bottle of water for Henry and took them to the front.

Helen had left, and the old man—I guessed he was somewhere in his late seventies or early eighties—was perched on a stool looking at a newspaper through a pair of thick black-rimmed eyeglasses that were perched way out there toward the tip of his long, meandering nose.

I put the two bottles on the counter.

The old guy used his forefinger to push his glasses onto the bridge of his nose and peered up at me. "That'll be two bucks even," he said.

I took out my wallet and put a five-dollar bill on the counter. I noticed that his eyeglasses were the kind with built-in hearing aids.

"Understand you been lookin' for Stoddard's old hunting camp," he said.

"That's right."

He clanged open his cash register, made change, and slapped the three bills down on the counter.

"Did you know the Stoddards?" I said.

"Can't say I really knew 'em," he said. "It was a long time ago." He frowned. "Arnold? Harold? Something like that. Owned a business of some kind over in Keene. Quiet folks. Pretty much kept to themselves. One day they up and moved away. Let's see, that was . . . my goodness, that must've been thirty, thirty-five years ago."

"You don't know Albert, then?"

"The boy?" He shook his head. "Guess he was a teenager when they left. Helen was mentioning him just now. Friend of yours, is he?"

I nodded.

"And you're looking for his camp."

"I am."

"Guess you talked to the Goff boys, eh?"

I smiled. "Do you know everything?"

"I guess I know just about everything that happens in this here town," he said. "Which amounts to nothin' much worth knowing." He grinned. His teeth were yellowish and a little large for his mouth. "I'm sure the Goff boys got you squared away."

I smiled. "They were very helpful."

"It's up to Limerick," he said. "The camp."

"Dub and Harris eventually showed me how to find it," I said. "It probably would've been easier if I'd asked you."

"Think they're Abbott and Costello, those two fellas. Some folks don't think they're so funny."

"I thought they were pretty funny," I said. I held up the water bottle I'd just bought. "You don't have some kind of container I can borrow so I can give this water to my dog, do you?"

"Guess I might," he said. He groaned, climbed off his stool, bent creakily under the counter, and came up with a plastic bowl.

"Thanks," I said. "I'll bring it right back."

The old man waved away that idea with the back of his hand. "Keep it," he said. "You might need it later."

"Well, thanks a lot."

"Hell, it's just a plastic bowl."

"Even so," I said. "It's very friendly of you."

102

"Guess I want you to think of Southwick as a friendly town," he said. "I'm betting the Goff boys had a little fun with you. Their idea of fun, anyway. Pair of clowns, them two." He held out his hand to me. "Names Farley, by the way. That's my first name. Farley Nelson. Lived in this town all my life. So'd my daddy. Me, I never saw no reason to go anywheres else. Never understood why anybody would. Nice town, Southwick. No place better on God's green earth, if you ask me." He grinned. "Course, I ain't ever been anywhere else."

I gripped Farley Nelson's hand. It felt like a hunk of tree bark. "I'm Brady Coyne," I said.

"Yep," he said. "Heard that already."

"Well," I said, "thanks for the bowl."

"Oh, I like dogs," said Farley. "Got two setters and a beagle and an old black Lab, myself. Usta hunt 'em, but last few years, my damn arthritis, mainly in my knees . . ."

I shifted my weight from one leg to the other and smiled and nodded while he told me about his ailments, and how good the partridge hunting used to be before the woods grew too tall, and how the cottontails had about disappeared—damn coyotes, he figured—and how nowadays the out-of-staters all came for the turkeys, and how he didn't do much hunting anymore. Still liked fishing, though. Had a bass pond dug out behind his barn, got a kick out of raising the fish and then trying to catch them, and I guess old Farley Nelson would've talked on and on if a gang of kids hadn't come in to pepper him with questions about the latest videos.

I used that as an opportunity to escape.

When I stepped outside, I saw that Helen was sitting on the bench in front. I nodded to her.

"Mr. Coyne," she said.

103

I stopped. "Yes?"

"Got a minute?"

"Sure."

She patted the bench beside her, and I sat down.

"That your dog?" She pointed at my car. Henry was sitting in the front seat looking at us.

"Yes. How'd you know?"

"Massachusetts plates. Hunting dog?"

"I guess he would be if I hunted," I said. "He's a Brittany. It's in his genes."

"Everybody hereabouts hunts. Bet Farley got your ear."

I smiled. "He seems like a nice guy."

She nodded. "He is. He'll talk your ear off, though." She looked away for a moment. "I was a bit short with you back at the office," she said. "I wanted to apologize."

I waved that sentiment away with the back of my hand. "You were doing business," I said. "I understand."

"It wasn't exactly that."

"No?"

"I knew the Stoddards," she said. "Didn't like them very much."

I shrugged. I figured if she wanted to tell me why, she would.

Evidently she didn't. "That's why I reacted the way I did when their name was mentioned," she said. "I don't like to be impolite, but I guess I was, and I'm sorry for it. I can tell you where their camp is."

"Thanks," I said. "I talked with the guys at the garage. They showed me on a map."

"Harris and Dub," she said. "Regular encyclopedias of information, those two."

"Did you know Albert Stoddard?"

"Just by reputation," she said. "He was about twenty years younger than me. He was a teenager when the Stoddards moved away."

"What was his reputation?"

Helen blinked at me. "I didn't mean it that way. I just meant, I didn't know him personally."

"Have you seen him recently?"

"Albert Stoddard?" Helen shrugged. "I don't suppose I'd know him if I did see him. What I remember is a skinny towheaded boy riding around the dirt roads on a three-speed bicycle. He must be, what, a forty, forty-five-year-old man now?"

"About that. He's a college professor."

"Imagine that," she said. "Are you looking for him?"

I smiled. "I'm just looking for his camp."

"It's in Limerick."

"Yes," I said. "That's what the Goff brothers told me." I stood up. "And I want to see if I can find it before it gets dark."

"Well, you better get started, then," said Helen.

I held out my hand to her. "It was nice talking with you."

"I just didn't want you to get the wrong impression," she said. "We're really a friendly town."

"That is my impression," I said.

I went to my car, and when I opened the door, Henry slinked guiltily into the back.

I poured half of the bottle of water into the bowl Farley Nelson had given me and put the bowl on the backseat. Henry licked the bowl dry, then lay down.

As I pulled away from the general store, I waved at Helen, who was still sitting on the bench.

She lifted her hand to me.

The truth was, I still hadn't made up my mind whether Southwick was a friendly town.

ELEVEN

The road out of Southwick angled northeasterly into Limerick, and I followed the Goff brothers' map in my head to the right fork and then the sharp right turn onto the dirt road at the stop sign, and fifteen minutes after I'd driven away from the general store in Southwick I crossed the little wooden bridge over the rocky streambed and turned onto the pair of ruts leading into the woods. If the Goff boys hadn't been funning me, that would take me to Albert Stoddard's hunting camp by the pond.

The roadway was old and rocky and the ruts were deep, and I had to steer my left-side tires onto the crown between them to prevent the undercarriage of my BMW from scraping against the rocks.

Goldenrod and grass grew in the roadway. I couldn't tell how recently any vehicle had been here, but it was obvious that it was not heavily traveled.

Well, Gordon Cahill's little Corolla had been here. Gordie had taken the photos to prove it.

And the photos showed Albert's Volkswagen. That made two vehicles before mine.

I drove in first gear, and the weeds and brush scraped against the sides of my car. Henry stood on the backseat with his nose pressed against the window, alert for partridges.

I crept along at about five miles per hour. The old roadway seemed to go on and on. It passed over the trickle of a brook, bumped up and down small hills, curved through woods and past grown-up meadows, and I guessed I'd gone over half a mile when it crested a rise and began to descend. Here the woods thinned into meadow studded with clumps of alder and poplar and juniper, and below me lay a little bowl-shaped pond nestled among the low wooded hills.

I stopped to take a look. Albert's camp crouched close to the pond in a grove of big pine trees. Gordon Cahill had taken his pictures from right here on the old roadway.

I keep a pair of bird-watching binoculars in my glove box. I took them out and scanned the scene. The green Volkswagen was nowhere to be seen. The place looked deserted.

I continued down the hill, pulled up in front of the camp, got out, and walked around it. The clapboards, once painted white, were now gray and flaking. Pine needles clogged the gutters, and a few bricks had fallen away from the top of the chimney.

Out back stood an unpainted outhouse. The door hung open. I peeked in. It was a two-holer. Most of the outhouses I'd seen—and used—had two or even three side-by-side seats, and I always wondered if, back in the days of out-houses, visiting them had been a social activity.

A half-empty roll of toilet paper sat on the wooden bench. The rims of the seats were gouged and splintered where porcupines, I guessed, had gnawed on them. They looked pretty uncomfortable.

Beside the house was a small barn with a caved-in roof. I slid open the door and went inside. Aside from an ancient tractor, a couple of oil drums, a rack of rusty gardening tools, and a stack of firewood, it was empty.

I prowled around the rest of the area. There was no green Volkswagen Beetle—or any other functional vehicle—anywhere, which, I cleverly deduced, meant Albert wasn't there.

I went back to my car, let Henry out, and he and I followed a path down to the edge of the pond. Beside the path at a little sandy beach, a red Old Town canoe lay overturned on a pair of sawhorses. I went over to it and brushed my hand over it. Some dried sand was caked on its skin.

I looked at the sand on the rim of the pond and saw a few grooves such as the keel of a canoe would leave if it had been launched or landed there. It was impossible to tell how recently they'd been made.

The canoe had been used sometime recently. The sand would've been washed off the canoe in the first rainstorm. I tried to remember. It hadn't rained for over a week, at least in Boston.

Henry waded in and started paddling around. I sat on the pine needles, leaned my back against the trunk of a tree, and watched him.

Albert, where the hell are you?

The sun was falling behind the mountains beyond the pond. Off to my right, half a dozen wood ducks wheeled in and splashed down. I glanced at my watch. It was a little after six. I had about half an hour of daylight left.

I called Henry in, and we headed back to the camp.

109

I stood at the foot of the steps leading up to the screen porch for a minute, pondering the pros and cons of breaking and entering. The outside screen door hung slightly ajar. I wouldn't have to do any breaking to enter the porch. I pulled it open and went in. Henry, of course, followed me.

A square table and four creaky-looking rocking chairs sat on the narrow porch. The wood on all the pieces of furniture was raw and rough, as if time and weather and heavy use had worn away their finish. It would be a nice place to sit and rock and look at the pond, especially at dawn and dusk when deer and turkeys would be active and bass or trout might be dimpling the water's surface.

I was tempted to sit in one of those rockers and try it, except here, on this porch and away from the open water of the pond, the shadows were creeping in fast. The woods already looked dark. I wanted to get on with it.

I tried the door that opened to the inside of the camp. It was unlocked. I pushed it open and stepped directly into the kitchen.

Entering, surely, though technically, at least, not breaking.

"Albert?" I said without expectation. "You here?"

If he was, he wasn't admitting it.

The shadows were even deeper inside. What light there was came from four small windows on two of the walls. I blinked a few times, and after a minute my eyes adjusted, and I saw that the entire downstairs of the camp consisted of a single room. The floor was cracked and faded yellow linoleum that was curling up along the edges. The walls were cheap old imitation pine paneling.

The kitchen had a soapstone sink with a hand pump. It was flanked by cabinets without doors that held glasses, mugs, plates, canned goods, pots, and pans. There was a blackened wood stove with a flat surface for cooking. The wood box beside the stove was empty. There was an oval dining table pushed against the wall. Four mismatched wooden chairs were pushed in around it.

The opposite end of the room was dominated by a large fieldstone fireplace. Facing it were two soft chairs, a big sofa, and a coffee table. On both sides of the fireplace, floor-to-ceiling bookcases had been built in, and they were stuffed with books.

A narrow, open stairway against the back wall led up to what appeared to be a sleeping loft over the kitchen end of the camp.

A Coleman lantern sat on the kitchen table. I lit it with my Zippo lighter.

My stereotype of a hunting camp included a mounted deer head over the fireplace and a stuffed mallard sitting on the mantel and a fox pelt tacked to the wall, but Albert's camp had none of these artifacts. In fact, what struck me was what the place was missing—personality, character, history, family. No old maps tacked on the walls, no ancient family photos or outdated calendars or old license plates, no fishing rods hanging on pegs, no stacks of board games on the shelves.

It struck me as the sort of place where a bunch of guys might come for a weekend to play cards and grill steaks and drink beer and escape women—which, come to think of it, probably fit Albert's needs perfectly. I wondered if he had a bunch of guys he liked to hang out with.

Or boys. Maybe he brought boys here.

I realized I didn't know Albert very well.

I took the lantern over to the stairs leading up to the loft. I hesitated at the bottom and said, "Albert, I hope to hell you're not up there."

111

No response. I went up the narrow stairway.

A grown man would have to stoop to walk around in the loft. I chose not to walk around. I could see everything from the top of the stairs.

Two bare mattresses lay directly on the floor. Otherwise, it was empty.

Albert, asleep or dead, was not there.

Finding Albert's body, I realized, was what I'd been expecting, and dreading.

I let out a long breath and went back down the stairs. Henry was waiting at the bottom with a where-the-hell-did-you-go look on his face.

I scratched his forehead and went over to the fireplace. I lifted the lantern and scanned the books in the shelves. It was an eclectic collection of novels and biographies, mysteries and westerns. None, as near as I could tell from a cursory look at the titles, had been published since about 1970.

Henry had crawled up on the sofa, and he was curled in a corner giving me his isn't-it-time-to-eat? look. I sat beside him, and when I set the lantern on the coffee table, I noticed that a book lay there along with a chipped white coffee mug and a big glass ashtray. Both the mug and the ashtray were empty.

I picked up the book. It was a biography of Henry Clay. I guessed Albert was reading it. His place was marked about two-thirds of the way through with a letter-sized envelope.

I slipped the envelope out of the book. It had been addressed to Albert at Tufts University. It was dated June 22 of this year and postmarked from Milford, New Hampshire.

It had been slit open. Inside were a couple of folded-up newspaper clippings. I took them out, laid them side by side on the coffee table, and moved the lantern closer.

They were obituaries—one for a man named Oliver S. Burlingame and the other for Mark Gorham Lyman.

I assumed—although I could've been wrong—that these clippings had been mailed to Albert in this envelope. Maybe not. Maybe he just used the envelope to keep them in. But either way, these obituaries apparently had some significance to Albert.

The typeface and bland formulaic style suggested they'd been cut from small-town newspapers.

I read the first one:

```
          OLIVER S. BURLINGAME


          Banker, Little League Coach


KINKAID-Oliver S. Burlingame, 45, died acciden-
tally March 19.


Mr. Burlingame was born April 12, 1957, in Pe-
terborough, New Hampshire, son of Anne (Stowell)
and Raymond Burlingame. He attended the St.
Paul's School in Concord, NH, where he was cap-
tain of the cross-country team and a member of
the rifle team.


Mr. Burlingame earned a B.A. degree in finance
and marketing from Northeastern University in
1980. He moved to Kinkaid in 1982 and began work
as a loan officer for the Kinkaid branch of the
St. Louis Savings Bank. He was the assistant man-
ager of the bank at the time of his death.
```

113

Mr. Burlingame was an avid skeet shooter and a
champion bass fisherman.

Family members include two daughters, Mary Ellen
Burlingame and Anne (Burlingame) Marvell, both of
Kinkaid.

Services are private. The family requests that in
lieu of flowers, donations in Mr. Burlingame's
memory be made to the St. Paul's School, Concord,
NH 03301.

Several things struck me. First was the word "accidentally," coupled with the fact that no medical facility was mentioned as the place he had died.

Second was the New Hampshire connection. Peterborough, where Burlingame was born, lay less than a half hour's
drive from both Southwick, where Albert Stoddard grew up,
and Limerick, where I now sat. And come to think of it,
Milford, where the envelope had been postmarked, was perhaps a half hour's drive east of Southwick.

I had no idea where Kinkaid was, though a good guess
would put it in Missouri, assuming the St. Louis Savings
Bank was a clue.

Third was the fact that in more than twenty years, Oliver
Burlingame seemed not to have made much progress in his
life. The leap from loan officer to assistant manager of the
same branch bank suggested perhaps one promotion. A man
of little ambition, or limited ability, or both.

Fourth was Burlingame's age. Albert Stoddard was about
forty-five, too.

114

Hm.

I turned to the other obit.

MARK GORHAM LYMAN

Sales manager, church deacon

BANGOR—Mark Gorham Lyman, 46, died suddenly on
April 2.

Mr. Lyman was born in Keene, New Hampshire, and
graduated from Bangor High School where he played
on the football and baseball teams. He served in
the United States Army where he attained the rank
of corporal. Upon his discharge he returned to
Bangor, where he became a salesman for Sprague
Electric. He was the regional sales manager at
the time of his death.

Mr. Lyman served as a deacon for the St. Anne's
Episcopal Church for sixteen years and was active
in the Bangor Community Theater.

He leaves his wife, Gail (Evans) Lyman, and one
son, Mark Gorham Lyman, Jr.

Funeral services will be held at 11:00 A.M. on
April 5 at St. Anne's Episcopal Church.

So. Burlingame died "accidentally," while this Mark Gorham Lyman died "suddenly." Keene, New Hampshire, Ly-

man's birthplace, was maybe a half hour's drive from Southwick. Lyman, like Burlingame, was about Albert Stoddard's age.

And the two men had died within a couple weeks of each other.

I started to reread the Burlingame obit—and that's when Henry jerked his head up, barked, uncoiled himself, and went skittering on his toenails across the linoleum floor.

He pressed his nose against the door and growled deep in his throat.

"Cut it out," I said to him.

He continued to growl.

I hastily refolded the two clippings, put them back in the envelope, and slid the envelope into my jacket pocket.

I picked up the lantern, went over to the kitchen door, and knelt beside Henry. "What the hell's the matter with you?" I said.

I thought of porcupines and skunks and raccoons. I didn't want Henry to tangle with any of those critters. Bird-dog genes might've flowed through Henry's veins, but he was still a city dog.

The Goff brothers had mentioned bears. Black bears, our New England species, were notoriously shy. Still, all bears were territorial. A Brittany spaniel would be no match for a bear.

I told Henry to *sit*, which he did, and to *stay*, which I knew he would do. Walt Duffy, his previous owner, had trained him well, and so far my haphazard commitment to discipline had not untrained him.

I opened the kitchen door and stepped out onto the screened-in porch. I held up the lantern and looked around. I saw nothing except the darkness under the pine trees, heard nothing except the soft early-evening breeze rustling the branches.

The light from my lantern didn't penetrate the dirty old screening very well, so I pushed open the screen door and started down the back steps . . . and then something hard smashed against the bony knob of my right ankle.

I yelped, felt myself falling, dropped the lantern, flailed my arms, and crashed onto the ground. I landed flat on my chest, and the wind blew out of my lungs.

The lantern flared and then died when it hit the ground. All was darkness.

I curled fetally on my side, grabbed my throbbing ankle with both hands, and tried to suck breath into my lungs. Sharp fiery pains were shooting up my leg and my chest burned. My mind whirled with confusing thoughts and images.

Then I became aware of movement close behind me, the merest whisper of sound—the smooth sole of a shoe scraping over a soft blanket of pine needles, and then the slow, calm exhale of a breath.

I sensed that someone was standing close to me.

I turned my head and looked up. The figure of a man, silhouetted against the silvery night sky, loomed over me.

"What's your problem?" I said. "Albert? Is that—?"

He kicked me in the ribs. He grunted with the effort.

It felt like I'd been shot. Red lights flared like sudden flames inside my head.

He put his foot on my chest and rolled me onto my back. Then something pressed hard against the middle of my forehead. It felt like the side-by-side ends of two sharp, slender metal pipes cutting a figure-eight into my skin.

It took me just an instant to realize what it was.

It was the muzzle of a double-barreled shotgun.

I squeezed my eyes shut. I figured my head was about to be blown off.

Then the pressure on my forehead went away. The gun barrel traced a slow, sensuous line down the side of my face and over my chest and belly. It stopped at my groin and prodded me there.

My scrotum shriveled. I took a deep breath, started to speak—and that's when he smashed the gun barrel down on the very center of the top of my head, and white lights blazed for an instant before everything went black.

TWELVE

In the movies, when your hero gets whacked on the head, he might lose consciousness for five minutes or an hour or all night, whatever serves the needs of the story. When he wakes up, he shakes his head, grins ironically, leaps into his car or onto his horse, and sets off to chase down the bad guys. He's angry, maybe embarrassed, and he probably sports a manly dribble of blood running down the side of his face, but otherwise he's none the worse for the experience.

In real life, it takes a mighty blow to the head to knock you out for more than an instant. A blow hard enough to do that will leave you with a concussion, at minimum. More likely a fractured skull. It can kill you.

I was out for only an instant. He had hit me squarely in the sensitive center of the top of my head, and waves of pain radiated from that spot all the way to the tips of my fingers and toes.

Through the dizzy blur behind my eyes I watched his shadowy figure move into the the darkness, and a minute later I heard the engine of a vehicle start up. Then I saw headlights flash on and slice through the dark forest and disappear.

In the movies I would have growled an angry vow, spit blood and teeth out of my mouth, and then sprinted to my car and sped through the woods after the villain who'd bushwhacked me.

But this wasn't a movie.

It took an enormous amount of willpower just to push myself into a sitting position. My ankle was throbbing, and a sharp pain jabbed in my chest whenever I took a breath.

But mainly, my head just hurt like hell.

I crawled over to the steps that led up to the porch of the camp, rested my back against them, and squeezed my eyes shut. Everything hurt less with my eyes shut.

So I slumped there against the wooden steps with my eyes closed, waiting for the pain and dizziness to pass and drifting on weird images and disconnected thoughts . . .

The whole time he was hitting me, I kept thinking, he never said a word. For some reason that made it even more frightening.

Ten or fifteen minutes later I became aware of a bright light shining in my face.

I opened my eyes experimentally. The dizziness and blurriness seemed to have subsided.

I blinked and shielded my eyes with my hand.

Somebody was holding a flashlight on me.

"Move that thing, will you?" I said.

He moved the light a little to the side so that it wasn't shining directly in my eyes. I looked around. A police car, a

120

square SUV of some kind, had pulled up in front of Albert's camp. "Limerick PD" was painted on the side, and a light bar was attached to the roof.

The man with the flashlight wore a khaki-colored police uniform. The brim of his cap was pulled low over his forehead so that his eyes were in shadow. He had one hand resting lightly on the holster on his hip. "What's happening there, pardner?" he said. "You drunk?"

"No," I said. "I fell down and hit my head."

"You okay? Can you stand up?"

"Of course." I braced my hand on the steps and pushed myself to my feet. A wave of dizziness made me stagger and reach for the railing for balance. I took a deep breath. The pain in my head had subsided to a dull, deep ache.

The cop moved beside me and patted me down. He found me unarmed. "You fell down coming out of the camp?" he said. "That what happened?"

"That's right," I said. "Must've tripped on the steps. Lost my balance. Banged my head."

"Right," he said. "Who are you?"

I turned to face him. "My name is Brady Coyne. Who are you?"

"Huh?"

"I asked your name," I said.

He blinked at me. "Munson. Officer Paul Munson. Looks to me like you've been snooping around inside the camp. Is that right?"

I thought, absurdly, that while he couldn't nail me for breaking and entering, he had me dead to rights for breaking and exiting. "I came up from Boston to see if Albert Stoddard was here," I said.

"Let me see your wallet," said Officer Munson.

I moved my hand to my hip pocket.

"Slowly," he said.

I withdrew my wallet with my thumb and forefinger and handed it to him.

He moved over to his vehicle, flipped my wallet open, and shined his light on my driver's license. He shined his light back on me. "So what do you want with Mr. Stoddard?"

"I'm a lawyer," I said. When in doubt, give 'em a non sequitur. "It's business."

"Lawyer, huh?" he said. "Mr. Stoddard in some kind of trouble?"

Officer Munson looked like he was playing dress-up in his khaki-colored uniform. He had a smooth, pink face and clear blue eyes. Sometime when I wasn't looking they'd made puberty a qualification for becoming police officers and brain surgeons and had started distributing Glocks and scalpels to children.

"I don't know if he's in trouble," I said. "I was hoping to ask him."

"Friend of his, are you?"

"Yes."

He narrowed his eyes as if he'd just made a smart deduction. "So you're his lawyer and his friend both, then."

I shrugged. "I can't really talk about it. I've already told you too much."

"So was he here?" said Officer Munson. "Mr. Stoddard, I mean?"

Somebody had been here. He'd whacked my ankle and kicked my ribs and poked at my testicles and smashed the top of my head with the barrels of a shotgun. It could have been Albert.

I considered briefly explaining to this small-town cop how

I'd been assaulted. But that would require other explanations that I couldn't ethically give even if I wanted to—to Officer Munson, or to anybody.

"No," I said. "Nobody was here." I looked hard at him. "Have you seen Mr. Stoddard around lately?"

"I'll ask the questions, sir," he said. "You got a key for this place?"

"No."

He narrowed his eyes at me. "You said you fell coming out. That means you went in. What'd you do, break a window?"

"The door was unlocked," I said. "I opened it and went in."

"No, sir," he said, "that's not what you did. Mr. Stoddard keeps the place locked."

I shrugged. "I don't have a key, and I didn't break a window. Take a look if you want." I suddenly remembered Henry. "Look," I said. "My dog's inside. Do you mind if I let him out?"

"What kind of dog?"

"Brittany spaniel. He might want to sniff your pants, but he's gentle and loving."

"If he tries to bite me, I'll shoot him."

"Fair enough," I said. I went back onto the screen porch and opened the door.

Henry was sitting there. He cocked his head and narrowed his eyes at me. It was the look he always gave me when I returned home after going someplace without him.

I patted his head. "Sorry about that," I said. "Come on. Heel, now."

He followed me off the porch. I went over to my car and opened the door. "Get in," I told him.

He got in.

"How'd you do that?" said Officer Munson.

"Do what?"

"Get your dog to obey like that?"

"I'm firm and consistent with him," I said. "Dogs are like children."

"I've got two hounds," he said. "They pay no attention to anybody. Gotta keep 'em chained outside."

"That explains it," I said.

"So you didn't answer my question," he said.

"Which question was that?"

"Mr. Stoddard. You said he was in trouble."

"I didn't say that. You inferred it. I just said I was looking for him. What about you?"

"Huh?"

"Have you seen him lately?"

"Just because I haven't seen him," he said, "that doesn't mean he hasn't been around. You sit over there for a minute." He shined his flashlight at the porch steps. "I've got to call this in, have them run your plates, see what we're going to do."

"What do you mean, *do*?" I said.

"You were trespassing, sir. I caught you red-handed."

"Red-handed," I said. "Wow."

He frowned at me. "Pardon?"

I shook my head. "Nothing. Go ahead. Check me out. I hope it won't take too long."

"Oh, we've got computers," he said.

I went over to the steps, trying not to limp, and sat down.

Officer Munson slid behind the wheel of his cruiser and used his two-way. He left his door open so he could keep an eye on me.

124

Ten or fifteen minutes later I heard him say, "Okay, right. Ten-four." He looked over at me. "You're free to go, sir."

I started to thank him, then decided not to. "Tell me something," I said.

"Sir?"

"Why did you come here."

"Here to Mr. Stoddard's camp, you mean?"

"Yes. Did you get a call?"

"A call?" He shook his head. "Why would there be a call? Who'd call?"

"Are you saying you just happened to drive all the way down this particular dirt driveway at this particular time on this particular evening just at the time when I happened to be here?"

He shrugged. "We keep an eye on all the unoccupied places in our jurisdiction."

"There must be dozens of them, huh?"

He nodded. "Oh, sure. Hunting camps, summer cottages, places up for sale."

"And you keep an eye on all of them?"

"Right. One of our main jobs this time of year."

"So this place here," I said, "it's on your rounds, is it? You come by here every day about this time?"

He laughed. "You kidding me? There's only six of us on the whole force. There's about three hundred square miles to cover in this town. No, we pretty much do it random."

"Random," I repeated. "So finding me here was just a lucky coincidence for you."

"Me, lucky?" He grinned. "You're lucky I'm not arresting you."

"And I do appreciate your leniency," I said.

"You go get into your vehicle now, sir. I'll follow you out,

125

make sure you don't get stuck. That BMW of yours, it's pretty sweet, but it sure wasn't made for dirt roads."

"That's very kind of you," I said.

"Protect and serve," said Officer Paul Munson, and I didn't detect the slightest hint of irony in his tone.

I drove out the long driveway and turned south on the paved road, heading home. The headlights of Officer Munson's cruiser followed me all the way to the town line, where in my rearview mirror I saw him make a U-turn.

I drove on for a few minutes before I remembered the envelope with the two obituaries that I'd found in Albert's camp. I patted my jacket pocket where I'd put it.

It wasn't there.

I figured the man with the shotgun had taken it.

I pulled to the side of the road, opened my glove box, found a pen and a pad of paper, and jotted down everything I could remember from those obituaries. I was pleased to observe that despite the throbbing on the top of my head, my mind was clear and my memory was sharp.

By the time I'd wended my way through the maze of dark country roads through some sleepy New Hampshire villages and found my way back to Route 101, it was approaching eight o'clock.

My head and ribs and ankle hurt, but aside from bruises that would be tender to the touch, I figured I was okay. No broken bones, none of the building nausea or persistent dizziness that were signs of a concussion.

126

He could have killed me if he'd wanted to. I wondered why he didn't.

I realized that my stomach was growling.

That reminded me that I hadn't eaten for a while, which reminded me that it was Evie's turn to take care of dinner.

Normally we eat around seven.

I assumed she got my message. I'd told her I might be a little late.

I was still two hours from home. By the time I got there, it would be later than anybody's definition of "a little."

I'd been a bachelor for a long time. I still wasn't in the habit of accounting for myself to somebody else.

Another way to look at it was: Being considerate took a conscious effort. It didn't come naturally to me.

Evie knew me pretty well, and she tolerated me better than I deserved. Still, after a while she'd probably start worrying, and worry had a funny way of evolving into anger.

I started looking for a telephone. Along that hilly stretch of Route 101 there wasn't much of anything except fields and trees, and it was another fifteen minutes before I spotted a pay phone outside a darkened gas station.

I pulled in. Henry, who'd been snoozing on the backseat, sprang to attention when the car came to a stop. It was way past his suppertime, too.

"Sit tight," I told him. "I'll be right back."

I dialed all the required numbers to charge the call to my card. The phone that Evie and I shared at our home on Mt. Vernon Street rang five times before her recorded voice answered. "You've reached Brady and Evie's house," she said. "We're sorry we can't get to the phone right now, but we do want to talk with you. Please leave your name and number and we'll get right back to you, we promise."

After the beep, I said, "Hi, honey. It's about eight, and I'm on the road somewhere in New Hampshire. Sorry about this. I got tied up. I've still got close to two hours before I get there. You better eat without me, if you haven't already. I'm a bad boy. Probably deserve a spanking."

I thought about telling her how I'd been assaulted and was lucky to be alive. But that would be a cheap play for sympathy, and it would serve no purpose except to make her anxious every time I went anywhere.

Besides, I didn't want to talk to her about the case.

So I said, "Henry sends kisses. Me, too." Then I hung up the phone and got back into my car.

Where the hell was she?

Okay, so she got the message I'd left at noontime, guessed I'd be home late, and decided to put in some extra time at the office. Evie's job was demanding and stressful, and she often worked late. But she always called, and when she said she'd be home by seven, or seven-thirty, or whatever, she always was.

It was more than she could say for me.

Sharing a house and a life with another person was turning out to be more complicated than I remembered.

Well, I had that spanking to look forward to.

I decided to retrace the route I'd taken in the afternoon, the route that Gordon Cahill had taken the night his car went off the road and exploded in flames.

It looked a lot different in the dark. No streetlights lit the way, and the trees arching over the road formed a black tunnel that blocked the starlight and moonlight from the sky. The road seemed darker and narrower and twistier and

128

spookier than it had in the sunshine, and I found myself checking my rearview mirror frequently.

Horowitz said that Cahill was a cautious man, and that's how I knew him, too. Gordon Cahill liked to be in control. He'd never drive too fast for the conditions, and he'd drink coffee if that's what he needed to stay alert behind the wheel at night.

I imagined him driving his little Corolla where I was now driving my BMW through the darkness, working on a new pun, maybe, or thinking about the case he was working on, or maybe just looking forward to getting home and crawling in bed with his wife, and then the headlights suddenly appearing in his mirror from around the bend, coming up fast behind him, and Cahill cursing, probably, at this impatient asshole who was now tailgating him on this narrow, winding two-lane road, and slowing down a little and easing to the side, inviting the bastard to pass him, and the vehicle, accepting the invitation, pulling out and easing up alongside . . . and then a shotgun poking out the window, and the explosion of the shot, and Gordie realizing that his front tire had been blown out, the steering wheel leaping in his hands, the little Corolla swerving off the pavement, out of control now, and Gordie standing hard on the brake pedal, his tires skidding and slewing through the sandy shoulder, and then the big tree trunk looming suddenly in his headlights, and the sudden hard, jolting collision . . .

No headlights came up fast behind me, and it wasn't until I emerged on the other side of the state forest into the village of West Townsend that I realized I'd been gripping my steering wheel so hard that my hands ached.

THIRTEEN

I pulled into my slot in the parking garage on Charles Street a little after ten. I had a headache. My chest hurt when I breathed, and a pain shot up my leg from my ankle when I stepped out of the car. I was hungry.

Otherwise I felt fine.

I limped down Charles to Mt. Vernon Street and up the hill to our townhouse. Henry stopped at most of the lampposts and fire hydrants along the way, which was fine by me. I wasn't moving very fast.

The light beside the front door was on, and the windows glowed warm and orange from the inside lights.

I opened the front door. "Honey?" I said. "We're home."

No answer from Evie.

Henry pushed past me and trotted into the kitchen. I followed him and found him sitting in the middle of the floor looking at me expectantly.

I checked the table. No note from Evie.

I opened a can of Alpo, dumped half of it into Henry's

dish, added a couple scoops of Iams and a dash of water, and set it on the rubber mat beside the sink.

Henry continued to sit there with his ears cocked and his eyes following me.

"Okay," I said to him.

He leaped up, charged over to his dish, and began gobbling. He usually ate around seven, too.

While Henry was eating I went upstairs. Our bedroom door was ajar and the light was on. I peeked in. Evie's bedtime novel lay on its open pages on her chest. Her reading glasses had slipped down to the tip of her nose, and her eyes were closed.

I went over and sat on the edge of the bed beside her. She was breathing softly through her mouth. I picked up her book, closed it on her bookmark, and put it on the bedside table. Then I gently slid her glasses off her nose and set them on top of the book.

I bent down, brushed her hair away from her face, and kissed her forehead.

She moaned softly, and without opening her eyes, she reached up a hand and pushed my face away.

"Hey," I whispered. "I'm home."

"I'm sleeping," she mumbled. "Go 'way."

I patted the mound of her hip under the blanket, turned off the light, and went back downstairs.

I went into my room, took the page of notes I'd made about the two obituaries out of my shirt pocket, added a couple of details that I remembered, and put it in the top drawer of my desk.

I sat there gazing up at the ceiling. I was trying to make connections.

Two men originally from the Southwick area. Both about

Albert Stoddard's age. The three of them must have all known each other.

Now two of them were dead.

So what?

Someone hadn't wanted me to see those obituaries. He'd beaten me and taken the envelope from me.

It was hard to imagine Albert hitting anybody. Still . . .

One thing, at least, seemed pretty clear: whatever was going on with Albert, it involved something more ominous than some mundane extra-marital affair.

Questions and hypotheses whirled in my poor aching head.

I wondered if Evie had gone to sleep angry. She'd be fully justified.

Living alone had been a lot simpler.

I dialed my voice mail. I had two messages, one from Roger Horowitz and one from Ellen Stoddard. Both wanted me to call them. Neither left a hint about what they wanted.

I didn't know if it was too late, but I called Ellen's cell phone anyway. It rang three or four times before she mumbled, "Yes?"

"It's Brady," I said. "If you're sleeping, we can talk tomorrow."

She cleared her throat, and then I heard the rustling of bedcovers. "You woke me up this morning," she said, "and now you're waking me up tonight. What is it with you?"

"I'm just returning your call."

"Does that mean you've got nothing to report?"

"I haven't talked to Albert," I said. "I suppose you haven't heard from him."

"No." She paused. "Damn him."

"Let me run a couple of names by you," I said.

133

"Names?"

"What about Oliver Burlingame or Mark Lyman? Ever heard of them?"

She hesitated, then said, "Um, no. Maybe if you gave me a context . . ."

"Men that Albert might have known," I said. "Maybe from when he was growing up."

"I don't recall his mentioning either of those names," she said. "If I'd met them I'd remember."

"You sure?"

"Jesus, Brady. I was sleeping. Give me a break. Why? What about these names?" Ellen sounded wide awake now.

I told her about the clippings I'd found in Albert's camp and how it appeared that they'd been mailed to him back in June. I left out the part about how Burlingame had died "suddenly" and Lyman had died "accidentally," and I decided not to mention how I'd been whacked on the head and the clippings had been taken from me. Those details would have only made her anxious.

"Hm," was all Ellen said.

"None of this rings any bells with you then?"

"No," she said. "These were not men I knew. If Albert ever mentioned either of them, I don't remember it. They grew up together, you think?"

"I don't know," I said. "They both had southwestern New Hampshire connections. Keene and Peterborough, where they were born, are near Southwick. The closest hospitals are in those towns, I'd guess."

"Hm," she said again. "So what do you make of it?"

"Just the obvious," I said. "Some old friend of Albert's, someone who also knew these two guys, mailed the obits to him at Tufts. It's something an old friend might do."

"And he took that envelope up to his camp with him, and three months later he's using it as a bookmark?" she said. "That's a little weird."

"I'll look into it," I said. "Um, you left me a message, asked me to call. Was there something specific?"

"Albert didn't show up for his classes today," she said.

"I know. I tried to reach him at Tufts."

"Well, that is emphatically not like him," said Ellen. "So I called to alert you to the fact that I am now officially worried."

"I'm sorry," was all I could think of to say.

"Where the hell is my husband?" I heard a catch in her voice. "This is starting to make me crazy."

"Maybe it's time to report him missing," I said.

"I thought of that. Jimmy says no."

"Jimmy, huh?"

"I know," she said quickly. "But Jimmy's only thinking about the campaign. How it would look. What would people think. I can't just blow him off. We've got the debates coming up next week, and . . ." Her voice trailed away.

"And?" I said.

She hesitated. "And . . . Jimmy says, whatever Albert's up to, it's what he's decided to do, and sending out the cavalry isn't going to change how he's feeling. I think Albert's sick of the campaign, that's all. He always hated it. He needs to get away from it. That's how Jimmy reads it, too. If it gets into the papers that Albert has jumped ship, Oakley's people will have a field day with it."

"Is that really how you read it, Ellen? That he's jumped ship?"

"I don't know," she said softly. "I guess so. It's the only thing that makes any sense."

135

"You *are* officially worried."

"It's just . . . I know Albert. Jimmy doesn't." She hesitated. "Find him for me, will you, Brady? I just want to know he's okay."

"Sure," I said. "I'll do what I can."

"You are a comfort," she said. "Thank you."

After I hung up with Ellen, I tried Horowitz, and I was relieved to get his voice mail. "It's Coyne," I said, "returning your call. It's about ten-thirty, and I haven't had dinner yet, so I'd appreciate it if you'd wait 'til tomorrow to get back to me."

I took my notes from the desk drawer and looked at them again. The words "suddenly" and "accidentally" kept jumping out at me. Gordon Cahill had also died suddenly, if not, technically, accidentally. I guessed his obit might euphemistically use one—or both—of those words to describe his death.

I went out to the kitchen. Henry had finished eating and was standing in the doorway whining. I let him out.

I hadn't eaten since noontime. Two Tupperware containers that hadn't been there in the morning now sat on the top shelf of the refrigerator. I took them out. One contained a chicken-and-vegetable stir-fry, already stirred and fried. The other held a big glob of rice, already cooked.

There was also a bottle of white wine, two-thirds full.

So Evie had not picked up dinner from the deli on her way home. She'd picked up the ingredients and cooked it for us.

Except I never showed up to eat it.

Evie wasn't much of a cook. She was pretty good at it when she decided she felt like doing it, but that only happened about once a month, when she found herself in a creative mood and envisioned a relaxed—and possibly amorous—evening of domestic togetherness.

I'd picked a bad time to show up three hours late for dinner.

It was close to midnight by the time I slid into bed beside Evie. She was lying curled up on her side facing away from me. She was wearing her long flannel nightgown—the one she wore to signal her lack of interest in lovemaking.

I hitched myself close to her, pressed my front against her back, hooked my arm around her, cupped her breast, and nuzzled her neck.

She moaned softly.

"Hey," I whispered.

"You okay?" she mumbled.

"I'm fine," I said. "Are you?"

"Mm." She rolled onto her back. "Gimme a kiss."

Her arms went around my neck. She tasted like peppermint.

"Dinner was great," I said.

She smiled without opening her eyes.

I moved the flat of my hand over her belly.

She reached down and pushed it away.

"Sorry I was late," I said.

"You lose," she said, and she rolled over onto her stomach and buried her face in her pillow.

FOURTEEN

I slept fitfully, and when I woke up, sunshine was stream-
ing through the windows and Evie had already left our
bed. It was nearly seven-thirty, an hour later than I usually
woke up.

I showered and shaved, pulled on a pair of jeans and a
flannel shirt, and went down to the kitchen, where I poured
myself the day's first mug of coffee, and looked out the back
window.

Evie was sitting at the garden table with Roger Horowitz.
Henry was lying on the brick patio beside her. Evie and Horowitz were sipping coffee and talking and watching the
birds flit around the feeders.

When I stepped outside, Henry scrambled to his feet and
came over. I gave his head a pat, then went to Evie, who
tilted up her cheek for a kiss, which I delivered.

"You're on the job early," I said to Horowitz.

"Wanted to catch you before Julie got you on the clock."

I sat at the table. "Sounds important."

He nodded. "Might be." He glanced at Evie. "We were

bemoaning the fate of the Red Sox," he said. "I say it's the damn bullpen. She says it's the manager."

"I say it's the Yankees," I said. "If they weren't around, we'd be in pretty good shape."

Evie stood up. "You boys have things to talk about besides baseball, I imagine, and I've got to go to work."

I smiled up at her. "Tonight's my turn."

She shrugged. "I'll try to call if I'm going to be late." She smiled at Horowitz, blew me a kiss, and went inside.

Horowitz watched her go, then turned to me. "She's pissed at you."

"You think so?"

"My system is fine-tuned for the signs," he said. "You know Alyse."

"Alyse always seems pretty easygoing to me."

"Sure," he said. "Evie seems the same way to me, too. Difference between knowing them and being married to them."

I sipped my coffee. "You didn't come here to talk about women or baseball."

He shook his head. "I wanted to, um, alert you."

"Alert me?"

He shrugged. "Warn you."

Involuntarily I touched my ribs, which hurt when I took a deep breath. In the shower I'd seen the purple bruise. It was in the shape of the toe of a boot. There was another bruise on my ankle. Like I needed to be warned.

But I didn't mention any of that to Horowitz.

I narrowed my eyes at him. "I hope you didn't use the word 'warn' around Evie."

"Give me some credit, Coyne."

"What do you want to warn me about?"

140

"I'm gonna tell you a couple things about Gordon Cahill you probably don't know," he said. "Needless to say—"

"I know," I said. "This is between you and me."

"I'm trusting you here, Coyne," he said.

"I understand. And if I need to be warned, I appreciate it. But there's no quid pro quo, Roger. I still can't tell you who my client is."

He waved that notion away with the back of his hand. "Don't worry about it."

"You saying what happened to Cahill had nothing to do with my client?"

"Nope. Didn't say that. Depends on who your client is, what he's up to, huh?" He cocked an eyebrow at me.

I shrugged.

"Anyways," he said. "You know how on TV whenever a car crashes into something, it explodes in a dramatic black-and-orange ball of flame?"

I nodded.

"You ever see that happen?"

"Besides on TV?"

He nodded.

I thought for a minute. "No," I said. "I've seen a few pretty bad accidents, but I've never seen a black-and-orange ball of flame."

"That's because," said Horowitz, "in the real world that hardly ever happens."

"So you're saying—?"

"We got the report on Cahill's car from forensics yesterday," he said. "Those little Corollas are tough. Only one way it could've gone up in flames like that." He arched his eyebrows at me.

"I don't like what I'm hearing," I said.

141

He nodded. "After Gordie got his tire shot and piled into that tree, somebody poured gasoline all over his car—inside and out—and touched it off."

"Jesus," I whispered. I blew out a long breath. "When it exploded, was Gordie—?"

"Was he alive? That what you're asking?"

I nodded.

"We're still waiting on the M.E. He'll tell us. You really want to know?"

I shook my head. "Not really." I peered at Horowitz. "So they shoot out his tire, then set his car afire. Not exactly subtle."

"Nope."

"Like they're trying to make a point."

He shrugged.

"Or," I added, "they're just not very bright."

"Or both," he said.

"So what are you thinking?"

Horowitz planted his forearms on the table and leaned toward me. "Gordon Cahill grew up in South Boston. St. Monica's parish. Ring a bell?"

"Sure. That's where Whitey Bulger grew up. The home of the Winter Hill Gang. Big-time Boston mobsters."

"Gordie didn't hang out with them. It's not like they were friends. Whitey Bulger's close to twenty years older than Cahill. Brother Billy's about fifteen. But Cahill was part of the neighborhood, part of that culture. The families all knew each other. They used to say, a young man grows up in Southie, he's got four choices. He works for Gillette, he works for the cops, he works on Beacon Hill, or he works for the mob."

"Whitey and Billy Bulger and Gordon Cahill," I said. "Be-

142

tween the three of them, they did everything except make razor blades."

"Those wiseguys Gordie busted in Haverhill back when he was undercover?" said Horowitz. "They did business with the Winter Hill Gang."

"A lot of blood on their hands."

"That's right. Drugs, extortion, loan-sharking, murder. You name it. They came down pretty heavy on the Winter Hill mob a few years ago. But those guys don't just go away."

"So you think . . . ?"

"It's not so much what I think," said Horowitz. "It's what I know. I know that Gordon Cahill had his name on the evening news for several months back there when he was testifying against all those shitbums. I know his testimony put away several of Whitey Bulger's old soldiers. I know that they've still got a lot of loyal friends in South Boston." He leaned close to me. "I also know," he said, "that guys like them have long memories. They place high value on loyalty, or their fucked-up version of it. Anybody from St. Monica's parish, cop or no cop, should be willing to die before he'd spill the beans against anybody from the neighborhood."

"Or be prepared to die if he did," I said.

Horowitz nodded.

"That was, what, ten, twelve years ago when Gordie worked undercover for the state cops?"

"Could be a hundred years. Doesn't matter. They never forget. Look," said Horowitz, "it's a theory, okay? Far as I'm concerned, a theory worth pursuing. But it doesn't mean I'm not interested in other theories."

"I really want you to solve this case," I said. "But I can't tell you who my client is."

He shrugged. "I came here to warn you, that's all."

"Even though I hired Gordon Cahill for some case that has no connection whatsoever to do with South Boston mobsters, you still think . . . ?"

"Look," he said. "Evie's a great kid, okay? Alyse thinks the world of her, and I do, too. She's way too good for you. But for some reason she seems to like you, and I don't want to have to come knocking on her door some night with bad news."

"I'll be careful," I said. "But even if some mobsters did kill Cahill for revenge or something, I don't see why they'd be interested in me."

"Just keep an eye on your rearview mirror, Coyne."

I remembered driving home the previous night through the Willard Brook State Forest. I was glancing into my rearview mirror the whole way.

Horowitz stood up, hesitated, then placed both hands flat on the table and pushed his face close to mine. "Anything you can tell me without violating your client's privileged status, I'd appreciate it, you know. Not even to mention your solemn duty as an officer of the court. This is now an official murder investigation."

I looked up at him. "Have you shared any of this with the New Hampshire cops?"

"New Hampshire?" He narrowed his eyes at me. "You want to elaborate on that for me?"

I shook my head.

"Any other suggestions?"

"Not right now."

"Okay. Good. Thanks." He turned and headed for the garden gate, which opened out onto the back alley.

"You're allowed to use the front door, you know."

"Parked in the alley," he said. "Didn't want to arouse the curiosity of your neighbors."

"Considerate," I said. "Thank you."

After Horowitz left, I went inside, refilled my coffee mug, and took it into my room.

I didn't know how to react to what Horowitz had told me. On the one hand, if a bunch of South Boston gangsters had killed Gordon Cahill out of vengeance for the testimony he'd given ten years earlier, it meant that the case he happened to have been on at the time was irrelevant.

Albert Stoddard was just some history professor who'd probably never set foot in South Boston.

On the other hand, Ellen Stoddard had been a hard-charging prosecutor for the D.A.'s office before she started running for the Senate. It occurred to me that she might have prosecuted a member of the Winter Hill Gang or two somewhere along the line.

I knew one thing for certain: Somebody had whacked me on the head and kicked me in the ribs and jammed the business end of a double-barreled shotgun against my forehead.

It was considerate of Horowitz to warn me. But I didn't need another warning.

FIFTEEN

I opened my desk drawer, took out the notes I'd made from the obituaries I'd found in Albert's camp, and read them again.

I glanced at my watch. It was a few minutes after nine. In Kinkaid, Missouri, where Oliver S. Burlingame lived and died, I figured it was too early to call.

But it was a few minutes after nine in Bangor, Maine. Not an unreasonable time to receive a sympathy call.

I called information, which informed me that Mark Lyman's wife, Gail, wasn't listed. The phone was still in her late husband's name.

I didn't like the idea of what I was going to do, but I did it anyway.

When she answered, I said, "Is this Mrs. Lyman?"

"Yes, it is," she said.

"Gail, right?"

"Yes, that's right. Do I know you?"

"I'm an old friend of Mark's," I said. "My name is Brady Coyne. I just heard what happened. I wanted to express my condolences."

147

She hesitated. "I don't recall Mark ever mentioning you."

"We've been out of touch for quite a while," I said. "Albert told me what happened."

"Albert?"

"Albert Stoddard?" I made it a question.

"Mark never mentioned any Albert Stoddard, either. How did you say you knew him?"

"Oh, back from our New Hampshire days. Albert and Mark and Ollie Burlingame and I. When we were kids. We all hung out together."

"I never heard of anybody named Ollie, neither," she said. "All that was a very long time ago. Mark's family moved away from New Hampshire when he was a teenager. He never talked much about his childhood."

"Well," I said, "like I told you, Mark and I, we pretty much lost touch after he moved away." I was making it up as I went along. So far, so good, I thought. "Still," I continued, "there are a lot of happy old memories, you know? So had Mark been sick or something?"

"Well . . ." She hesitated. "Your friend Albert didn't tell you?"

"All he told me was that Mark, um, passed away."

"Passed away. Ayuh. That's what he did, all right." She chuckled sourly. "Well, okay, Mr. Coyne. To answer your question, I guess you might say my husband was sick. One morning last April after I left for work, he loaded up his .30/06 and drove to some woods outside of town, and he stuck the muzzle in his mouth and killed himself with it. I'd say that's pretty damn sick, wouldn't you?"

"Oh, jeez," I said. "I didn't know that. I'm really sorry. How are you? Are you doing okay? That must've been a terrible shock."

"Oh, hell," she said. "I guess I wasn't that surprised. I

148

mean, you don't expect something like that to happen, but afterward, you look back, and you say, yes sir, the signs were all there, how could I've been so stupid?"

"He'd been depressed or something, huh?" I said. "That's pretty hard to imagine. I mean, back when we were kids . . ." I let the implications hang there like a question.

"I know," she said. "When I met Mark, fresh out of the army, he was this carefree happy fella, this handsome soldier, full of jokes and stories, always laughing." I heard her blow out a breath. "It all started falling apart last winter. I never saw it coming. One day he's fine, working hard, all involved in the church, the next day he's like this zombie, moping around, won't even talk to you. You think, well, he'll get over it. Winter's a bitch up here. Except he didn't get over it. He kept getting worse, and then he killed himself. I only wish he would've talked to me about it. I might've been able to help."

"Get him to a therapist, maybe," I said, just because it was my turn to say something.

"The money," she said after a minute. "I think it was all about money."

"Did he lose his job or something?"

"No, no. He was doing fine at work. I didn't even know about it until after he was dead and buried, when the lawyer was settling his estate. That's when we found out what he did. I can't forgive him for it. Depressed or not, I don't care. I'll be mad at that man for the rest of my days."

"What did he do?"

"He emptied out Mark Junior's college account is what he did. We've been saving and sacrificing for over sixteen years so Markie wouldn't have to go to the state school if he didn't want to. Now it's gone. All of it. Cleaned right out." She paused, then laughed softly. "Listen to me, will you? I don't

149

suppose you called up because you wanted to listen to my old sob story. What's done is done. I miss Mark and I love him. I truly do. But God help me, I'll be mad at that man 'til the day I die. I'm not proud of it, but there it is."

"Well," I said, "I guess under the circumstances anybody would feel about the same way." I hesitated for a polite beat, then said, "What did Mark do with that money, do you know?"

"Up in smoke. Gone. Who knows?"

"Did he gamble or something?"

"Oh, Lord," she said. "That's almost funny. Mark and I, we played cribbage for a penny a hole sometimes, and if I beat him for like fifteen cents, you'd think it was his life savings, and it'd take me a week to pry it out of him. Other than that, I don't think he ever even bet a beer on a golf match. Look—Brady, was it?"

"Yes. Brady Coyne."

"Well, Brady, I've really got to go fix my hair and drive off to my job now. It was nice of you to call, and I'm sorry I had to tell you what I told you. Best thing is if you can remember your old friend the way you knew him when you were boys." She laughed quickly. "Sure wish I could do that."

After we disconnected, I sat there looking out the window and feeling sleazy. I didn't much like dissembling, particularly to bereaved widows, and I especially didn't like the fact that it seemed to come naturally to me.

Gail Lyman, I tried to convince myself, hadn't needed much prodding. She probably spilled out her sad story to every political pollster and vinyl-siding salesman who cold-called her while she was eating dinner.

Except, of course, pollsters and salesmen didn't pretend to be childhood buddies of her recently self-deceased husband.

150

Well, I wasn't done. I still had Oliver Burlingame's "accidental" death on my mind. I decided to exhaust all other possibilities before I got involved in lying to one of his survivors.

I called Julie and told her I'd be in around noon, and all she said was, "Okay. Whatever. See you then."

Julie seemed to have resigned herself to my haphazard office hours, which scared me a little. Over the years I'd gotten used to being nagged about spending time in the office and accruing billable hours and scouting around for new clients. Julie had always taken her job seriously, and I knew it frustrated her that I sometimes didn't.

If I didn't pay her so well, I'd worry that she might go looking for a better boss.

I promised myself I'd put in a solid afternoon at the office and make Julie happy.

I went out to the kitchen and refilled my coffee mug. It was ten in the morning, which I figured would make it nine in Missouri.

Rand McNally helped me locate Kinkaid, Missouri, which appeared to be a suburb of St. Louis, and Verizon gave me the number for the Kinkaid branch of the St. Louis Savings Bank. I dialed it.

I waited through the recorded menu that listed all of my conveniently automated options, and I was rewarded, at the end, with an invitation to remain on the line and speak with an actual person, which I accepted.

"Good morning," she said after less than a minute. "My name is Marla. How may I help you today?"

"Good morning, Marla," I said, attempting to match her cheerfulness. "My name is Brady and I'm trying to get ahold of Ollie Burlingame."

151

She hesitated, then said, "I'm sorry, sir. Mr. Burlingame is no longer with us."

"Hm," I said. "See, I'm an old friend of his, and we've been out of touch for a while. Last I heard, he worked there. Do you know how I can reach him?"

"Mr. Burlingame, um, well, the thing is, he died."

"Oh, jeez. What happened?"

"I'm not sure I should—"

"This is terrible," I said. "Did he have a heart attack or something?"

"Actually, I heard it was a fishing accident," she said.

"No kidding." I paused for a beat. "Marla," I said, "the truth is, Ollie owed me money. Now what'm I going to do?"

"Get in line, I guess."

"I beg your pardon?"

She cleared her throat. "I'm sorry, sir. I really can't talk about it. If there's nothing else . . . ?"

"No, that's fine, Marla," I said. "You've been very nice." And I hung up before I found myself telling her more lies.

A quick trip down the Information Highway revealed that Kinkaid, Missouri, had a weekly newspaper called the *Kinkaid Current*.

The paper's on-line archives went back only a month, and I found no mention of Oliver Burlingame in them. But I did get the name of the editor—Tamara Quinlan—and a phone number.

I paused to ponder my strategy. What sort of lie should I tell this time?

I made up my mind, dialed the number for the *Kinkaid Current*, and Tamara Quinlan herself answered the phone.

I took a deep breath. "Ms. Quinlan," I said, "I'm calling from Boston and I'm looking into the death of one of your local people. Oliver Burlingame?"

152

"Why?" she said.

"Huh?" I said. "Why what?"

"Why are you looking into the death of this person?"

"Oh," I said, "well, this Burlingame was originally from New England, so there's the local angle. I heard some things, and I'm thinking there might be a story in it."

"Are you a reporter?"

"Oh, right. Sorry. Yes. Brady Coyne's the name."

"What paper are you with?"

"Actually," I said, "I'm a freelancer. Features, investigative stuff, you know? I do magazine work, too. So can you help me out with the Burlingame story? I checked your archives, but I didn't find anything."

"What did you hear about Oliver Burlingame, Mr. Coyne?"

"Call me Brady," I said. "What I heard was, he died in some kind of fishing accident and there might've been some money issues."

She was quiet for a minute. Then she said, "Well, I don't see any reason why I can't tell you what I know. First off, Burlingame drowned in the Calcasieu River down in Louisiana. This was back in March. He was one of those passionate bass fishermen, had the fancy boat, all the gear, traveled to tournaments and stuff. Bass fishing's pretty big in this part of the country, you know. March is a little early for the bass around here, I guess, so Burlingame went off to Louisiana for the weekend because the fishing was supposed to be good down there. That's the way I heard it."

"Drowned," I said. "How'd it happen?"

"Nobody really knows. They found his boat, and a couple days later they found him."

"No evidence of . . . ?"

"Foul play, you mean?" She chuckled. "I guess not. It's

153

unclear how thorough the police down there in Louisiana were, but they called it an accidental death."

"Did you follow up on that angle?"

"Me? Follow up? Ha. Look, we're just a small-town weekly. I'm my only full-time employee. Folks here in Kinkaid, they want to know what the mayor intends to do about property taxes and whether the sewer's going to come up their street and what the school board plans to do about the music program. I don't have the time or energy or resources to go muckraking. It'd be fun, but that's not what we're about here. So if you want to go raking up some muck, God bless you. You get a story, I can pay you ten dollars a column inch."

"Does that mean you think there's some muck in this story?"

"Well, you might want to check the money angle. There were lots of rumors flying around town. I actually thought about trying to write a follow-up story after we ran his obit, but I couldn't persuade anybody to talk on the record."

"How about off the record?"

"Off the record," she said, "Oliver Burlingame was apparently embezzling from the bank where he worked. They were going to fire him. If you can get confirmation of that, I'll buy your story."

"He died before they had the chance to fire him?"

"That's right."

"Convenient," I said.

"Yes, that's what I thought," said Tamara Quinlan. "People who knew him say Burlingame was about at the end of his rope. Off the record, they'll tell you he owed a lot of money, had a lot of pressure on him, and wasn't handling it very well. The people at the bank won't tell you anything, of course, on or off the record. Last thing they want made

154

public is that one of their employees—hell, their assistant branch manager—was dipping into the till."

"Who'd he owe money to?"

"He borrowed from friends, took loans from several banks, borrowed against his 401K and life insurance policies. He was tapped out."

"So what did he need that money for?"

"I don't know," she said. "I don't know anybody who knows. Even off the record, I couldn't find anybody who had a clue."

"What about the police? Were they involved?"

"Nope. The bank was handling the embezzling thing, if that's what it was, in-house. He died in Louisiana. No police case here." She hesitated. "My other phone's ringing."

"Can I call you again?"

"Sure. Sorry. Gotta go."

And she disconnected.

During my conversation with Tamara Quinlan, Henry had plopped his chin on my knee and commenced staring into my eyes. This meant he wanted to go outside.

So I picked up a legal pad and a felt-tipped pen, and Henry and I went out to the patio.

Our arrival panicked half a dozen mourning doves who'd been pecking fallen seeds from under the hanging feeders. Henry, who'd been bred for bird hunting, stared intently after the fleeing doves. Then he went looking for bushes to pee on.

I sat at the table and drew a line down the middle of the yellow sheet of paper. I labeled one column "Lyman" and the other "Burlingame." Then I wrote down what I knew about each man:

They were about the same age.

They'd both been born near Southwick, New Hampshire.

They'd both moved away sometime during their child-hood.

Both of them had been depressed shortly before their death.

Both of them had money problems.

Both of them had taken desperate actions to address those problems.

They died within two weeks of each other.

Both of them had died unattended deaths.

So what did all that have to do with Albert Stoddard? Why did he have copies of their obituaries? Who'd sent them to him?

The parallels between Albert and the two dead men were striking:

All three were in their mid-forties.

All had been born near Southwick, New Hampshire.

All of them had moved away from the Southwick area when they were teenagers.

Lyman and Burlingame were reportedly depressed. "Depressed" wasn't the word that Ellen or Jimmy D'Ambrosio had used to describe Albert. But depression manifests itself in any number of behaviors, including, maybe, Ellen's word "weird."

Okay. The questions I was left with were obvious:

Did Albert have money problems?

Had he taken desperate actions? Was one of his desperate actions murdering Gordon Cahill? Was another one kicking and slugging me and pressing a double-barreled shotgun against my forehead?

Or: Were we waiting to learn that Albert, like Lyman and Burlingame—and Gordon Cahill—had died an "accidental" or "sudden" death?

I went back inside, poured myself another mug of coffee

on the way through the kitchen, and took it into my office.

I found the manila folder that held the printouts of all the stuff Gordon Cahill had e-mailed to me the day before he died and took out the sheets that showed the last four months of Albert's bank statements. I'd already studied them. But that time I'd been looking for some New Hampshire connection.

Now I was looking for a clue that Albert had money problems, that he'd borrowed excessively, that he'd been paying off some large debt.

He'd withdrawn no large hunks of money. He'd written no particularly large checks, nor had he deposited any unusually large ones.

I felt that I was missing something, but I couldn't see it.

I tried to clear my mind of expectations and hypotheses.

And then I saw it.

May 15. May 30. June 15. June 30. July 15. On each of those dates, like clockwork, Albert had deposited $2,177.54 into his checking account. Biweekly paychecks, almost certainly. I did the crude math. After taxes and health and retirement deductions, it would amount to a little more than $3000 twice a month. It just about added up to a tenured college professor's pay.

On July 30, August 15, August 30, and September 15 he'd deposited nothing.

And the question was: If he suddenly stopped depositing his paychecks, what did he do with them?

Burlingame and Lyman had money problems. Now it appeared that Albert made three.

The word "blackmail" came to mind.

I called Ellen's cell phone and got her voice mail. "It's Brady," I said. "I've got a couple questions for you. Call when you get a chance, please. I'm home now and I'll be at my office this afternoon."

I had one more phone call to make before I changed into my lawyer pinstripe and went to the office.

"Evie Banyon," she answered. She sounded harried.

"It's your wayward roommate," I said.

"Oh," she said. "Brady. What's up?"

Oh, oh. When she called me "Brady" instead of "honey" or "sweetie" or "Big Guy," it meant either that she had people in her office or that she was angry with me.

"Are you busy?" I said.

"Always."

"Got people in your office?"

"No, Brady." I heard the exasperation in her voice.

"I was hoping we could have dinner together tonight."

"Wouldn't that be nice."

"I was thinking of Italian," I said, ignoring her sarcasm. "Let's go to the North End."

"You know I love the North End," she said. I thought I detected a softening in her tone. "You sure you can make it?"

"Me?" I laughed. "Why would you ask such a thing?"

"Ho, ho," she said.

"I'll make reservations for seven-thirty," I said. "Okay?"

"Sure. I'll be home by seven. Where?"

"You have a preference?"

"You know the North End better than I do," she said. "I trust you."

"I'm glad to hear that."

"I mean," she said, "I trust you when it comes to picking Italian restaurants in the North End."

"Well," I said, "that's something, anyway."

She called me "honey" when she said good-bye. That was something, too.

SIXTEEN

Nola's Trattoria was one of those little hole-in-the-wall Hanover Street Italian restaurants whose studied lack of pretention convinced tourists that they'd found the authentic Boston North End thing. The door off the sidewalk opened directly into the narrow rectangular dining room. There was a little podium inside the doorway where guests were greeted. Six tables were lined up along the left wall and eight along the right wall, with an aisle down the middle leading to the swinging kitchen doors. Fading murals on the rough plaster walls depicted Mediterranean vineyards and seaports and peasant villages.

When Evie and I walked in, Nick, the headwaiter at the podium, bowed and smiled at Evie, then turned to me and said, "Mr. Coyne. It's good to see you again. We have your table ready."

Aromas of garlic and oregano mingled with fresh-baked pastry and Romano cheese. From hidden speakers came a Resphigi tune. "The Pines of Rome," I think it was. Or maybe it was the fountains. Fat candles in glass containers burned on every table, and crisp white linen tablecloths covered them. All but two or three were occupied by diners.

Evie squeezed my arm. "I love it," she whispered. "Why didn't you ever bring me here before?"

Nick showed us to the front table by the big window that looked out on Hanover Street. He held Evie's chair for her, gave us menus, recited the evening's specials, turned and snapped his fingers. An instant later a pretty dark-eyed waitress came over with a bottle of red wine and gave it to Nick. He squinted at the label, then uncorked it and placed it on the table by my elbow. "Compliments of Mr. Russo," he said.

"Please thank Mr. Russo for me," I said. I fished one of my business cards from my pocket and slipped it to Nick. "And please tell Mr. Russo that I'd appreciate the opportunity to thank him personally."

He palmed the card. "Shall I give you a few minutes to decide what you want?"

"Yes, thank you."

When Nick left, Evie said, "You know these people?"

I nodded.

"Russo?" she said. "Is that Vincent Russo? *The* Vincent Russo?"

"Yep. Him."

"That Mafia guy? The mobster?"

"Yes. Russo owns this place."

She narrowed her eyes at me. "So why are we here?"

"A night on the town with my sweetie," I said. "This is a nice restaurant. Great food, fine wine, excellent service, understated ambiance. The ossobuco is special."

"We're patronizing some hit man?"

"Vincent Russo isn't a hit man," I said.

160

"So he hires them."

I shrugged. "He used to. He's retired."

"But we're here because of him, right?"

I reached across the table and put my hand on top of Evie's. "We're here," I said, "because I wanted to take you out to dinner. Because I feel bad that I couldn't call you last night, and because you ended up eating alone, and because you worried about me."

"I wasn't worried," she said. "I was angry. You could've taken me to a million places. But you chose this one."

"I do need to talk to Russo. He owes me."

Evie rolled her eyes. "Oh, great. Vincent Russo owes you. What does he owe you? You got somebody you need whacked?"

I smiled.

"So," she said, "does this mean you've done a favor for Vincent Russo? Are you in some kind of trouble, Brady?"

"No trouble, honey," I said. "And not a favor, really. I worked something out with him for a client a few years ago. Do you remember Mick Fallon?"

Evie looked up at the ceiling for a minute, then smiled. "Sure I do. Mr. Fallon was a patient at Emerson when I worked there. A great big man. That's when I met you. You came to visit him."

"Right. Mick had a gambling problem. Owed Russo a lot of money. I mediated their, um, dispute. Got it worked out so Mick would pay Russo what he owed him and Russo would refrain from whacking Mick. Good deal all around. They were both grateful for my efforts."

"Jesus," she said.

"Anyway," I said, "now Russo thinks he owes me, and he's eager to even things up. I am, too. It's not comforting,

161

having someone like Vincent Russo believe he's in debt to you, even if he is retired. So now I've come up with a way for him to even things up with me."

"I don't think I want to hear about it."

"Good," I said, "because I don't want to talk about it. Let's try the wine." I filled our glasses, then held mine aloft. "May the stars hit your eye like a big pizza pie."

Evie clicked her glass against mine. "That's definitely amore," she said.

A few minutes later Nick came with the antipasto and bread. I ordered the *ossobuco*, a choice that he endorsed with a nod, and Evie ordered the *seppie coi piselli alla romana*, which she pronounced with enthusiasm, causing Nick to smile broadly and bow deeply.

After he left, I said, "Squid?"

"Squid and peas," she said. "Roman style. Loose but accurate translation."

"I think you ordered it just because you liked saying it."

"So? I heard the way you said ossobuco."

"That's half the fun of Italian restaurants," I said. "It's way more fun than French restaurants. Waiters in French restaurants, they always roll their eyes and sneer at my accent. Italian waiters seem to enjoy my efforts."

"Your efforts are amusing," said Evie.

Nick brought a second bottle of strong red wine with our dinners, and after he took our plates away he delivered a platter of sliced melons and cheeses and two snifters of brandy. I was glad we'd decided to walk here to the North End from our place on Beacon Hill, even though my ankle was sore. By the time we finished this meal, I'd need the twenty minutes of autumnal night air to clear my head.

Evie and I were nibbling at the cheeses and melons and

sipping our brandy when Vincent Russo appeared beside our table. He looked older than I remembered him. He wore a white shirt and a red necktie and a dark suit. His shirt collar was loose around his throat, and his steel-gray hair had thinned considerably since I'd seen him last.

He held out his hand to me with solemn formality. When I stood up to shake it, he smiled and hugged me and kissed both of my cheeks and patted my shoulder.

I patted his shoulder, too.

"So good to see you again, Mr. Coyne," he said. "Welcome, welcome." He turned to Evie and bowed deeply. "Madame."

Evie smiled and held out her hand. Russo took it in his, bent to it, and kissed the air just above it.

"Evelyn Banyon," I said. "This is Vincent Russo."

Evie gave him her best smile. Evie's best smile would melt the heart of an IRS agent. Or a second-rate godfather.

"So, Nickie," said Russo, "he's treating you good, huh?"

"Excellent service," I said. "He's very attentive."

"He's a good boy," said Russo. "My nephew."

"You can be proud of him," I said. I gestured to an empty chair at our table. "Please. Won't you join us."

He smiled as if he hadn't expected an invitation and said, "For a minute only. Thank you." He sat down. "The food, it's okay, huh?"

"The food is excellent, as always," I said.

"It's wonderful," said Evie.

"Good, good." He waved his hand vaguely in the air, and Nick appeared instantly. "More brandy," said Russo.

He asked polite questions of Evie, who answered them politely. He asked after my boys, and I asked after his grandchildren.

163

Nick came and refilled our brandy glasses. Russo held his up, and Evie and I clicked ours against his. "Sante," he said, and Evie and I murmured, "Sante."

Russo reached over and gripped my forearm. "You are well, Mr. Coyne, huh?"

I held up my hand, palm down, and gave it a mezza-mezza wiggle. "Actually, I am grieving the loss of a friend, Mr. Russo. Perhaps you knew him? Gordon Cahill?"

I watched Russo carefully when I spoke Cahill's name. He didn't blink. His creased face and expressive mouth conveyed nothing but sincere sympathy, and his dark eyes remained blank. He shook his head slowly. "I am sorry," he said. "I did not know Mr. Cahill. It is never easy, losing a friend. The only thing worse is when it's family. This was, um, un-expected, then, huh?"

I nodded. "An automobile accident."

"Ah," was all he said, and then the subject switched to the Celtics. Russo loved professional basketball players.

A few minutes later he drained his brandy glass and pushed himself back from the table. "A pleasure to see you again, Mr. Coyne. We will do it again when I can sit with you longer. We will have some serious conversation." He turned and bowed to Evie. "Your presence, Ms. Banyon, brings joy to my restaurant. You will return, huh?"

"I certainly hope so," she said. She watched Vincent Russo hobble away, then turned to me. "So who's Gordon Cahill?"

I flapped my hand. "Friend of mine. He died."

"That's why you were so upset the other day. You couldn't tell me about it."

"That's right. It had to do with a client."

"But you can tell Vincent Russo about it?"

"I'm not telling Russo anything. I'm asking him."

She narrowed her eyes at me. "That's why Roger Horowitz showed up at seven-thirty this morning, isn't it? Something to do with Gordon Cahill's death."

I nodded.

"Horowitz is a homicide detective," she said.

"You're a pretty good detective, too, honey."

She gave me a quick, humorless smile. "Your friend Gordon Cahill was murdered, then."

"Yes," I said. "It looks that way."

"So," she said, waving her hand at the seat where Vincent Russo had been sitting, "are you gonna tell me what that— that verbal pantomime was all about?"

"Well," I said, "I asked Russo to find out what he could about what happened to Gordon Cahill, and I told him I wanted to know if it's linked to organized crime. He said he'd look into it and share what he finds out with me, provided it doesn't incriminate him or any of his family."

"*That's* what you guys were saying?"

"More or less. Yes."

She smiled and shook her head.

"You don't speak directly with Vincent Russo," I said. "Especially in front of a woman."

She looked up at the ceiling for a moment, then said, "And what if what he finds out *does . . .* ?"

"Incriminate him or someone in his family, you mean?"

"Yes."

"He'll make it clear that it would be in my best interest to stop thinking about Gordon Cahill."

"And will you?"

"Stop thinking about Cahill?"

She nodded.

"Sure," I said.

165

"Yeah," she said. "Bullshit."

I reached for her hand. She let me hold it for a minute, then drew it back and reached for her wineglass.

"Don't worry about me, honey," I said.

"You keep saying that." She hunched her shoulders and shivered. "He's so gallant." She pronounced it as if it were a French word, with the accent on the second syllable. "So warm. Charming, almost."

I nodded.

"Except his eyes," she said.

"You awake?" murmured Evie a few hours later.

"Mm," I mumbled. "Barely. You tuckered me out, honey."

She chuckled deep in her throat. She was lying on her side facing away from me. My arm was around her hips, and her butt was pressing back against me.

"Why were you limping?" she said.

"Was I limping?"

"Yes. And you've got a nasty bruise on your side. What happened?"

"Nothing," I said. "I fell down."

I slithered my hand up and cupped her breast. She took a quick breath, then reached up, covered my hand with hers, and held it tight against her.

"He's a scary man," she said.

"Russo?"

"Mm."

"Don't worry," I said. "He likes me."

"I doubt if that man really likes anybody."

166

"He loves his family passionately," I said. "He certainly seemed to like you."

"He's smooth, all right. But the way he looked right through me with those . . . those eyes of his. Such cold, bottomless eyes. Lizard eyes."

"I just need information," I said. "Either he has it or he doesn't, and if he has it, he'll either share it with me or not. Whatever, that will be the end of it. Then we'll be even, and both Vincent Russo and I will feel better."

"Jesus," she murmured.

Evie was quiet for so long that I found myself drifting back to sleep. Then she said, "I *was* worried."

"You mean last night? When you made a nice dinner and I didn't show up?"

"I tried to be angry," she said, "but I couldn't do it. Not until you got home and I knew you were okay. Then I could let myself be angry."

"How about now?" I said.

She let out a long sigh. "Go to sleep," she said. She squirmed herself back against me. "I'll let you know."

I smiled in the darkness. I knew I'd never understand women. I figured it was about time I gave up trying.

SEVENTEEN

I spent Thursday morning in court, and afterward I had the cabbie drop me off in front of Manny's Deli in Copley Square. When I walked into my office fifteen minutes later, I had a paper bag tucked under my arm.

Julie looked up from her computer and made a show of sniffing the air.

"Lunch," I said. "Let's go."

I went into my office. Julie followed me.

I cleared the fishing magazines and catalogs off the coffee table, plopped down the bag, and began removing the plastic containers from it. California avocado-and-mango salad. Pakistani cold curried chicken. Cuban rice with beans and baby shrimp. Maryland crabcakes. Alaskan salmon salad. An American Coke for me, a Diet for Julie.

She sat on the couch and began prying the tops off the containers. "What is this," she said, "some kind of international peace offering?"

"I didn't realize a peace offering was called for," I said.

"A peace offering is always called for." She gestured at the

169

containers of food. "Is there some kind of theme here?"

"No theme," I said. "Just stuff I thought you might enjoy."

"What happened to our tuna sandwiches and dill pickles and potato chips?"

"Oh," I said with a vague wave of my hand, "I just thought, something different for a change . . ."

Jule narrowed her eyes at me. "Why?" she said.

"What do you mean, why?"

"You're about to tell me you're taking tomorrow off, aren't you? Long weekend in Maine? Some fishing thing? Softening me up? Is that it?"

"Hell, no," I said. "Nothing like that. Maybe just a few hours this afternoon, but these crabcakes are special, aren't they? Did you try that red sauce? Manny had about a dozen different sauces for them, but . . ."

Julie was grinning at me. "You don't have to do this, you know."

"Do what?" I said.

"Ply me with food and drink."

I shrugged elaborately. "I wasn't plying you. I'm offended that the idea would even occur to you. I just thought, we have tuna sandwiches every day, and Manny's got all this great stuff, so why not—"

"Brady," she said, "you are the lawyer. If you want to abandon your practice for an afternoon, leave the people who depend on you in the lurch, you can just do it. It's best, of course, to inform your secretary in advance so she can make up excuses for you when clients and judges and other attorneys call. But that's optional. Because you *are* the lawyer."

"I am, aren't I," I said.

She sighed. "Where are you off to this time?"

"New Hampshire."

"Fishing?"

I smiled. "In a manner of speaking."

After Julie and I finished our lunch, I called Evie's office at Beth Israel. I expected to get her voice mail, but she answered on the second ring.

"It's me," I said. "Your very own sweetie."

"Hi, sweetie," she said. "What's up?"

"Wanted you to know I might be late tonight. Didn't want there to be another failure of communication."

"Okay," she said. "How late?"

"I don't know. I'd rather not mention a time."

Evie chuckled. "Which is it? You want me not to worry, or not to be angry?"

"Both," I said. "Either. I'm just trying to be considerate."

"You find that difficult?"

"Yes," I said. "But I'm working on it."

I walked home from the office and changed into jeans and a flannel shirt. Then I whistled up Henry, and he and I strolled down Charles Street to the parking garage.

It was a little after two-thirty when I turned onto Storrow Drive in downtown Boston.

Two hours later I pulled up in front of the Goff brothers' garage in Southwick, New Hampshire.

The red sign hanging in the office window said "CLOSED," and the doors to both bays were down. A tow truck was parked in front of one of the bays. "Goff's Garage" was stenciled on its door, along with a telephone number.

171

I got out of my car and peered in through the office window. All the lights were out. From somewhere inside the building a radio was playing.

I backed away and looked up at the second-floor windows. It didn't appear that any lights were on behind the curtains up there, either.

I walked around behind the building. The back yard, if that's what it could be called, was littered with rusted car bodies. Beyond them, on the edge of the woods, an ancient mobile home, the kind made of shiny aluminum with rounded-off corners that was intended actually to be pulled behind an automobile, was half buried in the weeds.

I continued my circuit of the house. A back door opened into the office, and when I looked through the window, I saw that an inside stairway led up to the apartment on the second floor. There were several narrow basement windows. I assumed they once had been glass, but now there was no glass. They were covered from the inside with plywood. Vehicles were lined up in a big lot beside the building, apparently waiting to be repaired. Many of them had obviously been in accidents. I suspected the Goffs rented their space as a holding area for wrecks while they waited for insurance appraisers to come and examine them.

I finished my circuit of the building and concluded that Harris and Dub Goff had called it quits for the day and were not home. So much for the stereotype of hardworking country folks.

This was disappointing. The Goff brothers had lived their entire lives in Southwick. I'd hoped to ask them if they remembered Oliver Burlingame and Mark Lyman.

My next stop was the general store, where I found Farley Nelson, the garrulous old-timer, at the cash register. He smiled when he saw me, showing me his extra-large teeth.

I smiled back at him, went to the cooler, snagged a bottle of water, and took it to the counter.

"That's a buck," said Farley.

I put a dollar bill on the counter.

"So howya doin'?" he said.

"Good," I said. "You?"

"Holdin' my own," he said. "Got your dog with you?"

"He's in the car. This"—I touched the bottle of water—"is for him."

"Need another bowl?"

"Still got the one you gave me the other day. Which I appreciate."

"Well," he said, "it's gettin' to be that time of year. My setter smells it in the air. Bird season. She's gettin' itchy. Bet your feller is, too."

"I don't hunt with him."

Farley Nelson craned his neck and looked out at my car, where Henry was pacing the backseat. "Brittany, huh?" he said. "Hell, don't matter whether you hunt him or not. He's a hunting dog. It's in his blood. Don't matter how old he is, or how he's been trained, or if he's ever done it before. It's bred into him. You put him in the woods, he'll go hunting."

"Look, Mr. Nelson," I said. "I was wondering—"

"Farley," he said. "Call me Farley, for goodness' sake. Makes me feel old, being called Mister by a grown-up."

I smiled. "Farley, then. I was wondering if you could spare a few minutes to talk with me."

"Don't see why not. What's on your mind?"

"I was thinking maybe we could find someplace where we wouldn't be interrupted."

He glanced at his wristwatch. "I'm supposed to get off at

five, actually, if that Jennifer girl shows up on time. She's on the soccer team, has practice every day she don't have a game. What's on your mind?"

"I wanted to test your memory about some people who might've lived here in Southwick a long time ago."

"Like Albert Stoddard, you mean? The fella you were asking about the other day?"

"Well, yes," I said. "Him and a couple others."

"No promises," he said. "My memory ain't what it used to be."

"Neither is mine," I said.

"Feel like buying an old coot a cold beer?"

"Of course."

"Why don't you meet me across the street." He pointed out the front window of the store. "I'll be along soon as Jennifer gets here to relieve me."

"At the inn?"

"They got a nice pub," he said. "Usually pretty quiet this time of day. If they don't get backed up with folks waiting for a table, they'll let you sit there all evening if you want to, just sippin' away at one beer."

Just then a woman appeared from somewhere in the back of the store. She was juggling a box of Cheerios, a bunch of carrots, a head of lettuce, a can of Maxwell House coffee, and a six-pack of beer. "How's that arthritis today, Farley?" she said as she dumped her groceries on the counter.

"I ain't complaining," said Farley.

"Turned over a new leaf, then, did you?" she said.

I lifted my hand to Farley. He nodded and jerked his head in the direction of the Southwick Inn across the street.

I went outside and let Henry out of the car. He squirted

174

on a few bushes while I emptied the bottle of water into his bowl.

He came over, drank it all, peed once more, and then I let him back in the car. I told him I'd be gone for an hour or so and he should guard the car, then crossed the street and went into the Southwick Inn.

The floorboards were wide and burnished and warped with age. The ceiling rafters were dark and low, and the woodwork was layered with two centuries of paint. There were pewter sconces on the walls and gingham curtains in the windows.

A thin, half-bald man was sitting at a rolltop desk with his back to the low counter inside the front door. When the bell dinged behind me, he swiveled around and looked at me. "Can I help you?"

A midwestern accent. Wisconsin, I guessed. He was wearing a white shirt and blue jeans and a red bow tie and round, silver-rimmed glasses.

"I'm meeting somebody in the pub," I said.

He pointed across the hallway with his thumb. "Grab a seat. I'll be with you in a minute."

The pub was a smallish room in the front corner of the inn. There were six stools pulled up to the bar and five tables lined up against the front wall by the windows. A dark oil painting of a clipper ship dominated one wall.

I took a corner table by a window that looked out onto the street. A minute later the half-bald man came in. "What can I get for you?" he said.

"A beer, I guess. Got anything local?"

"Want to try a Double Bag?"

I smiled. "Double Bag? What's that?"

"It's an ale."

"You recommend it?"

He nodded. "Oh, absolutely. Excellent. Brewed over in Vermont."

"Sounds good, then."

He went behind the bar and came back a minute later with an open bottle and a chilled glass mug.

"What do I owe you?" I said.

"Oh, we'll figure that out when you're done. You said you were meeting somebody?"

"Farley Nelson, from across the street."

"Ah. Farley."

"Are you the innkeeper?" I said.

"Yep. Jeff Little." He held out his hand.

I shook it. "I'm Brady Coyne. From Boston."

Jeff Little seemed in no hurry to get back to his roll-top desk, and he ended up sitting with me and telling me about how he'd cashed out of a dot-com start-up in Oregon less than six months before it crashed and burned, just lucky, it wasn't as if he saw it coming, and he came to New England looking to buy himself a bed-and-breakfast, prowled all over Maine and Vermont before he heard this inn was for sale, fell in love with the area, and the rest, as they say, is history.

"So how long have you been here?" I said.

"Two years next Christmas."

"You haven't run into a man named Albert Stoddard, by any chance?"

He frowned. "Stoddard. Rings a bell. Oh, right. That Democrat, the woman who's running for senator down in Massachusetts."

"Right," I said. "Same last name."

"Don't know any Albert," he said. "I know most of the

people in town, though not all of them by name." He smiled. "It's a pretty small town."

"Albert doesn't live around here," I said. "I just thought he might've dropped in for a beer or dinner sometime recently."

Little shrugged. "He might've, but if he did, he didn't introduce himself. Sorry."

A phone started ringing in the other room.

"Gotta get it," he said. "How's that ale?"

"Good," I said. "Strong."

He smiled and waved and left the room.

Farley Nelson came in a few minutes later. He went behind the bar and came back with a bottle of Budweiser.

He sat across from me and peered at me through his thick glasses with the built-in hearing aids. "So you met Jeff, eh?"

I nodded. "Seems like a nice guy."

"Local folks've been slow warming up to him. Usta be, this pub'd be jumping on a Thursday night." He waved his hand around, indicating its emptiness.

"Has Jeff done something wrong?" I asked him.

"Nope. He's a nice, friendly fella. Food's better than ever. Folks just liked Lou and Ginger, that's all, and they got it in their heads that if Jeff Little hadn't come along, Lou and Ginger would still be here running the place." He took a swig of his beer. "As if it wasn't them who put it up for sale." Farley smiled. "Been catching some nice bass from my pond lately. You like bass fishing?"

"Sure. They're a lot of fun on a fly rod."

"You oughta try my pond sometime."

"I'd like that."

"That probably isn't what you wanted to talk about, though, huh?"

177

"I always enjoy talking about fishing." I smiled. "But you're right. I was wondering if the names Mark Lyman or Oliver Burlingame might ring any bells with you."

He stared up at the ceiling for a minute, then looked at me and nodded. "I remember them."

"They were from around here, then?"

"Yes, sir. Both Southwick boys."

"What do you remember about them?"

He flapped his hands. "Nothin' special. Normal boys, they were. Oliver—they called him The Big O, sarcastic, don't you know—he was a scrawny little feller, one of those quiet kids you hardly notice. Lived with his mother out near the river. They moved away . . . hell, I can't recall when that was. Seems to me the boy was in high school. I'm thinking the mother got married or something, but I might be thinking about somebody else. The other one, the Lyman boy, I remember him a little better. Markie Lyman. He was always into something or other. Got ahold of some booze and ran his old man's pickup into a stone wall when he was in eighth grade, I remember that. Totaled the truck and not a scratch on the boy." Farley Nelson squeezed his eyes shut for a moment. When he opened them, he said, "All that was a long time ago. Hard to imagine them as grown-up men."

"You remember Albert Stoddard, don't you?"

"Sure. Those boys ran together. There were a couple others, too. All of 'em, about the same age. Hell, in Southwick if you're a boy, you gotta look pretty hard to find some fun."

"Aside from Mark Lyman taking his father's truck for a joy ride, what did they do for fun?"

"They fished, they hunted, they chased girls, they played touch football out behind the grammar school. Pretty much what boys do." He squinted at me. "I'm not helping you

178

much, I guess. You oughta talk to the Goff brothers. They know everything, and they've got better memories than me."

"I stopped by their garage," I said. "It was closed."

Farley Nelson chuckled. "Those two fellas got more money than King Farouk. They don't feel like working, they don't work. That's okay, provided your vehicle ain't parked there waiting for new brake pads or something. Hell, in the winter, early spring, they generally just close down the shop, take a couple months off, go somewhere where it's warm. I guess that's what you can do when you haven't got a wife or kids."

"I'll see if I can catch up with the Goffs," I said. "But I appreciate what you've told me. It does help." I paused. "Was one of those boys a ringleader, do you recall?"

He frowned. "Actually, I seem to recall there was another boy. I can almost picture him...." He shook his head. "Can't remember his name. He was maybe a little older. Big, good-looking kid. Always struck me, he was the one who had all the ideas, got them in trouble, and the others, they just went along with him." He squeezed his eyes shut for a moment. "Damn. His name, it's right there. If you said it, I could tell you if that was him, but damned if I can think of it."

"What kind of trouble?"

Farley Nelson blinked at me. "Huh?"

"You said this other boy got them in trouble."

"Oh, hell," he said, "just what boys get into, I guess. I'm not remembering anything particular."

"It might help me if you could recall his name," I said.

He scratched his head. "You know," he said, "it's one of those things, if you try looking straight at it, it's always out there to the side, and no matter how quick you move your

179

eyes, it always jumps away. I'll think about it, but I bet it'll occur to me sometime when my mind's on baseball or fishing or something."

"If it should happen to pop into your head," I said, "I'd like to know it." I reached into my wallet, took out one of my business cards, and slid it across the table to him. "Call me anytime. My home number's there."

He put on his glasses and squinted at the card. "You're a lawyer, huh?"

I nodded.

"So these questions, you planning to use them in court or something?"

"No, no," I said. "This is personal, not business."

"You never said why you wanted to know these things," he said.

"Like I said," I said, "it's kind of personal. Anyway—"

At that moment a uniformed policeman strode into the pub. It was Officer Paul Munson. He seemed to fill up the room with his bulk and his importance.

He came over and stood beside our table. "Farley." He touched the bill of his cap. "How you doing?"

Farley gave him a quick two-fingered salute. "Officer Munson. This ain't Limerick, you know. You've strayed a ways out of your jurisdiction."

Munson turned to me. "What brings you back to our neck of the woods?"

I smiled at him. "Just having a beer with my friend here. That's okay, isn't it?"

"Just so you're not breaking into people's houses."

"Oh, I've put all that behind me," I said. "I've reformed."

Munson smiled uncertainly, then looked at Farley Nelson. "He's pulling my leg, right?"

"I'd say he was," said Farley.

Munson turned back to me. "Well, sir, I recognized your vehicle. I saw it out front, and that's why I came in here, and I guess if I hadn't of, the Southwick officers would've done it pretty soon. We're keeping an eye on you."

"It's probably a good idea," I said.

"Son," said Farley to Munson, "me and Mr. Coyne here, we're trying to have a quiet beer, and you're coming mighty close to harassing us, you know that?"

"Harassing?" said Munson.

"Police harassment," said Farley. "Ain't that right, Brady? Mr. Coyne, here, he's a lawyer."

"I know that," said Munson.

"*Are* you harassing us?" I said.

He shook his head. "I don't mean to be."

I looked at Farley. "He's not technically harassing us."

"Coulda fooled me," said Farley Nelson.

"Unintentional," I said. "Public nuisance. Annoyance. Pain in the ass. Not harassment."

Munson frowned, looked from me to Farley and back at me, shuffled his feet, touched his holster, glanced at his watch, then said, "Well, all right. Gotta go." And he turned and left.

"You do something to antagonize that boy?" said Farley.

"No," I said. "I think he got antagonized all by himself."

EIGHTEEN

When I woke up on Friday, I remembered that I'd left a message on Ellen Stoddard's cell phone a couple days earlier asking her to call me, and she hadn't done it.

So while Evie was taking her morning shower, I poured the day's first mug of coffee, brought it into my room, and tried Ellen's cell phone again.

When she answered, I said, "It's Brady. Did you get my message the other day?"

"Yes. Sorry. I meant to get back to you, but I got sidetracked. There's a lot going on."

"I thought you were worried about Albert."

"Don't you dare judge me, Brady Coyne."

"I'm sorry, Ellen. I didn't mean it the way it sounded."

I heard her sigh. "What was it you wanted?"

"I wanted to ask you about Albert's finances."

"What about them?"

"Well," I said, "it appears that he never deposited his last four or five paychecks in his checking account."

"And?"

It was my turn to sigh. "Look," I said. "If you want me to stop doing this, just say the word. I'm concerned about Albert, and I thought you were, too. You and Jimmy asked me to try to find out what's going on with him. That's what I've been trying to do."

"Well, you can stop worrying," she said. "Albert's okay."

"Oh," I said. "Hm. Well, I'm glad to know that. You might have told me. Did he come home?"

"No. But I talked to the secretary at the history department. Albert called yesterday, said he'd be in next Tuesday."

"He's sick?"

Ellen laughed. "Not likely. He's just taking the week off. He's done that before. Tenured professors, they pretty much do what they want. They want some time off, they call in sick, wink, wink."

"And it doesn't concern you that he's playing hookey for a week? That doesn't raise questions?"

"Of course it does," she said. "The fact is, I had myself worked into a state where all I wanted to know was that he was alive. I convinced myself that even if he'd run off with one of his students or something, it would be okay. And you know what? It *is* okay. Now that I know he's all right, I don't care what he's doing. Now I can go back to thinking about my campaign."

"Well, that's good, I guess," I said. "What's Jimmy say about it?"

"Jimmy works for me."

"I was only thinking," I said, "that a week ago you were both concerned enough to retain me to hire a private detective to find out what Albert was up to."

"I've changed my mind about that," she said.

"Ellen," I said, "will you humor me for a minute?"

"For just about one minute," she said. "You caught me trying to eat breakfast and put on my makeup at the same time. You think that's easy, try it sometime. What's your question about Albert's paychecks?"

"He seems to have been depositing them in his checking account every fifteenth and thirtieth of the month. Then in July he stopped doing that. I'm wondering why. Does he get paid through the summer when school's not in session?"

"Yes."

"Well, I'm wondering what he did with those summer paychecks. He didn't put them in the bank."

"What difference does it make?"

"Does Albert have any money problems?"

"What do you mean?"

"Gambling debts? Bad investments? Has he bought any Italian shotguns lately?"

Ellen paused for a minute. "I couldn't really tell you. As far as I know, Albert doesn't gamble, and he has no interest whatsoever in the stock market. He really has no interest in money, period. He's always had enough, and he's never worried about it or wanted more. That's just the way he is. Albert and I keep our finances separate. We chip in for mutual expenses. The house, mainly. Otherwise, he lives his life and I live mine, and here and there our two lives intersect. We've always done it that way. I don't see why it matters."

I decided not to tell her that Oliver Burlingame and Mark Lyman, whose obituaries I'd found in Albert's hunting camp, both had money problems, and then they'd died—"suddenly" and "accidentally."

Maybe it was coincidence.

But I doubted it.

"It probably doesn't matter," I said. "I'm glad he's okay, and I'm sorry to bother you."

"No, Brady," she said. "I'm sorry. I don't mean to be unappreciative. It's just that I'm under mountains of pressure with these debates coming up, and all this Albert business doesn't help. Now that I know he's all right, I'm just going to try to not think about him. Whatever he's up to, it'll all make itself clear sooner or later. Meanwhile, I've got an election I'm trying to win, and that's what I need to focus on. Is this terribly insensitive of me?"

"I guess not," I said. "I'm envious. It's nice that you can compartmentalize like that. I wish I could."

She laughed quietly. "It *is* insensitive. Selfish, you might say. I know that. It's a gift and a curse. It enables me to concentrate on the job at hand no matter what's going on around me. But it's not a particularly admirable trait. Anyway, thank you for everything. Really. When this damn election is over, win or lose, I intend to treat you and Evie to prime rib at Locke Ober's. If we're lucky, we can persuade Albert to join us."

"That will be nice," I said. "I'll hold you to it."

Six months after John and Carla Barrera bought their Victorian dream house in Chelmsford, the north corner under the living room collapsed. A couple of upstairs windows shattered, the living-room floor split open, and a house-wide crack you could stick your fist through opened along the roofline.

When they called in a builder, he told them that the sills

were rotten and the foundation was crumbling. He gave them an estimate of $175,000 to jack up the house, rebuild the foundation, replace the sills, and repair all the rest of the damage.

John Barrera was a high school math teacher. Carla was an RN working a night shift at an assisted-living facility. They'd both worked hard and saved for ten years to accumulate the down payment for their first house. Now they were expecting their first child.

Their homeowner's insurance didn't cover the collapse of their house. They'd tapped out their borrowing power on their mortgage.

It was the kind of case I loved. There were plenty of villains to go after and a really nice couple to defend. The previous owners might have known about the rotten sills and disintegrating old foundation. If they did, they'd lied when they put the house on the market. I intended to find out.

The seller's realtor, at minimum, had been slipshod and at maximum, had also lied. The Barreras' own realtor had been irresponsible, the home inspector they'd hired had surely done an unprofessional job, and the bank's appraiser had likewise failed to see what, according to the various experts I'd sent out to look at the house, should not have been that hard to see.

I wasn't overlooking the possibility that money had changed hands. Bribery would make it a criminal case. But my aim was to negotiate a substantial enough settlement for the Barreras to repair their wounded house and have a big chunk left over.

John and Carla were prepared to sue. So was I. It would be fun to figure out who the main villain was and haul him to court and argue it before a jury. I doubted we'd end up having to take it that far, but the mere threat of it was powerful.

I spent Friday morning on the telephone with the lawyers of the various potential defendants in the case, and I'd just hung up with one of them when Julie tapped on my door.

"Enter," I called.

She entered and stood there in the open doorway. "Um, Mr. Coyne?"

I couldn't read the look on Julie's face. It seemed to be halfway between bewilderment and amusement. She only called me "Mr. Coyne" in the presence of adversaries or brand-new clients that we didn't know very well.

"What's up?" I said.

"There's a, um, gentleman here to see you."

I gestured for her to close the door, then crooked my finger at her. She came over and stood beside my desk.

"What is the name of this gentleman," I said, "and does he have an appointment, and what does he want?"

She glanced back in the direction of our reception area. "He says his name is, ah, Paulie?" She made it a question.

"Big guy," I said. "Silk suit. Diamond on his pinkie finger."

"Yes, that's right," said Julie. "Very big. He didn't mention a last name, and I didn't insist. He does not have an appointment. He said he came to, quote unquote, get you. He seemed to be under the impression that you were expecting to be gotten. I told him you were busy. He said he'd wait, but he didn't have much time, he's double-parked out front, his boss is a busy man. What the hell does that mean, get you?"

I smiled. "It's okay. Send him in."

188

She shrugged, turned for the door, then stopped. "*Get you?*"

I shooed her away with the back of my hand.

A minute later she ushered Paulie into my office. I stood up, went around my desk, and held out my hand. "Good to see you again," I said.

For a two-hundred-fifty-pound bodyguard with a nine-millimeter weapon under his armpit, Paulie had a limp hand-shake, and he avoided eye contact. A shy, respectful man. "Mr. Russo," he said, "he's waiting, Mr. Coyne. He don't like to wait. He's gonna blame me, he thinks he waited too long."

Paulie was wearing a shiny gunmetal-gray suit, a charcoal shirt, a white necktie, and lilac-scented cologne. I'd run into him a few times at Skeeter's back when he was breaking kneecaps for Vincent Russo. If I'd ever heard his last name, I'd forgotten it. Since Russo's "retirement," I'd heard that Paulie had been promoted to head bodyguard and chauffeur.

I took my suit jacket from the back of my chair and slipped it on. "Let's go, then," I said.

I told Julie I expected to be back in an hour or so, then followed Paulie out of my office building to a black Lincoln Town Car that was double-parked at the curb.

"I thought Mr. Russo liked the Mercedes," I said.

Paulie opened the back door for me. "Since nine-eleven," he said, "Mr. Russo buys nothing but American."

"A true patriot," I said.

Paulie pulled out onto Boylston Street, cut over to Storrow Drive, slid onto Cambridge Street at the rotary, and fifteen minutes later he stopped in front of Nola's Trattoria on Hanover Street. He got out and opened the back door for me.

A CLOSED sign hung in the door to the restaurant, and the

blinds had been lowered over the front window. Paulie used a key to let us in.

Vincent Russo was sitting at the corner table in back near the kitchen. He was sipping a glass of dark red wine and eating fried calamari with his fingers. He stood up when I approached, wiped his fingers on a linen napkin, and held out his hand.

I shook it. "I appreciate your seeing me," I said.

He flicked my gratitude away with the back of his hand. "It's what friends are for, Mr. Coyne. Please. Sit down, huh? You had lunch?"

"Yes, thank you." It was a lie. I wanted to spend as little time with Vincent Russo as possible.

He filled a glass to the brim with wine and pushed it across the table to me. He held up his glass.

I clicked mine against his, took a sip, and set it down.

"I have made inquiries," he said.

I nodded.

"Gordon Cahill."

"Yes," I said. "Gordon Cahill."

"Before he was a private investigator," he said, "he was a policeman."

I took another sip of wine.

"This Cahill was no enemy of ours," said Russo. "But there were those who considered him a traitor, huh?" He arched his bushy gray eyebrows at me.

"May I speak candidly, Mr. Russo?"

"By all means." He waved his hand around, taking in his restaurant. Paulie was sitting at a table in the front of the room reading a newspaper. "There are just the two of us here." He meant that the place wasn't bugged. Paulie, apparently, didn't count.

"It wouldn't even occur to me that what happened to my friend was in any way connected to a man of your reputation," I said carefully. "But what Gordon Cahill did several years ago, the testimony he gave, it unquestionably angered certain other people."

Russo's hooded eyes were watching me without expression.

"Whitey Bulger," I said. "Steven Flemmi. John Connolly. The Irish mob."

"Those men," said Russo, dismissing them with a backhanded gesture. "They are nothing to me." Russo put his forearms on the table and leaned toward me. "I have made inquiries, Mr. Coyne. I know that the state police—your friend Horowitz—they are asking questions. If they had the sense to ask me, I would tell them. They are wrong in what they're thinking."

"They're wrong," I repeated.

He looked at me without blinking.

"I mean no disrespect," I said, "but you are certain of this?"

He narrowed his eyes and pressed his lips together, then leaned back in his chair and shrugged.

"I'm grateful for your candor, Mr. Russo. May I ask you another question?"

He raised one hand about an inch off the table, then let it drop, which meant that one more answer and he would consider us even.

"I want to know who did this to my friend," I said. "They poured gasoline on him, Mr. Russo. They burned him alive."

"That is a terrible thing." He shook his head. "It shows great disrespect." He stared at me for a moment, then said, "Amateurs, huh?"

191

"Amateurs did this?"

He bowed his head.

I took another sip of wine, then pushed myself away from the table and stood up. "I appreciate your time, Mr. Russo," I said. "And I'm grateful for your information." I held out my hand to him.

He reached over and, without standing up, gripped it quickly. "Paulie will drive you back," he said.

I nodded, then turned and started for the door.

"Hey, Mr. Coyne," said Russo.

I turned.

"Bring Miss Banyon back for dinner, huh?"

This, I understood, was not an invitation. It was a demand. Having me accept his invitation was Russo's way of being assured that I respected him. It meant that now, in his mind, he had more than paid off his imaginary debt to me.

Now, by his calculation, I owed him. That's the way he liked it.

A gesture of respect was no small thing.

"Of course," I said. "Evie enjoyed her meal the other night. We'll be back very soon. Thank you."

"Next time you call and make your reservation," he said, "you be sure and tell Nickie you're bringing Miss Banyon. We'll cook something special for her, huh?"

"We'd both like that," I said.

As Paulie wheeled the Town Car through the narrow one-way Boston streets, I thought about my conversation with Vincent Russo.

I knew better than to take what he'd told me at face value. However courteous and helpful he might appear to be, he was a lifelong criminal who'd lied, cheated, bribed, threatened, maimed, and murdered his way to the top of the North End food chain. Truth was just another weapon for a man like Vincent Russo. If telling the truth served his interest, he'd tell it. If it didn't, he'd lie with equal sincerity. That's how it was in his culture, and the fact that he was more or less "retired" from the "business" didn't change anything.

If Russo had agreed with Roger Horowitz, if he'd told me that Irish Mafia from Southie had exacted its overdue revenge on that rat Gordon Cahill, I would've been tempted to believe it. Telling me that would've been a risky thing for Russo to do. It would've been a violation of the time-honored code. Men like Vincent Russo feared and respected other mobsters, even their rivals, far more than they feared or respected the police, never mind some lawyer.

But I had not heard what I wanted to hear. I'd hoped Russo would confirm Horowitz's hypothesis. I would've felt better if Russo told me that Gordon Cahill's murder was the work of Whitey Bulger's Winter Hill Gang, their vengeance for Gordie's undercover work and testimony more than a decade earlier.

Now I was left with the possibility, if not the likelihood, that Gordie's death was connected to a case I'd hired him to do. That made it my responsibility.

NINETEEN

L ater that afternoon I was gazing out my office window trying not to think about Vincent Russo when Julie buzzed me. "There's somebody here who wants to see you," she said.

"Who is it?"

"Mrs. Cahill," said Julie. "If you have a minute."

"Of course I've got a minute," I said. "I've got several minutes. You know I'm in here daydreaming."

I got up and went out to the reception area.

Donna Cahill, Gordie's wife, was a plump, pretty woman somewhere in her late forties. I'd only met her a couple of times. She looked older than I remembered.

She stood up when she saw me. She was wearing a gray business suit and an off-white silk blouse and high heels and a big shoulder bag. I had the impression that she'd dressed up for this occasion, as if she thought her appearance would make some kind of difference.

I went over to her and held out my hand. "I'm sorry about Gordie," I said.

"Yes. Thank you." She took my hand and smiled quickly. "I wondered if I could talk with you for a minute. I know I don't have an appointment, but . . ."

"You don't need an appointment," I said. "Would you like some coffee or something?"

"Your secretary already offered," she said. "I'm fine, thank you."

We went into my office. Donna sat on the sofa with her knees pressed together. She rested her big shoulder bag on her lap and tugged at the hem of her skirt.

I sat in the chair across from her. "How are you doing, Donna?" I said to her.

She looked out the window for a moment, then returned her eyes to me. "I guess I've been waiting for that late-night knock on the door ever since we got married," she said softly. "All that time he was with the state police? Even during the past ten years or so, when he was working private, presumably easy, safe, boring stuff, it never left me, that feeling of impending doom. It never went away. It didn't make for a particularly happy marriage." She looked up at me and smiled. I saw no irony in her smile. I guessed that in better times she had smiled often and easily.

"I can understand that," I said.

"Actually," she said, "I guess Gordon was happy enough. Anyway, all those years, they pretty much prepared me for what happened Sunday night. I'd played it out in my head a thousand times. So how am I doing? I'm doing about the way I imagined I'd be doing. Kind of numb, I guess."

I nodded. There didn't seem to be anything to say about that.

"He was doing what he wanted to do," she said after a minute, "what he was good at. I loved him, but I resented

196

the hell out of his job." She waved her hand, dismissing the importance of her own feelings. "Anyway, it seems like even now, after he's dead, his damn job is still haunting me."

I noticed that she'd taken pains with her makeup, especially around her eyes. In spite of her denials, I suspected she'd done some crying.

I put my elbows on my knees and leaned toward her. "What can I do, Donna? How can I help?"

"Gordon always said you were the one lawyer he could trust. He said if he ever needed a lawyer, you'd be it." She arched her eyebrows at me.

"I trusted him, too," I said. "Gordie was rock solid. Even if he did inflict me with some awful puns."

She smiled. "I want to do what's right. I guess I want to hire you. I need some advice."

I waved my hand. "You don't need to hire me. What's the problem?"

She was quiet for a moment. Then she said, "You know Roger Horowitz."

"Sure."

"You know how—how dogged he can be, then."

I smiled. "I certainly do."

"Gordon and Roger were old friends from his state police days," she said. "We used to socialize with Roger and Alyse. Now Roger's investigating Gordon's death. Roger tells me he was murdered."

"He told me that, too," I said carefully.

"He wants me to give him permission to go through Gordon's files and records. He thinks he'll find something that will lead him to the murderer." She paused. "I'd like him to catch whoever did this, of course. But . . ."

"But those files contain confidential information," I said.

197

She nodded. "Gordon always said confidentiality was an absolute in his work. He said it was the same as a doctor or"—she looked up at me—"or a lawyer." She shrugged. "Anyway, I don't quite know what to do. Roger says Gordon's dead, so it's up to me. He says I don't have any obligations to anybody. What do you think?"

"I'm probably the wrong person to ask," I said.

"I know he was working on something for you," she said. "I think that makes you the right person to ask."

"I don't know for certain if that case has anything to do with what happened to Gordie," I said.

"You think it might?"

I nodded. "It might."

She looked up at the ceiling. "Roger implied it had something to do with that testimony he gave ten or twelve years ago. He was hinting about mobsters, revenge. Like that. I think he was trying to scare me."

"Horowitz is a good man," I said. "He's just trying to solve a crime."

"I'm asking for your advice," Donna said.

"I can't be objective," I said. "My professional relationship with my own client is at stake, and as much as I want Gordie's murderer brought to justice, and even considering the possibility that there's a connection, I have refused to share any confidential information with Roger Horowitz. But that doesn't make it the right thing for you."

She shook her head. "Oh, I think it does. It's what Gordon would want, don't you think?"

I nodded. "Well, if you want the truth, I guess I do, yes. I think he would consider it a betrayal if you or I divulged confidential information about his clients to anybody."

"Even if it meant his murderer would go free?"

198

"That's a tough one, all right." I shrugged. "My situation is different from yours."

"He kept all his records locked up in his office in our house," she said.

"What about the office on St. Botolph Street?"

She shook her head. "That's just where he met with clients, did his research, played on his computer, used the phone. He didn't feel it was secure."

"I know Horowitz did some snooping around there."

"Well, I'm sure he didn't find anything," she said. "That's why he wanted to snoop around our house. I told him I had to think about it. He mumbled something about a search warrant."

"Typical," I said. "He's bluffing."

"So you think I'm on solid legal ground?"

"Legal or moral?" I said.

"Moral is my own problem," she said. "I'm not asking for your help with that. I want to know about legal."

"You could make a compelling case either way," I said. "On the one hand, you, as Gordie's wife, have no legal obligation to his clients. You could turn his files over to the police and let them worry about the confidentiality issue. On the other hand, the significance of those files doesn't change just because Gordie isn't here to protect them. They're still confidential. The people who confided in him still have every right to expect their privacy to continue to be honored."

Donna Cahill was smiling at me. "Could you repeat that?"

"Well," I said, "all I meant was, a lawyer could argue it either way. Which, of course, is typical of lawyers. Which I guess is what I was doing, come to think of it. You should do what feels right to you."

"So it *is* a moral issue."

199

I shrugged.

"Roger said he'd be back," she said, "looking for those files. I'm going to tell him no."

"You going to tell him you consulted with an attorney," I said.

"Sure. Why not."

"If you want to see Roger Horowitz blow his stack," I said, "just tell him it was me you consulted with."

"I wouldn't mind seeing Roger blow his stack." Donna smiled. "I've got something of yours," she said. She opened her shoulder bag and pulled out a manila envelope. "I found this on Gordon's desk. It's got your name on it."

"We were going to get together Monday morning," I said. "He probably planned to give it to me then."

"Yes, well . . ." Gordon Cahill's Toyota Corolla hit the tree in the Willard Brook State Forest on Sunday night, she was thinking.

I was thinking that, too. The timing of it was striking.

She handed the envelope to me. "One less confidential thing for me to worry about."

I took the envelope. It was sealed with cellophane tape. Cahill had scrawled "Coyne" on it with a black Magic Marker.

There was something else scribbled on the envelope, this in blue ballpoint pen. It said: "Leave no tern unstoned."

I looked up at Donna.

She smiled. "I guess he was working on another pun."

"I thought some of them were actually pretty clever," I said. "Though I never admitted that to Gordie. I think he enjoyed hearing you groan when he told one of his puns."

She shrugged. "He was a clever man, all right."

I put the envelope on the coffee table. "Thanks for this."

She stood up and smoothed her skirt over her thighs. "Well, I won't take any more of your time," she said. "Thank you for listening. Thank you for your advice." She gave me a little half smile. Then she suddenly turned her head away, and I heard her mumble, "Oh, shit."

I stood up and went to her side. I touched her shoulder. "Donna?"

She turned and put her forehead on my chest. "Roger told me he didn't want me looking at Gordon's body. Wouldn't even let me see a picture of him."

I put my arms around her. Cahill's body was a cinder, Horowitz had told me.

"He brought Gordon's watch and his wedding band and his wallet over for me to identify," she said. "They were in a big yellow envelope. The ring and the watch were half melted. They had to cut them off him. The wallet was charred." Her arms went around my waist and she hugged herself against me. "Thinking about what happened to him . . ."

I patted her shoulder. I felt useless. I couldn't think of anything to say.

"He kept his wallet in his hip pocket," she murmured. "He was sitting on it, and it got burned anyway. The money in it was ashes. I keep trying to imagine it . . ."

I made sympathetic noises in my throat and held on to her.

"I swore I wouldn't cry," she mumbled. "Gordon always told me I had to toughen up."

"I'd say you're plenty tough," I said.

"Just putting up with all his stupid puns." She chuckled softly into my shirt. "Oh, hell, Brady. I miss him."

"Me, too," I said.

After Donna Cahill left, I went back into my office, sat at my desk, and opened the envelope that Gordie had intended to give me. It contained two computer printouts of newspaper articles.

The headline for the first one read: "Search for Local Boy Given Up." The date at the top was October 22, 1971.

JAFFREY-After nine days of intensive searching by local and state authorities, specially trained rescue dogs, and an estimated seventy-five volunteers, the hunt for the teenage boy who got lost on Mount Monadnock on Columbus Day was suspended.

Robert Gilman, 13, of Southwick, was hiking the popular Parker Trail on the east slope of the mountain when an early-season blizzard separated him from the rest of his group.

According to State Police Lieutenant Francis Conway, the weather impeded the search efforts from the beginning. In addition to the Columbus Day blizzard, which left nearly a foot of snow on the mountain, another storm three days later dropped seven more inches. "Snow on the mountain in October isn't that unusual," said Lt. Conway. "Two major storms within three days of each other like that is pretty rare, though. The snow made it really hard for the dogs."

Conway indicated there was no immediate plan to resume the search.

I'd read somewhere that Mount Monadnock was the most-climbed mountain in the United States. It was one of those geologically old, round-topped, worn-down eastern mountains where casual hikers could follow well-marked walking trails to the summit in the morning, have a leisurely picnic, and descend in the afternoon. You could see Monadnock's peak from some of the hilly roads in Southwick, New Hampshire.

The headline for the second clipping read: "Boy's Body Found on Monadnock." It was dated July 16, 1972.

```
JAFFREY-Andy and Rebecca Gilman's nine-month
nightmare ended Saturday afternoon when hikers
discovered the couple's teenage son's body at the
bottom of a ravine off the Marlboro Trail on the
west side of Mount Monadnock.

Bobby Gilman, who would have turned fourteen in
three weeks, became separated from his friends in
a freak snowstorm last Columbus Day. Rescue work-
ers and volunteers searched for over a week be-
fore giving up.

The boys who were with Bobby that day told police
that they had been playing in the woods about
halfway up the mountain just off the heavily
traveled Parker Trail on the east slope when the
heavy snow squall suddenly enveloped them. They
headed down the trail, and only when they arrived
at the bottom did they realize that Bobby wasn't
with them.
```

"We found the boy's body on the opposite side of the mountain from where he got lost," said Jaffrey Police Sergeant Adam Becker. "We figure he must have gotten disoriented in the storm and the darkness, and he ended up wandering several miles in the wrong direction. It appears that he fell into the ravine and hit his head and broke his leg. If he'd just stayed where he was, the rescue teams would have found him for sure. It's a tragedy."

Bobby Gilman was an honor-roll student. He played the clarinet in the Southwick junior high school band and was a member of the French club. Funeral arrangements are indefinite pending the release of his body.

I tilted back in my chair and looked up at the ceiling. I was thinking of Andy and Rebecca Gilman. How do parents ever learn to live with such a thing?

I read the two stories again. The names of the boys who'd been with Bobby Gilman the day he got lost on the mountain were not mentioned. If they had been, I was willing to bet that Oliver Burlingame, Mark Lyman, and Albert Stoddard would've been among them.

If I was right, those boys must have lugged around a load of guilt all those years.

Mark Lyman, for one, had ended up taking his deer rifle into the woods shooting himself with it. Maybe he never did quite learn how to live with it.

Maybe Oliver Burlingame had gone to Louisiana and jumped off his bass boat.

And now Albert was acting, in Ellen's word, "weird." Guilt over something that happened thirty years ago?

If so, why now?

And what did Bobby Gilman's death on Mount Monadnock in 1971 have to do with Gordon Cahill's murder?

Julie and I usually close up shop a little early on Friday afternoons, so I got home before Evie. I changed into my weekend clothes, then took Henry down to the Common so he could stretch his legs.

When we got back, I snagged a Sam Adams from the refrigerator, took it to my room, and checked my voice mail.

I had one message: "Mr. Coyne, this here is Farley Nelson up to Southwick. I was thinkin' maybe you'd like to come on up here tomorrow, give them bass in my little pond a try. They've been bitin' awfully good lately. I'll be around all day. If you can make it, just come on up. Don't forget your fly rod."

He didn't leave his number, but I hit star-69 and retrieved it.

I dialed it, and when his answering machine picked up, I said, "Farley, it's Brady Coyne. Thanks for the invitation. I'll be there. Late morning sometime, assuming that's okay with you. If you get a chance, call me back. I need directions to your place."

I thought it would be fun to get to know Farley better, and maybe even to catch one of his largemouth bass on a fly. I was also looking forward to testing his memory about a Southwick boy who died on Mount Monadnock over thirty years earlier.

Evie and I were sipping Bloody Marys in our patio garden and watching the late-summer sky grow dark. We were debating whether to go out to eat or have takeout delivered. Neither of us had the energy to cook.

Henry was sprawled under the table listening closely to our discussion. He'd already eaten, but he was always attentive when the subject was food.

We'd pretty much agreed on takeout and had narrowed it down to pizza or Chinese.

I refilled our Bloody Mary glasses. "Tomorrow's Saturday," I said to Evie.

"Thank God."

"Feel like driving up to New Hampshire with me?"

She took a long thoughtful sip, then said, "Why?"

"Well, the foliage has started to turn. It's supposed to be a nice day. There are always antique shops . . ."

She was grinning at me. "Antique shops? Come off it, Brady Coyne. You hate antique shops. And since when did you want to go driving around looking at foliage?"

I shrugged. "I've got to go back up there, talk to someone. I thought you might like to come along."

"And do what?"

"Keep me company. It is a pretty drive."

She reached across the table and grabbed my hand. "Honey," she said, "don't worry about me, okay? You've got business to do, and if you've got to do it on a Saturday, that's fine. I understand. I'm a big girl. I'll give Mary a call, see if she wants to play." She gave my hand a squeeze. "Bring Henry. He enjoys foliage."

"I wouldn't do it if weren't important."

"I believe you," she said. She stood up. "I need a jacket. I'm getting chilly. Want anything inside?"

I shook my head.

Evie went into the house. I reached down and scratched Henry's forehead. I was thinking about Bobby Gilman stumbling around a mountainside in the dark with a blizzard swirling around him.

When Evie came back, she said, "Hold out your hands and close your eyes."

I did.

She put something into my hands. "Don't open 'em yet," she said. "Guess what?"

I closed my hands on it. "I know what this is," I said. "It's a damn cell phone." I opened my eyes and looked at Evie. "I hate cell phones."

"Tough," she said. "This is for me, not you. This is for when you're on the road or held up in court or off fishing or wandering around in New Hampshire somewhere and you realize you're going to be late and you know I'm about to start worrying about you, or you think maybe I'm already getting angry with you. This is so you can call me and tell me you're okay and you're going to be late and you love me. Just keep it with you, okay?"

"Okay," I said. "But I'll never use it."

"You'll use it to call me," she said.

"I guess so," I said. "But I'm not going to give the number to anybody. I don't want the damn thing jangling in my pocket."

"I've got the number," she said. "If it jangles, it's me, and you better answer it."

"If you tell Julie I've got a cell phone," I said, "I promise, I'll heave it off the Longfellow Bridge."

She smiled. "It's a deal. What about pizza?"

TWENTY

I was in my car heading north by nine on Saturday morning, with my brand-new cellular telephone riding on the seat beside me. Evie had insisted I leave it turned on. She assured me that if it rang, it would be her voice I'd hear when I answered it—so I better answer it.

I left Henry sitting inside the front door with his head cocked to the side and his brown eyes accusing me of abandoning him. I tried to convince him that I'd be back, but he wasn't buying it.

It was one of those breezy late September New England mornings—cloudless sky, a hint of frost in the air, dead leaves swirling alongside the road. The closer I got to Southwick, New Hampshire, the more splotches of crimson and gold I saw along the roadside. Flocks of migrating blackbirds perched on the telephone wires, and chipmunks and squirrels scurried around collecting acorns and beechnuts.

Foliage would be approaching its peak in Vermont's Northeast Kingdom. Over the next few weeks it would spread southward.

As I approached the village of Southwick, I came to the Goff brothers' garage. Both bays were open, so I pulled up in front and got out. I was eager to get a look at Farley Nelson's bass pond, but I had some questions that Harris and Dub Goff might be able to help me with.

On the radio inside the garage Ray Charles was singing "Georgia on My Mind." A Dodge pickup truck was parked in one of the bays. Masking tape outlined the headlights and windows and chrome, and it sported a brand-new coat of spray-painted blue primer.

An old Volvo station wagon was up on the lift in the other bay, and Harris Goff was working under it with a socket wrench. He was wearing his faded old Red Sox cap backward and whistling along with the radio.

I didn't see Dub.

I stood in the doorway and cleared my throat, and when Harris Goff didn't turn around, I stepped into the bay and said, "Mr. Goff."

He turned his head and squinted at me. "Hey," he said. "Boston."

"Wonder if I could talk with you for a minute," I said.

He waved his socket wrench at me. "Hang on a minute."

I went outside to the Coke machine, fed it a dollar bill, and got a can of root beer.

Harris Goff came out wiping his hands on a greasy rag. "You find Stoddard's camp okay the other day?"

"Your directions were impeccable. Thank you."

"Impeccable." He grinned through his scraggly black-and-gray beard. "Didn't get stuck in the mud, then?"

"Nope. No problem." I smiled. "I'd like to run a name by you."

"Go ahead."

210

"Bobby Gilman."

He looked off into the distance. "Haven't heard that name in a long time," he said slowly. "Twenty-five, thirty years, I bet."

"What can you tell me about him?"

He shrugged. "Not much. Just what I heard. He died. Me and Dub were off to college when it happened. All I know is, Bobby Gilman was just a kid. Got lost in the woods over on Monadnock, snowstorm blew in. They didn't find his body for close to a year. It was pretty big news hereabouts. Not many kids from Southwick die. Not many kids in Southwick to start with."

"He was a Southwick boy then?"

He nodded.

"Did you know him?"

"Me?" He shook his head. "He was about ten years younger than me."

"I understand he was with some friends when he got lost."

"That was the story."

"Do you remember who those friends were?"

Harris Goff scratched his beard and peered at me. "You got a lot of questions today, Boston. Why're you interested in some boy who died thirty years ago?"

"I can't tell you that," I said.

He grinned. "Lawyer business, huh?"

"Yes. Does the name Oliver Burlingame ring a bell?"

He frowned. "Should it?"

"He was a Southwick boy. About Bobby Gilman's age. He might've been one of those friends he was with."

He shook his head. "Like I said, I was off to school when that happened. I didn't know them boys."

"Never heard of Oliver Burlingame, then?"

211

"Can't say I have."

"They called him The Big O."

He shrugged.

"What about Mark Lyman?"

He looked up at the sky for a moment, then said, "Nope. Not him, neither. Sorry."

"But you knew Albert Stoddard," I said.

"Didn't know Albert," he said. "Knew the family. There was a sister. Older than Albert. Closer to my age. She had a reputation, if you know what I mean." He winked. "That's why I remember Albert. Them Stoddards had more money than most. Old man owned a plumbing supply place over to Keene, got himself a new Buick every other year. My mother used to say the Stoddards put on airs."

"Albert was about the same age as Bobby Gilman and Oliver Burlingame and Mark Lyman."

"I'd expect those boys were friends, then," said Harris Goff. "Southwick was even smaller back then than it is now. Anybody your own age, you go to school with 'em from the time you're five or six. You don't have a big choice when it comes to who your friends are."

"What happened that day Bobby Gilman got lost on the mountain?" I said.

"Hell, Boston. I told you, I wasn't there. Bunch of boys playin' in the woods up on the mountain, blizzard blows in, they all head down, and when they get to the bottom, one of 'em ain't there. That was the story."

"There must have been talk about it."

He shrugged. "I suppose there was."

"Rumors," I said. "Accusations."

"I don't know nothin' about that," he said. "Me and Dub were off to school, didn't hear much about it." He shrugged.

212

"Don't mean to be rude, Boston, but if I don't get that damn tie rod fixed on Mrs. Hart's old Volvo by noontime like I promised, she'll write another one of her bitchy letters to the newspaper."

"Sorry," I said. "I'll let you get back to work."

"Wish I could've helped you," he said. "Always like to help lawyers."

I smiled. "Thanks for your time. Say hello to your brother for me."

"Don't drive too fast, Boston." Harris Goff winked at me. "Rumor has it the police've got their eye on you."

Farley apparently hadn't checked his answering machine, because he hadn't called back with directions to his place. So I stopped at the general store. A tall teenaged girl wearing pigtails and a University of New Hampshire sweatshirt was behind the counter. An elderly woman in overalls and a pink hat was counting change into the girl's hand.

I got a bottle of orange juice from the cooler and stood behind the woman in the pink hat. The girl at the cash register was putting cans of cat food into a paper bag.

After the old woman left, I put my potato chips and juice on the counter.

The girl looked at me and smiled. "That it?"

I nodded and handed her a five-dollar bill.

She gave me my change. "Want a bag for that?"

"No, thanks," I said. "I wondered if you could tell me how to get to Farley Nelson's house?"

"You a friend of his?"

I smiled. "He invited me to see his bass pond."

She nodded as if that was the answer she'd expected.

"How well do you know your way around here?"

"Not very well."

She came from behind the counter and pointed out the front window at the road that ran past the store. "Head out that way," she said, "past the cemetery, three, four miles 'til you pass the lake. You want to take your . . . let's see"— she closed her eyes, consulting her memory—"it'll be your third . . . no, your fourth right after the lake. Look for the dirt road. It's really just a driveway. No street sign or anything. You go up a hill after you cross a little brook, and it's there on your right. Mr. Nelson's place is down the end, about half a mile in. Old white farmhouse with a big porch in front, red barn out back. It's the only house on the road. Been in their family for about a hundred years. Used to be a real pretty place. Nice view of the mountains. Mrs. Nelson always grew flowers, had a big vegetable garden. She made great apple pies. The Nelsons always brought stuff to the farmer's market on Saturdays. He's still got some sheep. She died a couple years ago."

"Sounds like you know him pretty well," I said.

"Everybody knows Mr. Nelson," the girl said. "He's an awfully nice old man. His family used to own half the town. He made loads of money, selling off the land. Donated a lot of his property for conservation, too. My dad says Farley Nelson has got bales of money piled up in his hayloft."

"But he works here?" I said.

"Oh," she said, "he doesn't do it for the money. He does it because he misses his wife. They were real close. He just likes to be around people. He's always inviting folks out to his house. Some people around here aren't very patient with him. He does talk a lot sometimes." She smiled. "But he's a nice man. Lonely, that's all."

214

The "three or four" miles the girl at the general store had mentioned turned out to be a little over six. Country miles are longer than city miles. I almost missed the dirt driveway that angled back to the right at the top of the hill after I'd crossed the brook, because by then I'd begun to think I'd already driven past it.

I turned in. The roadway was bordered on both sides by stone walls, and it was so narrow that in places brush scraped against the sides of my car. It dipped down, crossed the same brook I'd crossed on the paved road, went up a hill, and ended in Farley Nelson's farmyard.

A mud-spattered red pickup truck and a dark green Ford Explorer, both several years old, were parked side by side in front of the barn. A few sheep grazed in a rocky pasture off to the left, and as I sat there in my car, a dog—he looked like a cross between a Labrador retriever and a black bear—came lumbering out of the barn, barking gleefully.

When I got out of my car, the dog stopped barking, stood there stiff-legged, and looked at me. His tail swished back and forth, which everyone thinks is a sign of friendliness, but really signifies happiness, which isn't necessarily the same thing. Some dogs get very happy at the prospect of biting a human buttock.

This big black furball didn't strike me as the biting type, though, so I scooched down and held out my hand. He came over cautiously and gave it a sniff. If he was disappointed that it didn't hold a Milk-Bone or something, he kept it to himself. He circled slowly around me, snuffling greedily at my pants and shirt. I guessed he caught Henry's scent on me.

I stood up. "Where's your boss?" I said to the dog.

He looked at me, then lay down in the dusty driveway, put his chin on his paws, and closed his eyes.

Okay, so he wasn't telling.

I stood there in the sunshine and looked around. Through the trees behind the house I caught the glint of sun on water. Farley's bass pond, I guessed.

I assumed he'd come wandering out to see what his dog was barking at. But he didn't, so after a minute or two, I went over to the barn. The door was open. I stepped inside. "Hey, Farley," I called. "It's Brady Coyne. You in there?"

No answer.

I went around to the front of the house, climbed the three or four steps onto the porch, knocked on the door, and waited.

No sound came from inside.

I circled around the house, and out back, on the sunny southern side overlooking a weedy one-acre pond and facing a view of distant mountains, were two wooden Adirondack chairs. Farley Nelson was sitting in one of them. He wore a red-and-black checked wool jacket, baggy blue jeans, and scuffed work boots. His eyes were closed and his chin was on his chest. His gnarled hands rested on a folded newspaper on his lap.

I smiled. The old guy was sound asleep. When you're eighty-something, you've earned the right to take a nap whenever and wherever you want.

I imagined Farley and his wife sitting out here toward the end of a sunny summer's day having a drink and watching the dragonflies buzz around the pond and the shadows slither out of the woods and creep up the sides of the distant mountains.

An empty coffee mug and an ashtray with a cigar butt stubbed out in it sat on the wooden table beside him, along with his black-rimmed eyeglasses with the built-in hearing aids. No wonder he hadn't heard his dog barking or me calling his name.

My first impulse was to tiptoe away and let him sleep. But he had invited me to visit him. The girl at the general store had mentioned how lonely the old guy was, how he missed his wife, how much he enjoyed having company.

I figured he'd be disappointed if I didn't wake him up.

So I cleared my throat and said, "Farley?"

He didn't stir. I wondered how deaf he was.

I said his name again, louder this time, and when he didn't respond, I gripped his shoulder and gave it a gentle shake.

"Hey, Farley," I said. "Wake up."

His arm was rigid in my hand. I touched his cheek. It felt as cool as the early-autumn air.

Farley Nelson wasn't going to wake up.

TWENTY-ONE

I sat in the Adirondack chair beside Farley Nelson. I wondered if he'd just decided that this was as good a day as any to die, that the time had come to join his wife. I wondered if he'd known it was coming and brought his newspaper and coffee and cigar out here on this pretty September morning to wait for it to happen.

Heart attack, I guessed. Maybe a stroke.

I hoped it had been quick and painless and peaceful for him.

After a while, I got up and went to the back door of his house. It was unlocked, so I went in.

I found the telephone on the kitchen wall, dialed 911, and told the Southwick police dispatcher that I was at Farley Nelson's house and that Farley had died.

She asked if I was sure he was dead. I said I was pretty sure.

The dispatcher told me to wait right there and not touch anything.

I went outside and leaned against the side of my car, and

a few minutes later I heard sirens in the distance. The sirens grew louder, and then an emergency wagon pulled into the driveway, and right behind it was a police cruiser.

Two EMTs, both athletic-looking guys somewhere in their late twenties or early thirties, jumped out of the wagon.

I pointed behind the house. "He's back there," I said.

They went around to where Farley Nelson was sitting in his Adirondack chair.

There were two uniformed cops in the cruiser, a burly fortyish man and a younger dark-haired woman. The woman followed the EMTs out back.

The burly cop came over to me. "Sergeant Somers," he said. He held out his hand.

I shook it. "Brady Coyne."

"You found him, huh?" he said.

I nodded.

"Friend of his?"

"Yes."

"Nice old fella," said the cop.

"Yes, he was."

He took out a notebook. "I've got to ask you a couple questions, okay?"

"Sure."

"It'll only take a minute."

"That's all right."

He found a pen in his pocket and turned some pages in his notebook. "I need you to spell your name for me and give me your address and phone number."

I did.

"Your business?"

"I'm a lawyer."

He nodded as if he already knew that. "So how come you came here to Mr. Nelson's house today?"

I shrugged. "He invited me up. He wanted to show me his bass pond."

He smiled. "You're a fisherman?"

Before I could reply, Sergeant Somers's partner, the female officer, came out from behind the house and said, "Hey," and jerked her head for him to join her.

"Excuse me," he said, and went over to where his partner was standing.

They conferred for a minute, and then Somers came back to me. "I'm afraid I'm going to have to ask you to wait here with us, sir."

"What's going on?"

"A state police officer will be here. He'll want to talk with you."

The dark-haired female officer had gone to the cruiser. She was sitting in the driver's seat with the door hanging open, and she was talking on the two-way radio.

I turned to Sergeant Somers. "Can you tell me why they want to talk with me?"

"No, sir. I can't."

I could only think of one reason: There had to be a question about how Farley Nelson had died.

Somers remained with me but showed no indication that he was interested in more conversation. I guessed he was leaving the questions to the state police.

After a few minutes the female officer slid out of the cruiser. "They're on their way," she said to Somers. Then she went back to the rear of the house.

Ten or fifteen minutes later a New Hampshire state police

cruiser pulled into the farmyard and stopped beside the Southwick cruiser. A uniformed trooper got out from behind the wheel and stood there beside his vehicle. A tall guy with bushy gray hair got out from the passenger side. He was wearing a dark suit with a white shirt and a pale blue necktie. He headed straight for the rear of Farley Nelson's house.

After a few minutes, the gray-haired guy came back to where Somers and I were standing. "Sergeant," he said, "come on over here."

Somers followed him over to the state police cruiser where they conferred.

While they were talking, another car drove in. A sixtyish bald man got out of the passenger seat. The gray-haired state cop went over, said something to the bald man, and pointed toward the back of the house. I heard him say, "Doc." I guessed the bald man was the coroner. A minute later Sergeant Somers and the coroner went around to the back of the house.

The state police officer in the suit came over to me. "Looks like a damn used-car lot, huh?"

I nodded. Seven vehicles were now parked in Farley Nelson's farmyard.

"You're Brady Coyne?" he said.

I nodded.

"Lawyer from Boston, huh?"

"Yes."

"I'm Lieutenant Bagley," he said. He did not offer his hand. "I'm with the Major Crimes Unit out of the A.G.'s office in Concord."

"Major Crimes," I repeated.

"I understand you found the body."

"That's right."

"You were here to go fishing?"

I nodded. "Farley invited me up to see his bass pond."

"That's it?"

I smiled. "I like fishing. Farley seemed pretty proud of his pond."

"He invited you by telephone?"

"Yes, that's right. He called sometime yesterday afternoon."

"And you left him a message asking for directions."

I nodded. They'd listened to Farley's answering machine.

"That was"—Bagley glanced at the notepad he was holding—"at five-ten P.M.?"

"That sounds about right."

"Did he call you back?"

"No."

Bagley shrugged. "Let's start with where you've been and what you've been doing since then."

I told him. When I mentioned Harris Goff, he asked if I could pin down the time I stopped there and how long I'd stayed, which I tried to do. When I told him about stopping at the general store in Southwick for directions, he asked me the name of the girl behind the counter—which I didn't know—and what I'd bought there and what time I'd left.

He asked me how I knew Farley Nelson. I told him about my two previous visits to Southwick, about meeting him at the general store on Tuesday, and about how he and I had had a beer at the Southwick Inn on Thursday.

Bagley nodded as if he already knew that. "And were these occasions merely social?"

I shrugged. "The first time I bought water for my dog. He gave me a bowl. We talked about dogs."

"And the second time? At the inn?"

I shrugged. "I was asking Mr. Nelson about some people he might have known thirty years ago."

"I'm all ears, Mr. Coyne."

"It was about a couple of men who died last spring."

Bagley arched his eyebrows.

"Their names were Oliver Burlingame and Mark Lyman. I was asking about them in connection with a client of mine, and I can't say anything more about it."

"Did Mr. Nelson give you any useful information?"

"No, not really." I hesitated. "You think somebody murdered Mr. Nelson, don't you?"

"I'm quite certain of it," said Bagley.

I shook my head. "I saw his body," I said. "At first I thought he was having a nap. He was an old man. His hearing aid was on the table. I thought he just . . ."

Bagley touched his Adam's apple with his forefinger. "He was garroted, Mr. Coyne."

I looked at him.

He nodded.

"Jesus," I whispered.

"Looks like they used rope. The thin nylon kind." He held up his hand and spaced his thumb and forefinger about the diameter of a pencil apart. "Clothesline, maybe."

I blew out a breath.

"Doc Erb will pin it down for us," he said, "but I'm guessing it happened sometime last evening."

"The rigor," I said. "The temperature of the skin."

"You touched his body?"

I nodded.

"What else did you touch?"

I thought for a minute. "I went into the barn, called his name. Don't think I touched anything. I patted his dog. I sat

224

in the chair beside him for a few minutes. When I realized he was dead, not sleeping, I went into the kitchen and used the phone. Then I came back out here. That's all."

Bagley paused for a minute. "Naturally," he said, "I'm curious to know if Mr. Nelson's apparent murder is in any way connected to you and those two men you were asking him about the other day."

"I don't know." I hesitated. "Lieutenant, I'm a lawyer. I have a client."

"And you can't tell me who your client is or how he might be connected to any of this, I suppose."

"That's right," I said. "I can't." I paused for a moment. "Look. You should talk to Roger Horowitz. He's a homicide detective with the Massachusetts state police."

"Fill me in, Mr. Coyne."

I told him about Gordon Cahill's death the previous Sunday night in a burning car in the Willard Brook State Forest just a few miles south of the New Hampshire border. I told him that I'd hired Cahill on behalf of my client and he might or might not have been working on that client's case when he died. I told him that Cahill might have been coming back from Southwick, New Hampshire, that night, that ten years ago he had done undercover work for the Massachusetts state police, that he had testified in court against some Boston mobsters, that Horowitz and Cahill were old friends from those days, and that Horowitz was investigating Cahill's murder.

Bagley watched me with narrowed eyes as I talked, and when I finished, he said, "So it all goes back to your client."

"I don't know," I said.

"First your private investigator," he said, "and now Farley Nelson. You've been snooping around here asking innocent

225

people questions because you think your client had something to do with what happened to the PI. And now you've gotten this old man killed, too."

"I hope to hell that's not it," I said.

He arched an eyebrow. "You got a better explanation for what happened here today?"

"I don't have any explanation whatsoever for what happened here today," I said. "I don't know who killed Farley."

At that moment the two EMTs, along with Sergeant Somers and his dark-haired female partner, emerged from behind Farley Nelson's house. The EMTs were pushing a gurney on wheels. A dark blue plastic body bag lay on top of it. It was zipped up tight, and lying there on the gurney, it looked too small to contain a man's body.

Lieutenant Bagley and I watched them load Farley's body into the back of their wagon. Then they got in, backed around, and drove out the driveway.

The bald coroner appeared a minute later. Bagley went over and talked with him and then stood there in the driveway while the coroner got into his car, backed out, and drove away.

Then Bagley came back to where I was standing. "Doc Erb estimates it happened sometime between six and midnight last night. Figures old Farley died of a heart attack."

"Brought on by having a rope pulled tight around his neck," I said.

Bagley nodded.

"That would make it murder."

"Yes," he said.

"You already knew that," I said.

He shrugged. "You never know for sure."

Sergeant Somers came over and stood in front of Lieutenant Bagley. "Shall we secure the area, sir?"

Bagley nodded. "Forensics are on their way." He looked up. "Now what?"

A blocky SUV was pulling into the driveway. I thought I recognized it, and when I saw the logo and the words "Limerick PD" stenciled on the side, I was sure of it.

Officer Paul Munson got out, looked around, then came over to where Bagley and Somers and I were standing. "I heard about it on the scanner," he said. "Happened to be in the vicinity. Anything I can do?"

"We're all set," said Sergeant Somers.

Munson looked at me. "You again."

I nodded. "Me again."

He turned to Bagley. "What's he doing here?"

"You're out of your jurisdiction, Sergeant," Bagley said.

"I know this man," said Munson.

"We'll be in touch with you if we need your input," said Bagley.

Munson shrugged. "I just thought—"

"Thanks anyway," said Bagley.

Munson looked at me, then turned, got back into his vehicle, and drove away.

Somers went over to his cruiser, where his partner was waiting for him.

Bagley watched them for a minute, then turned to me. "The name Dalton Burke mean anything to you?"

I shook my head. "Should it?"

He reached into his jacket pocket, pulled out a sandwich-sized plastic bag, and held it up for me to see. Inside it was a wrinkled scrap of paper. "Dalton Burke" was printed in pencil on it. "It was balled up in his hand," said Bagley.

"Farley's hand?"

He nodded.

"Means nothing to me," I said. "Sorry."

"Oh, well." Bagley slid the plastic bag back into his pocket. "You can go, Mr. Coyne. I expect I'll want to talk with you some more."

I fished out one of my business cards. "That's got my home and office numbers on it." I remembered my new cell phone. I decided not to share that number with him.

He took the card, rubbed his thumb over the raised print, and stuck it in his shirt pocket.

I went around to the driver's side of my car and opened the door.

As I started to slide in, Lieutenant Bagley said, "Mr. Coyne."

"Yes?"

"I knew Farley Nelson," he said. "The old guy didn't have an enemy in the world."

Before you came along, he meant.

TWENTY-TWO

The road home from Farley Nelson's farm led me back through Southwick, and as I entered the village I realized that my stomach was growling. So I stopped in front of the general store, got out of my car, and went inside.

The same girl was behind the counter. Three or four people were gathered there, and they were all talking quietly. When I caught a look at the girl's face, I saw that her eyes were red.

I wandered around the back of the store and found a case with pre-made sandwiches wrapped in waxed paper. I chose a ham and Swiss cheese on rye, took a can of Pepsi from the cooler, and brought them to the counter.

The people who were standing there—an elderly woman and two younger men—stepped aside. I put my sandwich and Pepsi on the counter.

The girl pulled my purchases toward her and started to ring them up. Then she stopped and looked at me. "You're the guy who was here this morning, right? I gave you directions to Mr. Nelson's place."

"That's right."

"You found him, right? His body?"

I nodded.

"What happened?"

I shook my head. "He passed away. Heart attack apparently. That's all I know."

"People are saying he . . . he was killed or something."

"I don't know about that. The police are looking into it."

"Nobody would kill Mr. Nelson," she said. "He never did anybody any harm."

I nodded. "He seemed like a good man. I didn't know him very well."

"Everybody knows Mr. Nelson," she said. "Everybody's totally bummed."

I paid for my lunch and went outside. A knot of people had gathered on the sidewalk in front of the store. They were talking quietly, and when they saw me, they stopped and looked at me. It might have been my imagination, but I thought I detected accusation in their expressions.

I got into my car. My newish BMW with its Massachusetts license plates suddenly felt showy and conspicuous. I was an outsider in this little New Hampshire village, a foreigner, an intruder in a fancy car.

I backed out and pulled away. The folks in front of the general store watched me depart.

I drove slowly, heading home but in no particular hurry to get there, or to get anywhere, really. Farley Nelson's death was a weight in my chest. I couldn't shake the feeling that I was responsible for it.

Thinking about Farley led to thinking about Gordon Cahill. I felt responsible for what happened to him, too.

The road out of town followed the meanders of a rocky

little stream. I had noticed it every time I drove into and out of Southwick, and every time I saw it, I had the same thought: Trout lived in that cold, bubbly mountain water. Native brook trout. They would be small and spooky, and now in late September, which was their spawning season, the males would wear crimson spots as brilliant as drops of fresh blood on their backs and bright slashes of orange on their throats.

I spotted a narrow dirt side road that angled off the road I was driving on. It passed over the stream and disappeared into the woods on the other side. A good place to eat my lunch and ponder heavy thoughts.

I turned onto the dirt road, stopped just before the wooden one-lane bridge, picked up my ham sandwich and can of Pepsi from the seat beside me, and went down the sloping bank to the water's edge.

I sat on a boulder on the downstream side of the bridge, munched my sandwich, thought half-formed thoughts, and watched the water. The late-season currents swirled black and inscrutable around the rocks and flowed under the overhanging willows and alders. A few yellow poplar leaves drifted on the surface, brilliant spots of contrast against the dark water, and here and there an insect fluttered in the air and twirled in the eddies. I spotted none of those dimples or bulges that would betray a feeding fish, but the way an angler's subconscious mind works, I found myself studying how the top of the water moved, using those surface clues to imagine the unseen places below where trout might lie, and imagining myself easing into position so I could drift a fly to them.

Up at the head of the pool, the quick water funneled trout food through the narrow space between the granite bridge

231

abutments. The fish would line up along the seams between the fast and the slow water, and they'd gather in the area where the currents slowed and flattened out. Along the banks, in the soft water, they would lie in ambush and pick off whatever random edibles drifted along. A few fish would patrol the tail of the pool where the water quickened again, and there would surely be a trout or two lurking in the cushion behind that big midstream boulder—

"Hello, there." The voice came from behind me. It was a woman's voice.

I turned and shielded my eyes. It was Helen, the woman who worked at the real estate office. It had only been a few days ago when I met her.

It seemed like months.

She was standing in the dirt road looking down at me with her hands on her hips. She was wearing blue jeans and a flannel shirt and a red kerchief on her head. "Room for two fishermen in that pool?" she said.

"Come on down," I said.

She picked her way down the bank and sat on a flat boulder beside me. "Noticed your car," she said.

I nodded.

"Heard you were the one who found old Farley."

I drained the last of my Pepsi. "He was sitting in a chair in his back yard," I said.

"Stubborn old fool," said Helen. "The doctors told him he had to slow down. But would he? Hell, no. If he wasn't chopping wood or chasing his dogs around, he was getting up before the sun and lugging his old twelve-gauge pump gun through the woods to get to his deer stand." She shook her head. "He already had two heart attacks. They told him the next one would kill him."

I nodded and kept gazing at the moving water.

"Rumor going around he was murdered," she said.

I said nothing.

She shrugged. "Gossip gets going in this town, it takes a nuclear explosion to stop it. Old coot had a bad heart. It was going to happen sooner or later. I guess today was the day, that's all."

"I'm really sorry about Farley," I said. "I liked him a lot."

"He was looking forward to seeing you," she said. "Told me he was inviting you up, how you seemed interested in seeing his bass pond." She touched my arm. "Mentioned he remembered something he wanted to tell you."

"He didn't tell you what it was, did he?" I said.

"Nope. He was pretty proud of himself, though, I can tell you that. He worried about his memory, hated it when he couldn't recall something. I told him, you better write it down or you'll forget it again."

Dalton Burke's name. That's what he remembered. He had written it down.

"He didn't tolerate being told what to do," Helen said. "Ask him to do something, tell him it's for his own damn good, that's the last thing he'd do. Why do you think he smoked those smelly cigars, insisted on splitting his own firewood?"

I smiled. I had a vision of myself at eighty-something, if I lived that long, which was doubtful. I hoped I'd be splitting my own firewood.

"I'd say to him," Helen said, "let somebody else do it. You've earned it. And old Farley, he'd just grin, and he'd say, 'Live free or die, kiddo.' " She shook her head. "Stubborn old buzzard."

"You must've been pretty close to him," I said.

"He was my uncle, Mr. Coyne," she said. "I cooked for him when he'd let me, which wasn't often. Mostly he just wanted to be left alone, do things his own way. Damned independent old Yankee." She blinked. "I'm going to miss him, I'll tell you that." She wiped at her eyes with the cuff of her flannel shirt. "Anyway, all I wanted to say was, Southwick's a funny town, and when folks get ideas in their heads, it's hard to get 'em out, and you shouldn't pay any attention to them."

"What kind of ideas?"

"Well," she said, "you show up in town, a stranger, a lawyer no less, in your expensive car, and you talk with Farley a couple times, and next thing you know, Farley has his heart attack and it's you who finds him. You see?"

I smiled. "They blame me?"

"How folk's minds work sometimes," she said. "Just want you to know, my mind doesn't work that way. I feel bad, you're the one had to find him that way."

"Thank you," I said.

She stood up and wiped the dirt off the seat of her jeans. "I gotta go sell houses."

"Can I ask you something?"

She glanced at her wristwatch. "Okay."

"Does the name Bobby Gilman mean anything to you?"

"Well there's a name out of the past," she said. "What do you want to know?"

"I know Bobby Gilman got lost on Monadnock and they didn't find his body for nearly a year. I know he was from Southwick. I know it was thirty years ago." I shrugged. "Were there rumors about what happened?"

"Rumors?" She stared at the water. "Sure there were rumors. Small town like Southwick, there's always gossip.

There'll be stories about Farley circulating for the next week or two. Then folks will latch on to the next thing."

"What were the rumors?" I said.

"You shouldn't give credence to rumors, Mr. Coyne."

"I know that."

She was quiet for a minute. "Folks wondered what happened that day. How Bobby got separated from those other boys. How he ended up on the other side of the mountain. Why all those searchers with their dogs kept looking in the wrong place." She looked at me and shrugged.

"Those are questions, not rumors," I said.

"Some folks held those other boys responsible for what happened to Bobby Gilman, that's all."

"Any logical reason they should do that?"

"They were just your regular boys, Mr. Coyne. Maybe a little heedless, the way boys can be. So they lost track of Bobby out there in the woods in the snowstorm, or maybe in their hurry to get off the mountain they just forgot about him. You can blame them all you want, but they were just kids. It turned out to be a tragedy. But that didn't make those boys evil."

"People were calling them evil?"

"It's not even worth considering," said Helen. "I haven't thought about Bobby Gilman for years. I don't want to start now." She stood up. "I really do have to get going."

"What about Albert Stoddard?" I said.

She narrowed her eyes at me, then nodded. "Yes, he was one of those boys up on the mountain that day, if that's what you mean."

"And Oliver Burlingame and Mark Lyman?"

"Them, too."

"How about Dalton Burke?"

235

She opened her mouth as if she was going to say something. Then she closed it and nodded. "He was one of them, yes. They were just boys, Mr. Coyne. It was a long time ago. Best put to rest, if you ask me." She held out her hand. "Really, I've gotta go. I'm late."

I took her hand. "I'm glad you stopped."

She shrugged. "Thought you might be feeling bad."

"I was," I said. "Thanks."

Still am, I thought.

After Helen left I sat on my boulder. Dalton Burke. Farley Nelson had been proud of remembering that name. He intended to share it with me.

Well, he did.

I wondered if Dalton Burke had died recently, as Oliver Burlingame and Mark Lyman did—accidentally, or suddenly, or otherwise.

I watched the black water flow on by. No new insights presented themselves, so I got into my car and headed home.

Lieutenant Bagley had said that Farley Nelson didn't have an enemy in the world. That was obviously untrue. But it was possible that he hadn't had any enemies before I came along.

I didn't like thinking about that. I liked even less the fact that I couldn't share what I knew with the police.

Well, Bagley would undoubtedly get in touch with Roger Horowitz. They would compare notes. I guessed that between the two of them, they'd begin to find connections between the murders of Gordon Cahill and Farley Nelson. Things like that didn't happen coincidentally.

Albert Stoddard was the link, and I hoped Horowitz and Bagley would notice it.

Maybe Dalton Burke's name would help them.

I hoped so.

The more the police learned, the better I liked it. I wanted them to catch whoever had killed Farley Nelson. Maybe they'd locate Albert Stoddard. And if they scooped up Gordon Cahill's killer in the process, hooray.

I'd kept my client, Jimmy D'Ambrosio, out of it, and Ellen Stoddard, too. I'd done my job, and I fully intended to keep right on doing it.

No doubt I'd be hearing from Lieutenant Bagley again.

After I turned onto Route 101 heading east, I pulled to the side of the road and picked up my new cell phone, which had been riding on the seat beside me. I pecked out the number for Evie's cell phone and hit SEND.

When she answered, I said, "Hey. It works."

She laughed. "Welcome to the twenty-first century."

"Where are you?" I said.

"Believe it or not," she said, "I'm at the office. Quiet Saturday afternoon. I'm getting a lot of paperwork done."

"I thought you were going to get together with Mary, go to a museum or something."

"She couldn't make it. Now I'm wishing I'd gone along with you. Is it beautiful up there in New Hampshire?"

"It's pretty," I said. "But it's just as well you didn't come with me."

"Oh, oh," said Evie.

"I'll tell you what I can when I get home."

"On your way?"

"I am," I said. "I'll be there in an hour or so. How about you?"

"I want to finish up here," she said. "I'll be home for supper. Want me to pick up something?"

"No," I said. "I feel like cooking."

237

She hesitated. "What's this I'm hearing in your voice? You okay?"

"Sure," I said. "I'm fine."

"You sound like you could use a hug."

"Only one?" I said.

TWENTY-THREE

The nice thing about having a dog is, he's always thrilled to see you when you come home. No questions, no accusations, no worries, no anger, no sulking, no guilt trips. Just happiness.

Henry had spent the day snoozing in the sunshine in our walled-in garden, and when I went in through the back gate, he bounded over with his little stub tail whirring. I squatted down so he could lap my face, and I rubbed his ears and scratched his muzzle and patted his rump until he settled down.

After Henry and I had our reunion, we went inside. I microwaved a mug of the morning's coffee, took it into my cave, and tried Jimmy D'Ambrosio's cell phone.

When he answered, I said, "It's Coyne. We've got to talk."

"So talk."

"No," I said. "Face-to-face. Tête-à-tête. Mano a mano."

He hesitated. "What's this I'm hearing? You mad at me?"

"Exactly," I said. "Meet me at Washington's statue in an hour."

"Christ," he said, "I can't just—"

"It's three-thirty now," I said. "If you're not there in an hour, I'm calling Channel Seven."

"You can't do that."

"No? Tune in tonight at eleven."

He was quiet for a minute. Then he said, "Okay. Four-thirty. I'll be there."

From my bench beside George Washington on horseback I could watch the one-way traffic on Arlington Street, and I spotted Jimmy D'Ambrosio when he slid out of the taxi that pulled up by the entrance.

He looked around, saw me, waved, came through the open gate into the Public Garden, and sat beside me.

"So," he said, "what've you got? You track down Albert? He been a bad boy?"

"No. I've been looking for Albert. All there's been is dead bodies."

"Huh?"

"First Gordon Cahill," I said. "Our private investigator. Then, just this morning, I found a dead man up in Southwick, New Hampshire."

"Who's that?"

"Nobody special," I said. "Just a nice old guy who lost his wife a few years ago and worked in the general store because he liked being around people. Not an enemy in the world. That's what everybody says. I found him sitting in an Adirondack chair in his back yard. Real pretty vista. Meadows and mountains and patches of pretty autumn foliage, all gold and scarlet, you know? He'd been garroted."

Jimmy blinked. "Well, shit."

I nodded.

"So why're you telling this to me?" he said.

"Because two days ago I was asking this same old gentleman questions, trying to figure out what's going on with Albert Stoddard, and then yesterday he called me, invited me up, and when I got there this morning he was dead, and now the Major Crimes Unit out of the New Hampshire attorney general's office has a murder on their hands, and they're asking me how come I was the one who found the old guy's body, and goddamnit, I want to tell them."

"Well," said Jimmy, "you can't say anything about Albert."

"I can if you say I can," I said. "You're my client."

He shook his head. "I say you can't."

"They'll figure it out eventually," I said. "It'd be better if we went to them."

"Forget it, Brady."

I turned and pushed my face close to his. "I don't think you understand," I said softly. "Two men have been murdered."

He pulled back from me. "You can't prove there's any connection with Albert."

"Can't prove it," I said. "Not yet. But it certainly looks like there is. Meanwhile, there's a murderer—maybe two murderers—out there, and I feel like I've got important information. Look. I don't want to go to the media. I just want to tell the police what I know. They understand the importance of confidentiality. They can handle it."

Jimmy pressed his lips together and shook his head. "Can't let you do that," he said. "Can't take that chance."

I leaned back on the bench, lit a cigarette, and said nothing.

"You breach our confidentiality," said Jimmy, "I'll haul

your ass before the Massachusetts Bar Association so fast your balls will shrivel. There'll be a hearing, and I will give evidence, and they'll take away your license, and that'll be the end of your career."

"I don't take kindly to being threatened," I said.

"Me, neither," he said. "You threatened to air confidential information on television."

"I'm asking your permission," I said. "I just want to tell the police what I know. I want to help them catch a killer. If I tell them what Gordon Cahill was up to, that he was tailing Albert Stoddard, that Albert has a camp in Southwick, New Hampshire, where this old man was killed, it might help them."

"Permission denied," Jimmy said. "Look, Brady. Why don't you write up a final report for me, include a bill, send it to my office, okay?"

"You firing me?"

He shrugged. "Time to bring the investigation to a close, that's all. You're not getting anywhere that I can see. Albert's off somewhere being weird, but he's not causing the campaign any problems, and the media hasn't glommed onto him. Let's leave it lay right where it is."

"I'm worried something happened to Albert," I said. "Aren't you?"

"He called in at school the other day, told them he was taking the week off. Albert's okay. Ellen's not worried about him."

"I am," I said. "She should be."

Jimmy waved his hand. "Forget it. Case closed. Good job. Thanks a lot. Send me a bill."

I nodded. "Okay." I stood up. "See you later." I started to walk away.

"Hey," said Jimmy. "Wait a minute."

I stopped and turned to face him.

"Just because I'm not your client anymore," he said, "it doesn't mean . . . ?"

"Your secrets are safe with me forever," I said. "You're the one who's got to live with it. If you change your mind, let me know."

I pivoted around and walked away.

"After the election," Jimmy called to me. "We'll talk about it then."

I kept walking.

When I got home, I called Ellen Stoddard's cell phone. Her voice mail answered, inviting me to leave a message. I hung up and tried her home number. Voice mail there, too. So I said, "It's Brady. Please call me. It's important."

Then I redialed her cell phone and left the same message.

She called back a half hour later. "I'm kind of in the middle of things," she said when I answered. "What's up?"

"Jimmy just fired me. Wanted to be sure you knew."

"I didn't," she said.

"Is it okay with you?"

She hesitated. "Having him retain you to hire a private investigator was his idea in the first place," she said. "I pretty much go along with what Jimmy says."

I said nothing.

"The detective you hired is dead," she said. "So nobody's investigating Albert anyway."

"I am," I said.

Ellen said nothing.

"Have you heard from Albert?" I said.

"No, Brady. Not a word."

"And you're okay with that?"

She sighed. "Of course I'm not."

"But it's all about the election, huh?"

"That's unfair," she said. "Albert talked to the secretary at Tufts the other day, so I know he's okay. I don't know what he's up to, and I don't know why he hasn't tried to call me, at least, but Albert's done strange things before. It's not *all* about the election. But we do have an election, and I've got two debates to worry about among a million other things, and if I allowed myself to start worrying about Albert, I wouldn't get anything done."

"He's gone missing, Ellen."

"No," she said. "We just don't know where he is. There's a difference."

"You're not worried, then."

"I'm not allowing myself to worry."

"Well, okay, then. The only thing is, another man has been murdered."

She was silent.

"It might be connected to Albert," I added.

"Oh, dear," whispered Ellen.

"I intend to pursue it," I said. "It would be a lot easier if I could tell the police about Albert."

"What do you want to tell them about Albert?"

"Just that I've been trying to track him down. That I asked this nice old man some questions about Albert, and a couple days later he got murdered. That's all."

"What're you saying?" she said. "You think Albert killed somebody?"

"I don't know. I went up to his camp the other day. When I came out, somebody tripped me and kicked me and poked a shotgun at me and slugged me with it and left me unconscious. It was dark. I didn't see who it was."

Ellen was silent for a minute. "You don't think Albert would do something like that."

"Yes," I said. "I think he might."

"That's crazy," she said.

I said nothing.

"Albert couldn't hurt anybody," she said softly. "That's ridiculous."

"If you say so."

She hesitated. "Jimmy fired you?"

"Yep."

"Well," she said. "Whatever he says."

I laughed. "Just like that, huh?"

"Brady—"

"I've got a question for you, Ellen."

"What is it?"

"Does the name Dalton Burke mean anything to you?"

She was silent for a moment. Then she said, "I've heard that name. It makes me think of a baseball player, but..."

"That was Dalton Jones," I said. "He used to play for the Red Sox. Is that who you're thinking of?"

"No. I'm thinking of Dalton Burke." She paused. "I just can't..."

"A friend of Albert's maybe?"

"Yes. Right. Now I remember. A man named Dalton Burke called here looking for Albert. This was, oh, several months ago. I answered the phone. It was in the evening. Albert was at school. I wrote down the message."

"Do you remember what the message was?"

"Just for Albert to call him. He left a phone number."

"Do you have it?" I said. "The phone number?"

"No. I gave it to Albert."

"Burke didn't tell you what he wanted?"

"No. It wasn't much of a conversation. He asked for Albert, I said he wasn't home, could I take a message, and he gave me his name and number. That's it."

"Can you remember when this was?"

"It was probably the second or third week in May," she said. "I remember that Albert had stayed at school to grade final exams. He hates to bring work home with him."

"Did Albert ever mention talking with Dalton Burke?"

"Not that I recall."

"Did he say anything to you when you gave him the message?"

"Brady, this was four months ago."

"Do you remember anything else, Ellen?"

"No," she said. "This has something to do with what's happened to Albert, doesn't it?"

"I don't know."

"You'll keep me informed?"

"Maybe," I said. "Maybe not. Jimmy fired me, remember?"

After I hung up from Ellen, I opened my desk drawer and took out the notes I'd made about the two obituaries I'd found in Albert's camp. The envelope I'd found them in had been postmarked June 22, about a month after Dalton Burke called Albert.

Oliver Burlingame died "accidentally" on March 19.

Mark Lyman died "suddenly" on April 2.

Both of those events occurred before Burke called Albert.

I fired up my Mac, hopped onto the Information Highway, and typed in "Dalton Burke."

An hour later I knew several things about him.

He was born in Peterborough, New Hampshire, two years before Albert Stoddard was born.

He graduated from Brewster Academy in Wolfeboro, New Hampshire.

He earned a degree in business management at the University of Pennsylvania.

He owned Burke and Newfield Insurance Agency in Harrisburg, Pennsylvania.

And unlike Oliver Burlingame and Mark Lyman, Dalton Burke had not died.

TWENTY-FOUR

Monday morning I left my townhouse on Mt. Vernon Street, walked up Beacon Street to the Park Street T station, took the Red Line to Davis Square, and climbed the hill to the Tufts University campus.

At nine-thirty on a sunny Monday morning in late September, you'll find every college campus in the country virtually deserted. Students with nine o'clock classes have straggled into them by then, and those who don't have early classes are still in bed.

I spotted a Building and Grounds man wielding a leaf blower, and he pointed out the building that housed the history department. It was made of brick and covered with woodbine, a kind of ivy that turns crimson in the fall.

I went into the history building. Two women were looking at computer monitors in a small office on the left. I knocked on the open door, stepped into the room, and said, "Excuse me?"

They both turned around and smiled at me. One of them

appeared to be in her thirties. The other one was closer to fifty. They were both quite attractive.

The younger one said, "Can I help you?"

"Are you the history department secretary?"

She nodded. "We both are."

"Maybe you can help me, then," I said. "I'm looking for Professor Stoddard."

She shook her head. "He doesn't usually come in on Mondays. You can probably catch him tomorrow."

"Damn," I said. "I was really hoping to catch up with him today."

"Did you try him at home?"

I nodded. "No answer. That's why I'm here. It's rather important that I talk with him. I'm a lawyer . . ." I let that thought trail away, hoping to suggest that anything a lawyer might want with a professor was somewhere between very urgent and vitally critical.

"He was out sick all last week," she said. "As far as I know, he'll be in tomorrow. He's got a nine o'clock class."

"Sick," I repeated. "No wonder he wasn't answering his phone at home. How sick is he, anyway? He's not in the hospital, is he? Did he say what the matter was?"

"I don't know what he said," she said. "I didn't talk with him." She turned to the other woman. "Who talked to Dr. Stoddard when he called last week?"

The other secretary shook her head. "It wasn't me. When was it? Thursday, right? It must've been Emily." She looked at me. "We don't have any formal procedures when a professor calls in sick. We just tape a notice on the classroom door so the students don't have to sit around waiting."

"Who's Emily?" I said.

"One of our work-study students," she said. "She answers

250

the phone, does photocopying, filing, stuff like that." She glanced up at the clock on the wall. It was a little after nine-forty-five. "She should be here in about fifteen minutes. Would you like to talk to her?"

"Sure," I said. "That would be great."

She pointed. "The lounge is in there, if you want to wait. Help yourself to the coffee. I'll send Emily in as soon as she gets here."

The lounge furniture was a bit shabby, and the most in-teresting thing I could find to read was a newsletter from the American Historical Society. But there was an industrial-sized steel urn on a table in the corner, and the coffee was hot and strong, the way I like it.

A couple of minutes after ten, a blond girl stepped into the lounge. She was wearing a red-and-white striped jersey and tight-fitting, low-slung blue jeans that exposed her belly button. She wore a stud with a shiny gemstone in her navel.

"Sir?" she said. "Terri said you were looking for me?"

"Are you Emily?"

She nodded.

"Did you take Professor Stoddard's phone call last week?"

She frowned. "I gave Edie and Terri the message. He said he was sick and wouldn't be in for the rest of the week."

"Did he say anything else?" I said. "Did he mention what was wrong with him?"

She shook her head. "He didn't say."

"Did he say he'd be back this week?"

She bit her lower lip. "Um . . . no, I don't think so. He didn't say anything about this week."

I gave her my most earnest lawyer look. "Emily," I said, "it's quite important that I know exactly what Professor Stoddard said to you."

"Is he in some kind of trouble?"

"I really can't share that sort of information with you," I intoned solemnly. "I'm sure you understand."

"Oh, sure." She looked up at the ceiling for a moment, then said, "He didn't say much. It was kind of weird, actually. I mean, Dr. Stoddard is usually real friendly. When he's around, he always says hi, gives you a smile, makes a joke, you know? But all he said on the phone was that he was sick and wouldn't be in for the rest of the week. Formal-like, you know? As if he didn't even know me."

"That's all he said?"

Emily nodded. "Yeah. I remember thinking it wasn't like him, not to be friendlier." She shrugged. "It didn't even sound like him."

"What do you mean?"

"I don't know. His tone of voice, I guess."

"It didn't sound like his voice?"

"Well, I don't know. I guess it did." She frowned. "I don't think I ever even talked to him on the telephone before, so I don't know what he sounds like on the phone. I mean, it didn't really *not* sound like him. It was more like he was so all-business, in some kind of big hurry. Stressed about something, maybe. Dr. Stoddard isn't usually like that." She looked at me. "It was no big deal. I didn't think too much about it at the time. I just gave Terri and Edie the message."

"Emily," I said, "do you think you could remember exactly what Dr. Stoddard said when he called?"

She closed her eyes for a minute, then nodded. "When I answered the phone, he just said, 'This is Dr. Stoddard.' And I said something like, 'Oh, hi. It's Emily.' And instead of saying, 'Oh, hi, Emily. How're you doing?' like you'd expect, all he said was, 'I am ill. I won't be in for the rest of

252

the week. Please deliver my message.' And I think I said something like, 'I hope you feel better,' and he said, like, 'Thank you,' and then he hung up." She looked at me. "He must've been feeling really crappy. Usually he's a lot nicer than that."

"I'm sure that was it," I said. I stood up. "Thanks, Emily. I appreciate your help."

She hesitated. "I didn't do anything wrong, did I?"

I smiled. "Not at all."

I followed Emily back to the secretaries' office and asked them to have Albert call me if they heard from him. They promised they would, and I gave each of them one of my business cards.

I got back to my office in Copley Square via the MBTA a few minutes before my eleven o'clock appointment with Harriet Brubaker. Julie had prepared some documents for her to sign, and I had to go over them all with her, and by the time I finished explaining the language and significance of the documents to her, and after Harriet had her little cry on my shoulder, it was a few minutes past noon.

As soon as Harriet Brubaker left my office I called Jimmy D'Ambrosio's cell phone.

When he answered, I said, "Albert did *not* call in sick to the history department last week."

"What the hell are you talking about? Ellen talked to the secretary herself."

"Somebody called," I said, "but it wasn't Albert."

Jimmy was silent for a long minute. Finally he said, "You know this?"

"Whoever called," I said, "it wasn't Albert. It was somebody saying he was Albert. The girl who took the call told me it wasn't Albert's voice."

"Well," said Jimmy, "so what?"

"Do I have to spell it out for you?"

"No," he said. "I get it. You think this should convince me to give you permission to violate our confidentiality and talk to the police."

"If that wasn't Albert on the phone—"

"I'm not stupid," said Jimmy. "I understand the implications."

"So what do you say?"

"I say what I said the other day, what I've been saying all along, what I'm gonna keep saying at least 'til after the first Tuesday in November. I say no."

"I've got to tell Ellen," I said.

"What good would that do? You want to upset her?"

"She has a right to know."

"Listen," said Jimmy. "It doesn't matter what Ellen says. I'm the one who hired you, which makes me your client. Not her. I'm the only one who can give you the go-ahead to talk to the police. Which I'm not going to do. Okay? I'm not. Period. You can talk to Ellen if it'll make you feel better. I can't stop you. Just be sure you understand that it'll upset her to the point where she'll probably screw up the debates and lose the election. That what you want?"

"I don't give a shit about the election," I said. "Albert Stoddard is what I care about. Him and Gordon Cahill and Farley Nelson."

Jimmy hesitated, then said, "You think something's happened to Albert, don't you?"

"Yes."

254

"That wasn't him who called, huh?"

"No, I'm quite certain it wasn't."

"Any idea who it was?"

"Sure," I said. "It was whoever killed Cahill and Farley Nelson, that's who."

"I wish to hell you hadn't told me this, Coyne."

"I know," I said. "Now you've got to tell Ellen."

"If I don't," he said, "and she finds out I kept it from her, she'll never forgive me. Thanks a lot."

"Sorry," I said.

"Like hell you're sorry," he said. "You are a devious son of a bitch, you know that?"

"Compared to you, I'm a novice."

"Yeah," he said. "Thanks. That's a compliment." He was silent for a moment. "Okay," he said finally. "I'll talk to Ellen."

"Tell her I want to talk to the police about it," I said. "Tell her it'd be even better if she did it herself."

"Ellen already knows that."

"But she thinks Albert's okay."

"I'll see what she says," said Jimmy.

"You better tell her the truth."

"What, you think I'd lie to her about something like that? You think I'm some kind of heartless monster?"

"That's a rhetorical question, Jimmy D."

After I hung up with Jimmy D'Ambrosio, I tried the number for the Burke and Newfield Insurance Agency in Harrisburg, Pennsylvania, that I'd copied from the Internet.

When the woman answered, I asked to speak to Mr. Burke.

She asked me who was calling.

I told her my name was Brady Coyne, that I was a lawyer calling from Boston, and that it was important. "Tell him it concerns Albert Stoddard," I added.

"Stoddard?" She spelled it.

"That's right."

"Is this in regard to a claim?" she said.

"Right. A claim."

"I'll connect you with our claims department. Just—"

"No," I said. "I must speak with Dalton Burke."

She hesitated, then said, "Of course. One moment, sir. I'll see if Mr. Burke can come to the phone."

A moment later a deep voice said, "This is Dalton Burke. Mr. Coyne, is it?"

"That's right."

"How can I help you?"

"Tell me why you called Albert Stoddard."

"Who?"

"It was last May. You talked to his wife, left a message. Did Albert ever return your call?"

"What do you want, anyway?"

"Your two buddies, Burlingame and Lyman, are dead already. How come you're still alive?"

"I have no idea what you're talking about," he said.

"You do remember Bobby Gilman?" I said.

"Who are you?"

"You got a pencil?"

"Of course."

"Write this down." I gave him my office phone number. "Got it?"

"Yes."

"Write my name beside it. Brady Coyne. I spell it with a 'y.' Write the word 'lawyer' beside that. Keep in mind that

256

lawyers are people you can confide in. We are also officers of the court. You need to talk to a lawyer."

"This isn't funny, you know," he said. "Is this supposed to be some kind of joke?"

"After you think about it," I said, "and when you figure out that it's not in your interest to lie to me, call me."

"Mr. Coyne," he said, "with all due respect—"

"Never mind respect," I said. "I want answers. I want to know what happened on that Columbus Day on Mount Monadnock thirty years ago when you and Bobby Gilman and Albert Stoddard and Oliver Burlingame and Mark Lyman got caught in that snowstorm, and all of you came down except for Bobby."

He was quiet for a minute. Then he said, "You must have me confused with somebody else. I'm sorry."

"I'll be expecting your call," I said. Then I hung up.

TWENTY-FIVE

Randy St. George was my last appointment on Monday afternoon. Barbara Cooper, his wife's lawyer, had faxed over some changes she wanted to make in their separation agreement, and I needed to explain them to Randy and help him decide how to respond to them. He thought they were insignificant. I reminded him that nothing in any legal document—no comma, no conjunction, no passive verb—was insignificant. If these changes weren't significant, Attorney Cooper wouldn't have wanted to make them. It was my job, as Randy's lawyer, to understand their significance, however hypothetical, and then make sure he understood them, and then help him decide if we should let them stand. That's why he was paying me the big bucks.

Randy and I ended up deleting a couple of those changes and leaving the others, and when I ushered him out of my office a few minutes before five, I saw Roger Horowitz sitting in the waiting room. He had an attaché case on his lap and a frown on his face. His knee was jiggling up and down like a piston.

259

I did not acknowledge his presence.

Randy and I shook hands, and when he left, I turned to Julie, who was tidying up her desk the way she does when she's getting ready to leave for the day. "No other appointments, right?" I said.

She cast a quick glance past my shoulder in Horowitz's direction. "No scheduled appointments, no."

"Good," I said. "I'm going home then."

"Coyne," said Horowitz from behind me. "Quit fooling around. We gotta talk."

"Did you hear something?" I said to Julie.

She smiled.

"My imagination, I guess," I said.

"He's been here for half an hour," she whispered.

"Tough."

"He's not going away, you know."

"Please tell him," I said to Julie, "that even if I wanted to, I can't talk with him."

She craned her neck and looked over my shoulder. "Mr. Coyne can't talk with you, sir," she said to Horowitz.

"Tell him he's gonna talk to me whether he likes it or not," he said. "Tell him I'll follow him home, if that's what it takes. Tell him I'll convince Evie to let me in, and I'll spend the night sitting on the foot of their bed 'til he talks to me. Tell him I'm not going away. Tell him he doesn't want to piss me off any more than he already has. Might as well do it now."

Julie shrugged, then looked at me. "He says—"

"Got it," I said. "Thank you." I turned around to face Horowitz. "Nothing's changed, Roger."

"Everything's changed." He stood up. "Let's go into your office."

I arched my eyebrows at Julie.

She nodded.

"Tell him he's got ten minutes," I said to her. Then I turned, went back into my office, and sat at my desk. I left the door open.

I heard Julie say, "You've got ten minutes," and I heard Horowitz's sarcastic guffaw.

He came in, closed the door, sat in the client chair across from me, and put his attaché case on my desk.

"Evie tells me she got you a cell phone," he said.

I nodded. "She did. So what?"

"So gimme your number."

"Why?"

"In case I want to call you. Why else?"

"I don't want you to call me," I said. "I don't want anybody to call me on the damn thing."

"You should cooperate with an officer of the law," he said, giving me his wicked Jack Nicholson grin. "If you know what's good for you."

"I don't even know the number," I said. "Why would I want to call my own phone?"

"Turn it on. It'll show your number."

I shrugged, took the phone from my pocket, turned it on, and when my number popped onto the screen, I copied it down on a scrap of paper. Then I turned off the phone and slipped it back into my pocket.

I pushed the paper across my desk. Horowitz picked it up and stuffed it in his shirt pocket. "You oughta leave your phone turned on," he said. "In case somebody needs to get ahold of you."

"All these years without a cell phone," I said, "I've done just fine."

"Some people might disagree with that," he said. He took a deep breath, puffed out his cheeks, then blew out the breath. "I don't appreciate you advising the bereaved widow to not cooperate with me," he said.

I shrugged. "Advice is cheap."

"Yours is," he said. He flicked away that irritation with the back of his hand. "Anyway, I've been talking with Lieutenant Bagley from the New Hampshire state cops. I believe you made his acquaintance."

I nodded.

"He's with the Major Crimes Unit," said Horowitz. "In New Hampshire murder is considered to be a major crime."

"I guess it is most places," I said.

"I'm not sure how sharp this Bagley is."

"He seemed sharp enough to me."

"Sharp or not," said Horowitz, "Bagley's got a murder on his hands, just like me. Funny how you have managed to pop up in the middle of both of them."

"I wouldn't say in the middle, exactly," I said.

"Hell," he said, "you found one body. The other body belonged to a guy who was working for you."

"These are facts you don't need me to confirm."

Horowitz waved his hand. "Bagley and me, we've been comparing notes. The way you assumed we would when you gave him my name. You saved the two of us a lot of time finding each other. So thank you for that, anyway."

I shrugged. "I'm an officer of the court."

"Yeah," he said. "Good for you." He opened his attaché case, took out a manila folder, and put it on my desk. "You've been looking for a guy name of Albert Stoddard, who happens to be the husband of the Democratic candidate of our beloved Commonwealth for the U.S. Senate, whose

262

mother happens to be a client of yours." He arched his eyebrows at me. "Which goes a long way to explaining your reticence about your case."

"What do you want me to say?" I said.

He held up a hand. "All told, you've been up to Southwick, New Hampshire, three times in the past week. Asking questions of the townsfolk. Questions about Albert Stoddard, near as Bagley can determine, though he doesn't seem to have determined much else. One of those townsfolk was an old guy named Farley Nelson, who you found garroted in his back yard day before yesterday. Who you'd been conferring with at the local inn just a few days prior." He squinted at his notes. "Last Thursday, that was." He looked up at me. "Have I got that right so far?"

I nodded.

"Well," said Horowitz, "that's about all Bagley can seem to pry out of anybody. I got the feeling there's more, but like I said, I'm not sure how sharp he is."

I wondered if Bagley had talked to the Goff brothers, or Helen and Carol at the real estate office, or Paul Munson, the young cop. If he had, I wondered if any of them had mentioned Bobby Gilman or Oliver Burlingame or Mark Lyman. I wondered if he'd followed up with Dalton Burke, and if he had, if he'd had any more luck with him than I had.

"Now me," said Horowitz, "my first thought was that Gordon Cahill was killed by mobsters from the Winter Hill Gang. Revenge for his excellent undercover work ten, twelve years ago. It's still a pretty good theory, and I'm not inclined to abandon it out of hand. But then I hear from Lieutenant Bagley about this other murder, and it makes me think, hm, I wonder if Gordie was driving home from Southwick, New

263

Hampshire, when he had his tire shot and gasoline poured all over him. And if that was what he was doing, I'm wondering if he was up there for the same reasons you've been going up there lately." Horowitz arched his eyebrows at me.

"I'm not going to tell you who my client is or why they hired me or anything about them," I said, carefully—if ungrammatically—using the plural pronoun in order to avoid using a gender-specific singular one.

"I'm not asking for a name," said Horowitz.

"Then what do you want from me?"

He pounded his fist on my desk. "Dammit, Coyne. I want to know why you wanted to go to Albert Stoddard's hunting camp in the first place. I want to know if you found anything there. I want to know what went on between you and that Farley Nelson that got him murdered. I want to know what questions you've been asking those people in Southwick, New Hampshire. What I really want to know is, what's your theory on Gordon Cahill's murder, and what do you think its connection is to this other one."

I shook my head. "I gave Bagley your name, figured he'd do some snooping around, put two and two together, and so would you, and between the two of you . . ."

"Bagley hasn't come up with much. Says he's finding the local folks pretty unhelpful. He hasn't got any theories about his case. He says the old guy didn't have any enemies."

"That's obviously wrong."

Horowitz nodded. "Bagley figures you've got a theory."

I shrugged. "I really don't."

"He thinks you do."

"Maybe he's just not sharing with you."

Horowitz narrowed his eyes at me.

"Are you sharing with him?" I said.

He shrugged. "I'm sharing what I think should be shared, sure."

"Did you mention the Winter Hill Gang to him?"

Horowitz gave me one of his ironic smiles. "You're the one who's been talking with Vinnie Russo. You tell me."

"Russo said it was amateurs," I said. "Of course, he's not the most reliable witness."

"To answer your question," said Horowitz, "no, I didn't bother mentioning Whitey Bulger or the Winter Hill Gang to Lieutenant Bagley. They'd never kill some old farmer in his back yard."

"Well," I said, "I can't help it if you guys can't work out your petty territorial issues."

"You better not criticize the way I do my job, Coyne."

"Why not? You're criticizing the way I do mine."

"I'm just asking for your theory," he said.

I waved my hand. "Do you have a theory?"

He blew out a long breath. "Two murders," he said slowly. "Two different jurisdictions. Two different means. Two victims who apparently didn't even know each other. They don't look like they're connected. But then, lo and behold, there you are, in the middle of both of 'em. Can't be coincidence. So what we've got is two murders, one murderer, one motive. That's my theory."

I smiled. "It's a start."

"Albert Stoddard," he said. "You think he killed Cahill when you put him on his tail, and then he killed the old guy who was going to tell you about it. That it?"

"I should terminate this meeting right now," I said.

"But you won't," said Horowitz, "because you liked Gordie and you liked that Farley Nelson, and you feel responsible for what happened to both of them, and you really do

265

care about justice being done in spite of the fact that you're a pain in the ass." He reached across the desk and put his hand on my wrist. "Help us out here, Coyne."

I pushed his hand away. "I'm not responsible for what you guys figure out by yourselves," I said. "Good luck. I sincerely and profoundly hope you catch the bad guys. But I can't help you, and it's not fair that you should expect me to. I don't want to talk to you anymore. So please go away and leave me alone."

Horowitz opened the manila folder and pulled out some sheets of paper. "Got something for you to look at." He handed one of the sheets to me.

It was an eight-by-ten glossy black-and-white photograph, evidently taken at night. It showed the burned-out corpse of a small sedan. Its hood was sticking up at a cockeyed angle, and the left front tire was flat, and the window on the driver's side was smashed. In the photo, you couldn't tell what the original color of the car had been. The paint had peeled and blistered, and it was all charred and blackened.

I blew out a long breath. "Gordie's Corolla?" I said.

He nodded and handed me another photo.

I glanced at it, then pushed it away. "Jesus Christ," I whispered.

"Take a good look at it, Coyne," said Horowitz.

I didn't want to, but I couldn't help it. I pulled it to me and looked again.

This photo was in color. It showed what I could only surmise by its general shape had once been the upper torso and head of a human being. Like the automobile, the skin was blackened and charred and blistered. It looked as if it had half melted. The hair, nose, ears, lips, and eyes were cinders. The face was lumpy and unrecognizable. It was only vaguely human.

I put the photo face down on my desk. "I get your point," I said.

He handed me another photo. When I turned my head away, he said, "Go ahead. Look at it. It's good for you."

I couldn't help myself. I looked. This was also a color photo, although the dominant color was black. It showed Gordie's entire body. It had been deeply burned from head to toe. The skin was peeling away in places, revealing patches of yellow and red. Instead of fingers and toes, there were lumpy little blackened stubs.

I swallowed back the bile that rose up in my throat. "I hope to hell you don't plan on showing any of these to Donna," I said.

"You think she'd change her mind about cooperating with us if I did?"

"I think she'd hate you forever."

"I'm showing them to you," he said. "I don't care if you hate me forever."

"I've never seen anything worse," I said. "Doesn't exactly make me think fondly of you."

"You didn't see him in person," he said. "I did."

"I'm sorry."

"So now I'm having these dreams," said Horowitz. "About old Gordie. I keep seeing him this way." He tapped the photos. "We were really good friends, you know. He told the worst goddamned puns you ever heard." He smiled, and for once I saw no irony in it. "I'm worried I'm losing my objectivity."

"Is that why you shared these damn pictures with me?" I said. "Hoping I'd lose *my* objectivity?"

"Bet your ass," he said.

I shook my head.

"Give me something, Coyne."

"What? You know everything I know."

"Who hired you?"

I shook my head. "Go away, Roger. Leave me alone. And take your damn pictures with you."

"I'll take 'em," he said, "but don't you forget them."

"How could I?" I said.

Evie brought home take-out Chinese—Moo Goo Gai Pan for her, beef and broccoli with fried rice for me. She ate with chopsticks. I used a fork. Pretty much the difference between us right there.

Horowitz's photos haunted me—as he'd intended—and several times while we were eating I found myself holding an empty fork halfway to my mouth and staring off into the distance. Evie kept frowning at me, but she didn't say anything.

We had just put our plates on the floor for Henry to lick when my phone rang.

I made no move to answer it. Evie and I had a rule that we did not answer the telephone while we were eating.

"You might as well get it," she said. "Talk to *somebody*, anyway."

I arched my eyebrows at her.

She shrugged, then bent down for the dishes, which Henry had licked clean.

I went to my room and picked up the phone.

"It's Helen Madbury," said the voice when I answered. "From Southwick."

It took me a moment. "Oh," I said. "Helen. I don't think I ever heard your last name."

"It's my ex-husband's, actually. Did I interrupt your dinner?"

"We just finished," I said. "What's up?"

"Farley's funeral is Wednesday. I thought you'd like to know."

"Thank you," I said. "Where and what time?"

"One in the afternoon at the Congregational church. That's the white one right there in the village. He'll be buried in the cemetery across the street. I'm having a little reception at my house after the interment. You're invited."

"That's very kind," I said.

"Farley liked you," she said. "I assume you liked him."

"I did. I liked him a lot."

"Well," said Helen, "I hope you can make it."

"I'll try," I said.

After I hung up with Helen, I went back to the kitchen. Evie and Henry were not there.

I found them both upstairs. Evie had changed into her nightgown and was under the covers reading a paperback book. Henry was curled up beside her.

I sat on the bed. "You look like you're ready to go to sleep."

"Pretty tired." Evie licked her finger and turned a page in her book.

"Hell," I said, "it's only eight-thirty."

"Long day." She kept reading.

I didn't say anything.

Neither did she.

Finally, I said, "I just got invited to a funeral."

"Mm," she said. "That's nice."

"Farley Nelson," I said. "The old guy up in New Hampshire I was telling you about."

"You didn't tell me much."

"Well, I know. I—"

"Don't," she said. "I don't want to hear your lecture about the sanctity of client privilege again. If you can't talk to me, fine."

"Honey," I said, "listen—"

"No." She snapped her book shut and plucked her glasses off her face, then turned and looked at me. "If you think I don't understand, you're not giving me very much credit. You think I want you to tell me confidential secrets?"

"It's more complicated than that."

"No doubt," she said. "Listen, Brady. For the past week or so you've done nothing but mope around. You are monosyllabic on those rare occasions when you speak at all. Mostly, you avoid me altogether, as if you think I'm going to hound you until you divulge classified information."

"I wasn't aware of that," I said. "I'm sorry."

"You lie to me."

"I don't lie to you," I said.

"Oh?" She shook her head. "You come home with bruises on your body and you tell me you fell down. That's not a lie?"

"I didn't want you to worry."

"I'd appreciate it if you'd let *me* decide whether I should worry or not." She blew out a quick, exasperated breath. "It's not exactly what I dreamed about when I imagined my ideal relationship, you know. I mean, deciding to live with you, to buy this house with you, to . . . to share my life with you, it wasn't easy for me."

"It was very easy for me," I said.

270

She narrowed her eyes at me. "Don't do that, dammit."

"I'm sorry," I said. "You're right. That was glib. It wasn't easy for me, either."

"I envisioned a partnership," she said.

"We have a partnership. A good one."

"Not when you don't share your feelings. Not when something is obviously eating at you and you avoid me. Not when you lie to me whenever something happens to you. It makes me feel as if I'm the cause of it."

"You're not the cause of it," I said.

"Jesus," she muttered. "I *know* I'm not the cause of it. I'm telling you how I *feel*."

"Oh," was all I could think of to safely say.

"That was your cue to tell me how *you* feel," she said.

"I'm not very good at talking about my feelings," I said. "Never have been."

"What are you afraid of?"

"Afraid? It's not about being afraid of anything. It's just how I am."

"That's a damn cop-out, Brady Coyne. It's like saying, oh, well, I'm a child molester, but you shouldn't blame me. It's how I am."

I smiled. "That's an interesting analogy." I rolled onto my side and touched her face.

She turned away from me. "Don't."

"I'm sorry," I said lamely.

"Sometimes," she mumbled, "being sorry just doesn't do the job."

I lay back on the bed with my hands laced behind my head. I didn't know what to say.

After a minute, Evie turned to face me. Tears had welled up in her eyes. "I hate it that you make me whine," she said.

271

"I'm not a whiner. I'm a strong independent woman, dammit. Do you see what's happening to us?"

"It's not easy," I said. "We knew it wouldn't be easy."

"Maybe this was a mistake."

"This?" I waved my hand around the room. "Our place? Henry? Sharing our lives?"

She nodded.

"Is that what you think?" I said.

She looked at me with her wet eyes, then shook her head. "Sometimes I just don't know."

"It's hard," I said. "But it's worth it."

"Living alone is easier," she said.

"Oh, yes," I said. "It's way easier. Emptier, too. Remember?"

"I remember." She smiled softly. "Just tell me why you're so sad, Brady. Can't you do that?"

"Yes," I said. "I can do that." I took a deep breath and let it out slowly. "Roger Horowitz showed me some pictures today," I said. "They were . . . horrible. I can't get them out of my head."

"Pictures of what?"

"Gordon Cahill's body. It was burned beyond recognition."

"And you feel responsible, is that it?"

I nodded. "It's not rational. But I do."

"That's why Roger showed them to you?" she said. "To make you feel responsible?"

"Yes."

She reached over and squeezed my hand. "What else?"

"There's a lot of pressure on me," I said. "Horowitz is trying to get me to . . . to betray people who trust me. Part of me thinks I should do it. It's hard to know what's right."

"And how does that feel?"

"Feel?" I said. "It makes me sick to my stomach sometimes, is how it feels. It keeps me awake at night. It's what causes me to . . . to be inconsiderate of the people I love. It makes me not think very highly of myself."

She nodded. "So what about that funeral?"

"I don't like funerals."

"Are you going?"

"I don't think so."

"Because funerals make you feel bad?"

I nodded. "I guess so."

"You should go," she said. "Funerals are good. They help people get a handle on their feelings."

"Closure, you mean?" I said.

She shrugged. "Sure. Closure is a good thing."

"He was a really nice old guy," I said. "I mean, I hardly knew him. But I liked him."

"Tell me about him."

So I told Evie about Farley Nelson, how when his wife died he went to work in the general store so he could be around people, how everyone in the little town knew him and liked him, how he called me and asked me to go fishing in his bass pond, how he was murdered before I got there, and how I was the one who found his body.

Evie held my hand tightly in both of hers while I talked, and when I finished, she said, "You'll feel better if you go to his funeral."

"Think so?"

"Absolutely."

"Maybe I will, then."

Evie smiled. "See? That wasn't so hard, was it?"

"What?"

"Talking about your feelings."

"Is that what I did?"

"Sure."

"Don't tell anybody, for God's sake," I said. "I've got a reputation to uphold."

TWENTY-SIX

Wednesday dawned gray and sunless with a whiff of winter in the air. Perfect for a funeral.

Farley Nelson was on my mind.

Evie and I took coffee out to the garden, as we always did when it wasn't raining. We wore sweaters and held our mugs with both hands for warmth.

A downy woodpecker was hammering away at the suet feeder. Nuthatches and titmice were filching sunflower seeds from the hanging feeders, and a gang of goldfinches flocked on the thistle feeder. The finches had begun to don their more somber winter shade of olive.

I never tired of watching our birds.

"That funeral is today," I said to Evie.

"You're going, aren't you?"

I nodded. "I feel like I should."

"Yes, you should," she said. "Want me to go with you?"

"No, honey. That's okay."

Evie shrugged. "Up to you. I will, you know."

"I know. Thanks. I'm fine."

Henry, who had been snoozing under the table with his chin on my instep, lifted his head and looked at me. Sometimes I was positive he understood everything.

"You can't go," I said to him. "You don't own a good necktie."

At nine o'clock I called Julie and told her I'd be out of the office all day because I had to attend a funeral.

She said, "Likely story."

"Evie thinks I should go."

"Sure," she said. "Blame her."

Both sides of Southwick's main street were lined with parked vehicles. I found a place to leave my car in the lot behind the general store and walked from there to the Congregational church, a couple hundred yards down the street.

A police cruiser was parked directly in front of the church, and two uniformed officers were standing there. They sipped coffee from foam cups and nodded to the folks who were filing inside.

I recognized both of them—Officer Somers and his female partner, who'd been the first on the scene when I called about Farley Nelson. When I walked past them, they both nodded without smiling. The female cop said something to Somers out of the corner of her mouth, and I could feel their eyes follow me as I mounted the church steps.

I was the guy who'd found Farley's dead body. That made me a suspicious character.

Helen Madbury was standing inside the door greeting people. When I walked in, she gave me a hug. "Thank you so much for coming," she said. "It would please him to know you're here."

Mechanical words. I figured she was saying the same thing to everybody.

It was quarter to one, fifteen minutes before the service was scheduled to begin, but already the place was packed. I didn't know whether they were all Farley's friends, or if the citizens of Southwick just considered attending funerals to be their civic duty.

A lanky woman with short white hair and sharp blue eyes whom I'd never seen before handed me a program. Another relative of Farley's, probably. A younger sister maybe. I saw some family resemblance.

She also thanked me for coming.

When I entered the church, heads swiveled around to check me out, then turned to say something to the heads next to them. To most of the citizens of Southwick, I was a stranger.

Or maybe they all knew who I was. That Boston lawyer who'd been snooping around. The guy who'd found Farley's body.

I found a seat on the outside aisle in the back pew on the right. The organist was playing "A Mighty Fortress Is Our God." The townsfolk whispered among themselves. I didn't see any tears flowing. It was a somber occasion, but not a tragic one.

I spotted the Goff brothers about halfway to the front on the other side of the middle aisle. They weren't hard to spot. They were big men and seemed to take up a lot of room. They were wearing dark suits and appeared to have trimmed their beards.

They had their heads bowed, as if they were praying. I'd never seen Harris Goff without his baseball cap. His head was balder than his older brother's, and it shone pink in the muted light that seeped down through the stained-glass windows. Both Goff men looked older in suits and ties than they did in grease-stained overalls and ratty T-shirts and work boots.

A cluster of teenagers were sitting a couple rows in front of me. One of them was the girl who worked at the general store, the one who'd given me directions to Farley's place. The girls wore dresses and heels, and they looked like grown-ups. The boys wore suits and neckties, but they still looked like kids.

I spotted Carol, Helen's partner at the real estate office, and Jeff Little, the innkeeper, and a couple of other familiar faces that I couldn't place.

Otherwise, they were all strangers to me, even if I wasn't a stranger to them.

I sat on the hard wooden pew, rolled the paper program in my fingers, and hummed along with the organ music. I always liked those old Protestant hymns.

I tried to think about Farley Nelson, to remember him properly on this occasion, but I hadn't known him very well. My thoughts kept turning to Gordon Cahill. I'd known Gordie quite well. The horrible images from Horowitz's photos kept popping up in my head.

I wondered when they'd turn what was left of Cahill's body over to Donna. I figured a funeral and a burial would help her push on with her life.

After a while the organ stopped playing, and a gray-haired woman in the robes of a minister walked slowly down the aisle. When she got to the front I noticed that Farley's casket was already there.

The service lasted less than an hour. Some familiar lines of scripture were read, a few familiar hymns were sung, and the minister delivered a short but touching homily about Farley and the full and God-fearing life he'd lived. It was evident that she'd known him well, and her words almost convinced me that there was a God to whom we should give thanks for allowing us to know people like Farley.

Then Helen Madbury went to the front and talked without notes about her uncle. She told a few stories that evoked quiet laughter from the congregation and made it clear that Farley would be missed and remembered fondly and gratefully but without tears. At the end of her talk, Helen reminded us that Farley would be buried in the cemetery across the street. She hoped we'd all attend, and she invited everybody to her house for refreshments afterward.

I figured everybody but me knew where she lived.

We sang another hymn, and the minister delivered her benediction, and then six men, a couple of them about Farley's age and the others a generation or two younger, toted his casket up the center aisle while we all sang "Onward Christian Soldiers." Singing felt good, and I found that I remembered most of the words to all four verses.

The congregation recessed from the front to the back, so I was one of the last to leave. When I got outside, I saw that the sky had darkened and a few fat drops of cold rain had begun to fall. Typical.

The two police officers stood in the middle of the road, prepared to halt traffic, although there was none to halt, and the mourners were straggling across the street toward the cemetery on the hill. I followed along. Up front I could see the pallbearers leading the way.

We gathered in a big semicircle around the grave site. A

few umbrellas had sprung up. From where I stood in the rear, I couldn't see much, but I heard the minister recite the Twenty-third Psalm, words that never failed to move me. I was happy to observe that she stuck with the old poetic King James language. "Yea, though I walk through the valley of the shadow of death, I shall fear no evil. For Thou art with me."

Nowadays they say: ". . . you are with me." It would never sound right to my ears.

". . . and I shall dwell in the house of the Lord forever."

Then the minister's voice lifted, inviting us all to bow our heads and join in reciting the Lord's Prayer.

I bowed my head but kept my prayers to myself.

"Go in peace," said the minister, and the folks began straggling back down the hill to the road. I moved under one of the big beech trees that grew here and there in the cemetery, leaned against the trunk, and waited for the crowd to disperse.

By the time the last of them had reached the foot of the hill, the first of them were already in their cars heading north out of town—to Helen's house, I assumed.

I waited there under the beech tree until I was alone in the cemetery. Then I started walking up and down the rows.

I'd covered less than half of the two or three acres of gravestones when I found Bobby Gilman's. It was a simple, gray polished granite stone, and even though it had stood there for thirty years, it looked shiny and new.

ROBERT ALTON GILMAN
August 7, 1958–July 16, 1972
Beloved Son of Andrew and Rebecca
Thy Will Be Done

I noticed that they'd used the day Bobby's body was found as the date of his death. He'd been up on the mountain for nearly ten months by then. I supposed it was as good a date as any.

I pondered Bobby Gilman's fate for a minute or two, but had no new insights. He'd barely turned thirteen when he got lost on that mountain in the sudden October snowstorm. He was close to turning fourteen when his body was found. All the rest was mystery.

As I turned and started to leave, the gravestone next to Bobby's caught my eye.

REBECCA COLE GILMAN
December 6, 1936–October 12, 1972
Beloved Mother Of
Robert, Harris, and Lyndon
With God's Angels Now

It took me a moment to process this information.

Bobby's mother had died just three months after her boy's body was found—on the one-year anniversary of the Columbus Day when Bobby got lost on Mount Monadnock.

It was hard to believe that the date was a coincidence.

I guessed Bobby's mother had chosen October 12 as the day when she would join him in heaven.

Rebecca Gilman had two other sons besides Bobby.

Lyndon and Harris.

Lyndon was known by the nickname his kid brother had given him because he couldn't pronounce the word "brother."

Dubber. Dub.

Dub and Harris Goff.

Bobby Gilman had been their brother.

281

TWENTY-SEVEN

I glanced down the hill to the front of the church. A few stragglers were milling around down there. Among them were Harris and Dub Goff. With their thick beards and bald heads they were easy to spot. They were talking to Officer Somers and his partner. Limerick police officer Paul Munson was standing there with them. I wondered if he spent as much time in Limerick, where he belonged, as he seemed to in Southwick.

As I watched, Harris and Dub shook hands with all three officers, turned, and started across the street. They were heading in my direction.

I instinctively ducked behind the thick trunk of a stately old beech tree.

The Goff men stopped at a red pickup truck that was parked beside the road across from the church. Dub climbed in behind the wheel. Harris opened the other door, hesitated, and before he got in, he looked up. He was a hundred yards away, but it felt like his gaze bored directly into my eyes.

After a moment, he bent down, said something to his

brother, and got into the truck. I watched as it pulled away and headed north as all the other vehicles had gone, past the cemetery and out of town in the opposite direction from their garage. On their way to Helen's, I assumed, for the post-funeral reception.

I stayed where I was, behind the trunk of that big beech tree. I was feeling furtive. I'd learned something interesting— and maybe dangerous.

Bobby Gilman and the Goff men were brothers. When I asked Harris Goff about Bobby the day I found Farley Nelson's body, he could have told me. It would have been logical. The fact that he didn't struck me as enormously significant.

I'd decided what I had to do next, and I didn't want anyone to see me doing it.

I waited for Officer Somers and his partner and Officer Munson to get into their cruisers and drive away. They, too, were apparently headed for Helen's reception.

Munson drove away in the other direction. Back to Limerick, I assumed.

I lingered there in the cemetery for several more minutes. The streets were empty. The village of Southwick appeared deserted.

I looked at my watch. It was about ten after three. I figured the Goff brothers would feel obligated to linger at Helen's reception for at least an hour. To be on the safe side, I guessed I better finish what I had to do by four.

I followed the path down the hill and out of the cemetery. When I got to the main road, I turned right and headed back to the general store, where I'd left my car.

A CLOSED sign hung in the door of the store. Evidently the entire town had closed down for Farley's funeral.

I went around to the back. My car was the only one left in the lot. I unlocked it, took my new cell phone from the glove compartment, and slipped it into my jacket pocket. Then I locked up the car.

I eased around to the front of the store and looked up and down the main street. Not a single vehicle was on the move. Not a single person strolled on the sidewalks. Not a single light shone from the windows of the inn or the real estate office across the street.

Good.

I turned up the collar of my jacket against the chill. The rain had stopped about the time the minister bade us to go in peace, but the autumn air was damp and chilly, and the dark layer of clouds hung low and ominous overhead.

I walked quickly, and it took less than five minutes to get to the Goff brothers' garage.

The doors to the two bays were down. A CLOSED sign hung in the door to the office. No lights shone from any of the windows of the garage, or from the windows of the apartment on the second floor, either.

From somewhere deep inside the building, I heard muffled voices and music. I guessed the Goffs had left their radio turned on.

So far, I was quite certain no one had seen me.

I walked slowly around the side of the building. I didn't know what I was looking for. I wanted to be able to recognize it, whatever it was, when I saw it, so I tried to keep my mind empty of expectations and alert for anomalies. I wandered through the backyard and around to the big side lot where several dozen vehicles in varying states of disrepair huddled together. Smashed up rusty wrecks, most of them, although a number of them seemed to be in pretty fair shape.

Then I stopped. A newish black Volkswagen Beetle three rows back had caught my eye.

I stared at it. Something was out of place. An anomaly indeed.

What the hell was it?

It took me a minute to figure out what I'd noticed.

The inspection sticker.

Many of the vehicles in the lot bore no license plates, including that Volkswagen. But they all had inspection stickers on the windshield.

The sticker on that Volkswagen was rectangular and had been stuck in the bottom corner of the windshield on the passenger side.

The inspection stickers on all the other vehicles in the Goffs' lot were square and had been affixed to the top middle of the windshield behind the rearview mirror.

I checked the car nearest me, a ten-year-old Ford Taurus. The square sticker behind the mirror had been issued by the state of New Hampshire.

All of the cars in that lot had square New Hampshire stickers behind the mirror.

All except the black Volkswagen.

I edged around the vehicles and stood beside the Volkswagen.

The rectangular inspection sticker in the bottom corner of the windshield had been issued by the Commonwealth of Massachusetts.

Albert Stoddard was from Massachusetts. He drove a Volkswagen Beetle.

Except Albert's beetle was green. This one was black.

I walked slowly around the car, looking carefully. And

286

across the top edge of the right-side taillight I saw what I was looking for.

A torn strip of masking tape.

I took out my car keys, knelt down, and scraped away some of the black paint from the bottom of the right rear fender.

Under that shiny black paint was a layer of green paint.

This was Albert's car.

I blew out a breath. Okay. Up to this moment, it had all been hypothetical, a tenuous connection between Albert Stoddard and the Goff brothers based on my discovery in the graveyard that the Goff men were brothers, or half brothers, of Bobby Gilman, and that Albert might have been with Bobby on the mountain that Columbus Day over thirty years ago when the blizzard blew in.

Now the connection was concrete. Albert's car was here, in the Goffs' yard. They had repainted it to conceal its identity.

If the Goffs knew where Albert's car was, it was reasonable to conclude that they knew where Albert was.

I looked at my watch. Twenty-five minutes to four.

I gave myself twenty more minutes. Then I'd walk back down the main street to my car where it was parked behind the general store, and I'd get the hell out of Southwick, New Hampshire, and let the cops deal with it.

Before finding Albert's VW, I'd figured that if Harris or Dub caught me wandering around their property, I could talk my way out of it. If they had nothing to hide, I had nothing to fear.

But now I knew they *did* have something to hide.

Now, if they found me here . . .

I had no idea what they'd do. I didn't intend to be there to find out.

I had twenty minutes. I'd leave no later than five minutes to four. Assuming the Goff men lingered a courteous hour at Helen's reception, that would give me a cushion. I didn't want them even to see me walking along the sidewalk on the way back to my car from their place.

I remembered my cell phone.

I took it from my pocket, turned it on, and pecked out the number for Roger Horowitz's cell phone. He had given me this number a couple of years earlier. "Don't use it," he'd said. "If you do, it had better be good."

This, I figured, was good. This was what Horowitz wanted. This, if I wasn't mistaken, was about the murder of Gordon Cahill.

I pressed SEND and held the phone to my ear.

It bleated weakly, two or three pitiful little hesitant rings. Then nothing.

I looked at the little screen on the phone.

"Call failed," it said.

Great.

I stuck the phone back in my pocket. So much for modern technology. The damn thing worked fine when I didn't need it.

Okay. Twenty minutes.

Think, Coyne.

Behind the Goffs' house at the rear of the yard on the edge of the woods I remembered seeing an old aluminum house trailer. I went to it.

It was small as mobile homes go, no more than twelve feet long, with rounded corners that were supposed to give it an aerodynamic look. Unlike most so-called mobile homes, this model had been designed actually to be towed behind a vehicle.

Now it was up on cement blocks, and weeds and vines and briars grew against it.

I walked around the trailer. There were two small windows and a door on the side facing the woods. I tiptoed up and peered into the windows, but they were so dirty I couldn't see anything inside except shadows.

I tried the door. It wasn't locked, but the latch was rusty, and it took my full strength to turn it.

The door swung open with a loud metal-against-metal squeal.

I poked my head inside.

There came the quick, soft scurry of panicky rodents. Otherwise it was dead quiet.

I stepped inside. In the dim light that filtered in through the filthy little windows and half-open door, I could see that nobody had been in there for a long time. A thick layer of dust and a liberal scattering of mouse turds and scraps of half-chewed cardboard were scattered over the linoleum floor and the cheap built-in kitchen table and the Formica counters and the two narrow pull-down beds.

It smelled of must and dust and rot and abandonment.

"Albert?" I said softly. "Anybody here?"

Nobody answered.

I opened the cabinet doors, and the door to the tiny bathroom, and the doors to the two narrow closets.

Nothing.

I stepped outside into the Goffs' back yard.

I couldn't tell whether I was disappointed or relieved. I wasn't sure what I'd hoped to find.

A clue, at least.

Albert Stoddard's dead body at most.

Whatever it was, I hadn't found it.

Now what?

I went back to the house and walked slowly all the way around it. The cellar windows were boarded from the inside with plywood. The entire first floor of the building was occupied by the two bays with the auto lifts and the office to the garage. Two doors opened into the office area—one from the front, and one in back. I tried them both. Both were locked.

The radio or television that the Goff brothers had left on was loudest and clearest in the back right corner of the house.

I stopped there and pressed my ear against the wall. I decided it was a television. It sounded as if it was in the cellar.

Why the hell did they have a TV in the cellar?

Okay, maybe it was a finished basement. Maybe they had a den or a bar or a pool table down there, although Dub and Harris Goff somehow didn't strike me as the kind of guys who'd have a pine-paneled rec room in their basement.

I kept my ear against the wall, and in a moment when there was silence from the television, I thought I heard a different sound.

A human sound. A moan, or a groan, or a weak voice.

Then the television began blaring again.

My imagination? Maybe I'd heard the hum of an oil burner kicking on.

I listened some more, but all I heard were television noises.

Up to now I hadn't done anything wrong.

Now, I decided, I was going to break and enter Dub and Harris Goff's house.

If I was wrong, and if I got caught, I'd have some explaining to do.

What the hell. I was a lawyer. We lawyers are good at thinking on our feet.

Good at lying, some people would say.

An old wooden bulkhead was attached to the back of the house. I lifted one of the heavy doors and stepped down. When I pulled it shut behind me, the darkness was almost complete. I carefully felt my way down the five or six wooden steps that stopped at a metal door. I felt for the knob and tried it. It wasn't locked. I pushed it open and stepped into the cellar.

It was pitch-dark. I fumbled around on the inside wall, found a light switch, and flicked it on.

Four bare bulbs, no more than forty-watters, cast dim yellowish light into a shadowy, dank, cobwebby basement. It had a low unfinished ceiling, fieldstone walls, and a dirt floor. It was full of junk—old furniture, piles of lumber, a bench jumbled with hand tools, shelves loaded with paint cans, stacks of cardboard boxes, a disassembled motorcycle.

The television sounded louder down here.

I had to hunch over to walk under the ceiling beams. I followed the sound of the television to a closed door in the corner under the stairs that ascended up into the house. A small room had been walled in under the stairway.

I stood outside the door to this room. The television sounds came from inside.

The door was locked from my side with a simple sliding steel bolt.

I slid it open, turned the knob, and pushed the door open.

The first thing I noticed was the odor. It was vile, acrid, stomach-turning, and it permeated the air in that tiny room. I couldn't identify the smell. It reminded me of rotting garbage.

291

Aside from the dim, bluish light from the TV, the room was dark. The television sat on a low table against the left-hand wall behind the open door where I stood. It was playing something in black-and-white—judging from the sappy violin music, an old romantic movie.

I blinked a couple of times to adjust my eyes to the dimness.

Then, in the shadows against the wall to my right, I saw a figure huddled under a blanket on a cot. He was lying on his side, curled fetally, facing the wall, with his back to the TV.

He moaned softly.

"Albert?" I said.

He moaned again, but he didn't move.

I went over to him and touched his shoulder. "Hey," I said. "Hey, Albert. It's me. It's Brady Coyne."

He slowly rolled onto his back. His eyes flickered open, and he looked blankly up at me. "Brady?" he whispered.

His lips were swollen, and his eyes were narrow slits. He wore a week's growth of whiskers. Even though it was damp and chilly in the unheated basement, his face was sheened with perspiration.

It took me a minute to recognize him.

"Gordie?" I said. "What the hell are you doing here?"

TWENTY-EIGHT

Gordon Cahill's eyes blinked and his mouth moved, but his voice was too weak for me to hear what he was trying to say.

I turned off the volume on the flickering TV, then knelt beside him where he lay. "Say it again," I said.

"Pills," he mumbled. He pointed a shaky finger at the small table beside his cot. "Need one."

On the table was a half-filled glass of water and a plastic prescription pill bottle. I picked up the bottle and read the label. Morphine. For pain. Also good for inducing unconsciousness. Powerful, addictive stuff.

I shook my head. "No pills. We've got to get you out of here.

"No," he said. "Can't do it. My leg. Need a pill."

I peeled back the thin blanket that covered him, and I nearly puked at the stench of rot and decay that came up at me.

The bottom half of Gordie's right pant leg was black and oozing with dark blood and greenish pus. His leg had swollen so that it filled his pant leg like a fat sausage.

"What have they done to you?" I said.

"Busted it," he said. "Axe. My shinbone." He gestured vaguely to the corner of the room.

Standing on its head was a long-handled single-bladed axe. I went over and looked at it. The blunt end of the steel head was caked with dried blood.

I tried to imagine it. It made me shiver.

I went back, knelt beside Gordie, and pressed my palm against his forehead. His skin was afire.

My mind swirled with questions. But they could wait.

"Can you stand up?" I said.

He squeezed his eyes shut and gave his head a small shake. "No way. I can't hardly move. Just gimme a pill, for God's sake."

"Let me think," I said.

I had to get him to a hospital. Judging from the smell of his leg and the heat of his skin, the infection was coursing through his entire body. I was no doctor, but I guessed that he was pretty close to dying.

In his condition, he'd be a dead weight. I couldn't carry him very far—certainly not all the way to my car—even if he could tolerate the pain.

If the Goff men came back while I was there, I'd lose my chance to get Gordie out.

They'd probably bust my leg with the flat end of an axe, too.

I fished out my cell phone and hit 911. This time I didn't even get one halfhearted ring. "Call failed," it said on the screen.

"I've gotta go get you some help," I said to Gordie. "I'll bring an ambulance."

He reached out and clamped his hand weakly onto my wrist. "I don't care what you do," he mumbled. "Just gimme a damn pill."

He was probably addicted to the morphine. Given his condition, though, it was hardly the time to worry about that.

I opened the bottle, shook a capsule out onto my palm, picked up the water glass, and held them to him.

"Put it here," he said. He stuck out his tongue.

I put the pill on his tongue.

His throat worked, swallowing it. "Water," he said.

I held the water glass to Gordie's mouth and tilted it up for him. He took a couple swallows, then turned his head away.

I put the glass back on the table. "I'm leaving now," I said to him. "I'll be back."

He rolled away from me so that he was facing the wall.

I touched his shoulder. "Did you hear me?"

"Whatever," he mumbled.

I stood up and took one step to the door—and that's when I heard a door slam. Then there were men's voices and heavy footsteps on the floor overhead.

The Goff brothers had come home.

My first thought was to dart out through the bulkhead, skulk through the yard, and run back to my car.

But before I could move, I heard the cellar door open overhead. Then footsteps started down the stairs.

I pulled the door to Cahill's little cell closed and wedged myself into the corner behind the door. Maybe Goff, whichever brother it was, wouldn't even open the door. Or maybe he'd just peek inside, see that Gordie was passed out on the cot, and leave. Then I could slip away through the bulkhead.

The footsteps on the stairs descended. Then they stopped. He'd reached the cellar.

"Must be gettin' careless," he said from outside the door, as if he were talking to Gordie. "Left the lights on and your door unlocked. Don't suppose you walked out, did you?" He laughed. "Naw. Don't suppose you did that. You still alive in there, Mr. Detective, I hope?"

The knob on the door turned. I picked up the axe, held it at my shoulder, and pressed myself against the wall.

I was standing behind the door when it opened. The first thing that came into the room were the twin barrels of a shotgun, held about waist high.

When the hand and arm that held the fore end of the shotgun followed, I smashed down on them with the business end of the axe.

He yowled, and the shotgun clattered to the floor. I launched myself at him. In the bluish flickering light of the muted television I saw that it was Dub, the older one. I tried to hack at him again with the axe, but he rammed his shoulder against my chest before I could bring it down on him.

I staggered backward, smashed into the wall, and went down on the seat of my pants.

Dub Goff started at me . . . and a sudden explosion filled the little room. It sounded as if a bomb had gone off.

Dub seemed to be lifted up and blown backward, and I saw a patch of red bloom on the front of his thigh.

I glanced at Cahill. He held the shotgun propped along the length of his body on the bed. It was pointed at the open doorway. His finger was curled around the trigger. His eyes were wide and crazy.

"Don't shoot again," I yelled at him. "We'll need that second barrel."

He turned his head slowly and looked at me as if he'd never seen me before.

"Don't shoot," I repeated. "Give me the gun."

I went over to him and took the shotgun out of his hands. I held it at my hip and turned to face the door, where I expected to see Dub Goff lying in a puddle of blood.

But Dub wasn't there.

"You son of a bitch," came a growly voice from somewhere outside the room. "You shot my brother." It was Harris Goff.

"You better call an ambulance," I said, "before Dub dies."

"Fuck you, Boston. I shoulda put a hole in your head first time."

"Now's your chance," I said. "Come on in."

"No hurry, Boston." He chuckled. "You go ahead, stay right there with your detective buddy. Watch him die. It's gonna be slow and smelly. Me, I can wait. I got all the time in the world."

"You planning to let Dub bleed to death?"

"Dub's gonna be okay," he said. "He's tough. Pretty pissed, though."

"Nice try," I said. "But I saw his leg. It nearly got blown off."

"You got one shot left," said Harris. "If I was you, Mister Lawyer, I'd eat that barrel and pull the trigger right now, 'cause if I get there first, you'll wish to hell you did."

"I'm saving this barrel for you, Harris," I said. "The way it looks to me, you can wait out there while Dub bleeds to death, and I can wait here while Cahill dies, or else you can call an ambulance and save both of their lives. What do you say?"

"Dub ain't gonna die," he said, but I thought I detected a hint of uncertainty in his voice.

"You know what the femoral artery is?" I said.

"If you think—"

At that moment, a bell chimed from somewhere inside the house.

"There's your doorbell," I said.

"Fuck," muttered Harris.

"You better answer the door," I said.

Some shuffling sounds came from outside the room. Then the door to our little room closed, and I heard the deadbolt slide into place. "Sit tight, Boston," said Harris. "Don't go nowhere. I'll be back in a minute so we can continue this nice conversation."

Harris's footsteps clomped up the wooden stairs over my head. Then a door closed.

A moment later I heard faint voices from upstairs. Harris had answered the doorbell. Someone was up there.

"Cover your ears," I said to Gordie.

I glanced at him. He didn't move.

I moved to the back wall of the little room, leveled the double-barreled shotgun at where I figured the deadbolt was on the outside of the door, and pulled the back trigger.

The shotgun roared, and a fist-sized hole appeared on the edge of the door.

I dropped the shotgun, went to the door, and turned the knob. It swung open.

Dub Goff was sitting on the dirt floor outside the door, facing me. His back was pressed against a stack of cardboard boxes, and he was holding a big-bore revolver in his lap. It was pointing at me. I guessed it was a .45.

Blood was pooling under him, and his eyes looked droopy.

"Jesus, Dub," I said. "We've got to get you to a hospital, man."

For his answer, he put both thumbs on the hammer of his revolver and cocked it.

I ducked back into Gordie's little room just an instant before Dub pulled the trigger. The bullet left a hole you could stick your big toe through about head high on the wooden door.

A moment later heavy footsteps came clomping down the cellar stairs.

I picked up the empty shotgun by the barrels, held it against my shoulder like a baseball bat, and backed against the wall.

I heard movement outside the door.

"Mr. Coyne?" came a voice. "You in there?"

The two shotgun blasts inside that little room had half deafened me. But I thought I recognized that voice.

"Officer Munson?" I said. "That you?"

"Yes. Don't shoot me. I'm coming in."

TWENTY-NINE

A few minutes later an ambulance arrived and a team of EMTs took Gordon Cahill and Dub Goff away on gurneys and sped them off to the hospital.

Then a pair of state police officers took Harris Goff away in handcuffs.

Officer Somers was there, and he and Munson stayed behind at the Goffs' place to wait for the crime-scene people to arrive. Somers's young female partner, who said her name was Meredith O'Dell, drove me to the Southwick police station in her cruiser. I rode up front in the passenger seat, which assured me that I was not a suspect of any kind. Not that I should have been. Reassuring, nonetheless.

Officer O'Dell—she said I should call her Merrie—led me to a small conference room. She asked if I wanted coffee. I did. She returned a minute later with two mugs and sat across from me at a rectangular wooden table. She was drinking tea.

She told me her job was to baby-sit me and that neither of us was supposed to reveal information about what she called "this case" until the right people arrived.

I asked her if Cahill was going to make it. She shook her head. Either she didn't know or she wasn't going to share with me.

Her headshake could have meant Gordie was doomed, but I chose not to read it that way.

So we made small talk. She told me she'd been dating a patrolman in Keene, but she didn't think it would go anywhere. He wanted to be a big-city cop—his ambition was to join the New York or Los Angeles force—and she wanted to live on a farm and raise babies and chickens and goats.

I told her about Evie, my virtual spouse, and Billy and Joey, my two sons, and Henry, my dog.

Merrie O'Dell had a dog. She'd rescued it from the pound. It was mostly golden retriever, with a few drops of mastiff blood. It slept on her bed and took up most of the space.

I was on my second mug of coffee when the door opened and Lieutenant Bagley, the state cop from the Major Crimes Unit in Concord, came in.

Merrie O'Dell stood up and moved to the door. Bagley sat in her chair across from me.

"How's Cahill?" I said to him.

He shrugged, then looked over his shoulder and jerked his chin at Merrie. "Find out," he said.

She nodded and left the room.

Bagley folded his hands on the table and peered at me. "You've been busy, Mr. Coyne."

"If you want me to explain everything to you," I said, "I'm afraid I can't."

"Don't worry about it. Don't speculate. Just tell me what happened."

"I have a client to protect," I said.

He nodded. "I understand. We'll get an official statement

302

later, and then you can be as careful as you need to be. This is just between you and me, and I'd like to hear it all. I figure between what you know and what I know, we can figure this out."

So I told him everything. I began two weeks ago when Jimmy D'Ambrosio hired me, and I ended two hours ago when Officer Munson rescued me from the Goffs' cellar. "I don't know why Munson happened to show up when he did," I said, "but I hate to think of what would've happened if he hadn't."

Bagley smiled. "Munson had his eye on you. Ever since he happened upon you at Stoddard's cabin, he figured you for a suspicious character. He was lurking around after the funeral, keeping an eye on you, and when he saw you heading for the Goff brothers' house, he tailed you. He heard a gunshot, had the good sense to call for backup, and waited for Somers and O'Dell to get there. Just about the time the three of 'em knocked on the door, you fired the shotgun again. That got their attention. If you hadn't done that, they would've had no choice but to turn around and leave."

I nodded. "That was my intent."

There was a soft knock at the door.

Lieutenant Bagley called, "Come in."

Officer Merrie O'Dell poked her head in and beckoned to Bagley.

He stood up, left the room, and closed the door behind him.

Bagley was gone nearly fifteen minutes. When he came back, he sat down and looked at me. I couldn't read his expression.

"Your friend Cahill's in pretty bad shape," he said. "They've got him in ICU, loading him up with antibiotics.

They want to operate on that leg, but they can't until they get the infection under control." He shrugged. "That's all I can tell you."

I nodded. "Thanks."

"Dub Goff lost a hunk of muscle off his leg," he said. "He'll live. We've got a guard with him in the hospital. Assume you're interested, seeing as how you contributed to his condition."

"For the record," I said, "it was Cahill who shot Dub."

"Well, good for him." Bagley smiled. "I just talked with Lieutenant Horowitz. He was—shocked might not be too strong a word—that Gordon Cahill was alive."

"He thought Gordie got burned up in his Corolla," I said. "It must've been Albert Stoddard. I figure the Goff brothers killed him."

Bagley nodded. "The question is why."

"I've got a theory."

"Me," he said, "I've got something better than a theory."

"What's that?"

"I've got Harris and Dub Goff. They have both expressed enthusiasm about enumerating and justifying the things they've done. We're waiting 'til their lawyers arrive."

"Playing this one by the book, huh?" I said.

"We play 'em all by the book, Mr. Coyne."

Saturday afternoon three days after I found Gordon Cahill in the cellar of the Goff brothers' house, I was raking leaves and pulling dead annual plants out of our gardens on Beacon Hill when Roger Horowitz called.

"You got any beer in your refrigerator?" he said.

"Depends."

"You give me a Sam Adams," he said, "I'll tell you a story. Deal?"

"Sure," I said. "Good deal."

Horowitz knocked on the back gate fifteen minutes later. Henry went over and barked, and when Horowitz came in, Henry sniffed his cuffs. Horowitz bent down and scratched his muzzle.

I fetched a bottle of Sam Adams lager for each of us, and Horowitz and I sat at the patio table. Henry curled up underneath, plopped his chin on my foot, and went to sleep.

"Where's Evie?" Horowitz said.

"Shopping. She's running low on shoes."

He smiled. "Bagley and I have been talking with those Goff brothers. Their lawyers are advising them to cop a plea, so they've been more than cooperative. Inasmuch as you probably saved Cahill's life, I figured I should share the story with you."

"Tell me how Gordie's doing."

"Still in the ICU up there in Peterborough," he said. "Stable, they tell me. No visitors yet. He's all drugged up, in no condition to talk anyway. Donna drives up every day."

"He's going to be okay?"

"Looks like it. They're not sure about his leg, though."

I nodded. "I thought he was a dead man when I found him." I took a sip of beer. "So let's hear your story."

This was the Goff brothers' story as Roger Horowitz reconstructed it for me:

On the morning of October 12, 1971, five boys from Southwick, New Hampshire, piled into a '59 Buick owned and operated by the oldest of them, sixteen-year-old Dalton Burke. Albert Stoddard and Oliver Burlingame were fourteen, Mark Lyman fifteen.

Bobby Gilman, barely thirteen, was the youngest. The only reason Bobby got to tag along was because Dalton Burke's mother, who was friends with Mrs. Gilman, insisted the boys bring him. Bobby played in the junior high band and got good grades and didn't like sports. Everybody teased him. He didn't have any friends. The other kids called him a pussy.

They drove southwest from Southwick to Mount Monadnock. It took about half an hour. It was a crisp October day—bright sun, high skidding clouds, a wintry bite to the air.

The boys chose one of the less popular trails on the shaded western slope of the mountain. This one was marked by paint slashes on trees and boulders, and if you didn't pay attention, you could easily wander away from the trail. In some places you had to use your hands to pull yourself over rocks and up the steep parts of the trail.

The five boys had barely gotten halfway to the top of the mountain when Bobby Gilman started whining. He wanted to stop and rest. He was tired. He was thirsty. He was cold. He had a blister.

Oliver called him a baby.

Mark said if he couldn't stop bitching he should go back down by himself and wait at the bottom for them.

Bobby started crying. He said he didn't want to be left alone. He said if they didn't help him, he'd tell his mother.

Albert told him to shut up.

Dalton said they had to bring him along, because if they didn't his mother would be pissed.

So Bobby hobbled along behind the other four boys, and every fifteen minutes or so they had to stop and wait for him to catch up.

He never stopped whining.

It took them much longer to get to the top of the mountain than it would've if Bobby Gilman hadn't been along, and when they finally stood on the rocky summit, they saw that a black cloud bank was moving in from the northeast.

Dalton Burke squinted at the sky and said they better get back down. It looked like a storm was coming.

They'd barely reached the timberline when Bobby sat on a rock and took off his sneaker. His sock was wet with blood from a broken blister. When he saw the blood, he started crying.

Mark Lyman picked up Bobby's sneaker and tossed it to Albert Stoddard. Albert tossed it to Oliver Burlingame.

Oliver threw it into the bushes.

Dalton told Oliver to go fetch Bobby's sneaker and give it back to him. Dalton was the oldest, and besides, he had the car, so the other boys usually obeyed him.

Oliver found the sneaker and threw it at Bobby. It hit him on the head. Bobby picked it up and tried to put it back on, but it hurt too much.

About then it started to snow. It came on the edge of a sharp wind, a sudden white sheet of hard little kernels blowing almost horizontally, sweeping over the mountain-side.

Dalton Burke helped Bobby Gilman get to his feet. "We gotta get going," he said. "Forget about your damn sneaker. Let's move it."

"I can't," sobbed Bobby. "My foot hurts."

"Fuck him," said Oliver. "We're gonna have a fucking blizzard. Let's go."

"We can't just leave him," said Albert.

"Why not?" said Mark.

Dalton put his arm around Bobby's waist and helped him hobble over the rocks down the mountain. After about ten minutes, it was Albert's turn to help Bobby.

The temperature was dropping, and already, under the black clouds and in the thick driving snow, it was getting dark and the snow was starting to stick to the ground.

They were on a steep, rock-strewn section of the trail when Albert slipped on a slick boulder. He and Bobby fell down in a heap.

Bobby started crying again. "I hurt my leg."

"We're never going to get there at this rate," said Oliver. "We're all gonna freeze to death."

Dalton went to Bobby, grabbed the front of his jacket, and yanked him to his feet. "I'm sick of you whining like a fuckin' baby," he said.

Bobby scrunched up his face and cried louder.

Dalton started shaking Bobby. "Stop your damn crying," he yelled. "I can't stand it anymore. Just shut up."

Bobby kept crying.

So Dalton hauled back and slapped Bobby's face as hard as he could. Bobby slipped, staggered, waved his arms in the air, then tumbled backward off the boulder and out of sight.

The four other boys crept to the edge and looked down.

Bobby was lying there on his back amid a jumble of rocks in a crevasse about twenty feet below them. One of his legs was bent at an impossible angle underneath him.

Bobby wasn't crying. He wasn't even moving.

"Oh, shit," said Albert.

Dalton Burke slithered down to where Bobby lay. A minute later he looked up at the other three. "His head's all smashed in," he said. "He ain't breathing."

"You killed him," said Oliver.

"Not me," said Dalton. "All of us."

"What're we gonna do?" said Mark.

"We gotta get an ambulance or something," said Albert.

Dalton climbed back up to where the other three boys were. "No ambulance is gonna help him," he said. "It's too late. We killed him."

"*You* killed him," said Oliver again.

"No," said Albert. "He's right. We all did it. It's all of our faults."

"Shut up," said Dalton. "Lemme think."

The four of them crouched there on the boulder with the snow swirling around them and Bobby Gilman's body twisted on the rocks below them, and after a few minutes, Dalton said, "Here's what we do. We tell them we were climbing the Parker Trail, and—"

"That's over the other side of the mountain," said Mark Lyman.

"Exactly," said Dalton Burke.

"If they go looking there—"

"Exactly," said Dalton again. "That's the point, you idiot. We tell them we all got separated in the blizzard, and when we got to the bottom Bobby wasn't with us. That's all. Keep it simple. We waited for him to show up 'til it got dark, and then we thought about going back up there to look for him, but we decided it'd be better if we went for help. They'll go looking over there on the east side."

"They won't find him," said Albert.

"Exactly," said Dalton for the third time. "They might never find him. So we make a solemn vow, okay? We stick to our story for the rest of our lives. We promise never *ever* to tell anybody what really happened."

He held out his hand and the other three boys put their

hands over his the way they did in the huddle before going out to play a game of basketball.

"Promise?" said Dalton.

The other three nodded.

"Our secret," Dalton said. "Forever and ever. Say it."

"Forever and ever," said Mark Lyman and Oliver Burlingame and Albert Stoddard.

"Wow," I said.

Horowitz nodded. "Got another beer?"

I went inside, snagged two more bottles of Sam from the refrigerator, and brought them outside.

"Dub and Harris Goff," I said. "They were Bobby Gilman's brothers."

"Half brothers, actually," said Horowitz. "Same mother, different fathers. Old Man Goff got drunk and drove his pickup into a telephone pole when Dub and Harris were little. Rebecca Goff married Andrew Gilman a year later, and a couple years after that she gave birth to Bobby. Harris and Dub both claim they liked little Bobby, did their best to protect him. He was always a small, fragile boy. The apple of his mother's eye. She spoiled him." Horowitz took a swig of beer. "When Bobby disappeared, Rebecca shut herself in her bedroom and never came out. On Columbus Day a year to the day from when those boys climbed Mount Monadnock she swallowed a bottle of Valium. Dub and Harris were off to college when that happened. They worshiped their mother, knew she'd killed herself because of what happened to Bobby, and being the kind of men they were, they figured somebody had to be responsible for it. To men like the

Goffs, nothing just happens because it happens. They've got to have somebody to blame for everything."

"In this case," I said, "they were right."

Horowitz shrugged. "It festered with them for thirty years. It wasn't what happened to Bobby that upset them so much. It was their mother killing herself. Finally they decided to do something about it. Everybody in town knew who those boys were who were with Bobby Gilman that day. So the Goffs tracked down Oliver Burlingame in Missouri and got the story out of him. Then they went to Mark Lyman and Dalton Burke and Albert Stoddard and convinced all of them to give their versions. The one I told you seems to be their best synthesis of what happened that day."

"So they killed Burlingame and Lyman and Albert Stoddard," I said.

"First they extorted them," he said. "Told them they'd leave them alone and not report the story if they paid them money. They all sent monthly checks to the Goff brothers' post office box. It was a tidy income for the Goffs for a while. But they got greedy, kept demanding more. Finally Burlingame and Lyman refused to keep paying. So the Goff brothers tracked them down and killed them."

"What about Albert Stoddard?" I said.

"Last summer when the Goffs learned that Stoddard's wife was running for senator, they put the squeeze on him, threatened to go public with the story, ruin Ellen's chances to get elected if he didn't pay them more. For a while he endorsed his biweekly paychecks and sent them to the Goffs, but he knew he couldn't do that forever. So just a couple weeks ago he decided to have it out with them. He drove up to Southwick and holed up in his old camp, hoping to make some kind of deal. The Goffs claim they were working it out with Stoddard when Cahill showed up. Gordie already had most of the story, and there was no way they could make a deal with him. No one could make a deal with Gordon Cahill."

"So they killed Albert in Gordie's Corolla," I said.

"Yep," said Horowitz. "They tried not to make any of their murders look like murder. A fishing accident, a suicide, and a car accident. They thought they were pretty clever."

"Blowing out a tire with buckshot?" I said. "Then dousing him with gasoline? That's clever?"

"I didn't say they actually *were* clever," said Horowitz. "Just that they thought they were. They were quite proud of what they did to Albert Stoddard. Especially the skid marks on the road and the way they made the car hit the tree." He shrugged. "They did have us thinking it was Cahill in that Corolla, I'll give them that."

"Has the M.E.—?"

"Not yet," he said quickly. "They finally figured out to check his goddamn dental records." He shook his head. "Damn sloppy all around. The M.E. All of us. Rule number one: Don't make assumptions. Just because he was in Cahill's car, had Cahill's wallet in his pocket . . ." Horowitz tilted up his beer bottle, drained it, and slammed it down on the table. "Sloppy," he repeated.

"You want another one of those?" I said.

He waved the back of his hand. "Two's enough."

"So," I said, "who called Albert in sick at the history department? One of the Goff boys, huh?"

Horowitz nodded. "That was Harris. Guess they figured you'd stop looking for Albert if you thought he was just out sick."

"They figured wrong."

He smiled. "One would be tempted to observe that they aren't too bright. Except they did manage to carry off two murders without raising any suspicion."

"Burlingame and Lyman." I shrugged. "They killed old Farley Nelson because he'd figured out what was going on?"

"So they say," said Horowitz. "The old guy was going to tell you the story I just told you, or something close to it. He'd figured out it was the Goff brothers, and when they confronted him, he didn't try to hide it."

"Bastards," I muttered. "One of them kicked me and whacked me on the top of the head when I went to Albert's camp. He poked at my balls with the muzzle of his shotgun."

Horowitz nodded. "They mentioned that."

"Never said a word the whole time," I said.

He shrugged.

"So," I said after a minute, "what was their plan for Gordie?"

He shook his head. "Dub held his leg on top of a cement block, and Harris smashed his shinbone with the back end of an axe. Then they locked him in that room in their cellar, fed him morphine pills, and let the infection fester. They were waiting until Cahill was close to dead with that busted-up leg. Then they were going to dump him in the woods out behind Stoddard's camp, let him die. They figured by the time his body was discovered, everyone would assume he'd broken his leg out in the woods and died before he could crawl out. They liked what they saw as the irony of it."

"Sort of like what happened to Bobby Gilman," I said.

"Sort of," said Horowitz. "Close enough to it for Dub and Harris Goff."

"And what about Dalton Burke?"

He smiled. "Mr. Burke has been quite cooperative. He

313

confirms the Goffs' story pretty much the way I told it to you, except Burke claims it was Oliver Burlingame who actually gave Bobby Gilman that fatal shove." He shrugged. "We'll never know, really. Burke's the last living witness."

"So why didn't the Goffs kill Burke?"

"Simple," said Horowitz. "Dalton Burke makes a lot of money. He could afford to keep paying them. They were planning to squeeze him dry before they killed him. Saving the best for last was the way Dub put it."

"Is Bagley going to prosecute Burke for what happened to Bobby Gilman?"

He shook his head. "Don't see how. Thirty-year-old case. No evidence, no other witnesses. Me, I've got the Albert Stoddard murder to worry about."

"Are you worried?"

"I always worry," said Horowitz.

THIRTY

Two weeks after I found him in the Goff brothers' cellar, I was sitting beside Gordon Cahill's hospital bed in his private room in the Monadnock Community Hospital in Peterborough, New Hampshire. His right leg was encased in an ankle-to-hip cast. Three plastic bags hung on an aluminum rack beside him and dripped fluids through a transparent tube into an IV sticking into the back of his left hand.

His eyes looked hollow, and there were more wrinkles on his face and neck than I remembered. It looked like he'd lost a lot of weight. But there was a healthy flush on his cheeks, and he was smiling. He looked a thousand times better than the last time I'd seen him.

Donna had called me the day before and told me that Gordie had finally been moved out of the ICU. It had taken them ten or eleven days to knock down the infection. Then they operated on his leg. There would be two or three more operations, the doctors were saying. Gordie's shinbone had been splintered.

They were still weaning him off the morphine. The Goff

brothers had encouraged him to swallow as much of it as he wanted. He'd quickly become seriously addicted.

"So you're going to make it," I said to Gordie.

"They tell me it was touch and go for a while," he said. "They said if they'd got me a day later it might've been too late. You saved my life."

"I was the one who got you into it in the first place," I said. "It was the least I could do."

He smiled. "Good point. Thanks anyway."

I nodded. "I'm dying to know how you tracked down Albert Stoddard so fast."

"You want me to divulge my trade secrets?"

"I promise not to tell."

Cahill turned his head and gazed out the window. His room was on the first floor, and his window gave a pretty view over a rolling meadow to some distant hills. The low-angled afternoon sunlight played over the crimsons and golds of the autumn forests. The foliage was just at its peak. "Donna wants me to quit," he said after a minute.

I didn't say anything.

"She told me how unhappy she is," he said. "How she worries all the time. How she felt when Horowitz told her I was dead. How it was almost a relief." He turned and looked at me. "She says she refuses to go through that again. She says if I go back to investigating she's going to divorce me."

"What're you going to do?"

He shook his head.

"Sounds like a no-brainer to me," I said.

"Yeah, you're right. It should be. Except I really love the work, you know? It's what I'm good at. It's what I do. It's what I am."

"Is Donna serious, do you think?"

"Oh, yeah," he said. "She's serious, all right."

"So . . . ?"

"It was his tax returns," said Gordie.

"Huh?"

"Stoddard. His tax returns told me how to find him."

"Hell," I said. "I looked at them. I didn't see a damn thing."

"You're not a trained investigator," said Gordie with a smile. "Albert Stoddard deducted the property taxes he paid to the town of Limerick in the state of New Hampshire on his federal income tax returns. One phone call to a chatty woman in the Limerick assessor's office told me everything I needed to know."

"So you drove up there?"

"Yep. Found his place, saw his Volkswagen was there, took a couple photos on my digital camera. Finding Stoddard wasn't the problem. You hired me to figure out what he was up to. That's what got me in trouble."

"What happened?"

"I came home, spent some time on the Internet, then went back up there the next day. Sunday, this was. The Volkswagen wasn't there, so I hid my car and walked in through the woods. I thought I was being careful. I thought I might find some answers inside that old camp." He shook his head.

"The Goff brothers?"

He nodded. "They were waiting for me, as if they knew I was coming. Took me by surprise. Pointed a shotgun at me and hauled me back to their cellar. Then they busted my leg, and that's really the last thing I remember."

"How'd you figure out the Bobby Gilman connection?" I said. "Donna gave me those printouts."

317

"Something the woman at the Limerick assessor's office mentioned," he said. "The Internet has made the PI's job almost too easy. I could've done the whole job on my computer and telephone, never left my office."

"Maybe that's your answer," I said.

"To what question?"

"The question of your career and your marriage."

Cahill looked at me and cocked his head. "You mean, limit my work to sitting at a desk playing on machines?"

I shrugged. "You could hire other guys to do the legwork. Do you think Donna would go for it?"

"I've been a cop of one kind or another all my life," he said softly. "I like the action. I like dealing with people. Good guys and bad guys both. Playing with computers isn't exactly my idea of action. The real question is, would *I* go for it?" He shook his head. "Put it this way," he said. "The doctors wanted to amputate my leg. They said if they didn't I might die. I told them, fuck it. Without my leg I couldn't do what I do, wouldn't be who I am. Might as well die. So now I've got my leg. What good are two functional legs if you don't do legwork?"

I smiled.

"So what would you do?" he said.

"Doesn't matter what I'd do," I said. "But if you're stupid enough to pick your job over your wife, don't expect me to handle your divorce."

He turned his head and gazed out the window. "She's been here every day," he said. "Don't know what I'd do without her." He was silent for a minute. Then he looked at me and smiled. "So did you hear about the two Eskimos who were out in their kayak hunting walruses up around the Arctic Circle?"

318

"Gordie, damm it—"

"It was about zero degrees out there," he said, "and they were freezing their balls off, so they decided to build a fire. You can probably figure out what happened."

"I assume the fire burned a hole in their kayak and they sank," I said before I could stop myself.

"You got it," said Gordie. He arched his eyebrows at me. "And the moral of the story?"

"Here we go," I muttered.

"You can't have your kayak," he said, "and heat it, too."

At eight o'clock on the evening of the first Tuesday in November, Evie and I were snuggling on the sofa in our living room, sipping red wine and watching the returns. Evie had about as much interest in politics as I had in shopping for shoes, but her favorite shows had all been preempted by election coverage.

Albert's murder had been big news, of course. A few days after they realized Gordon Cahill was alive, the M.E. officially identified Albert by his dental records. There had been considerable embarrassment about their assumption that it was Gordie's burnt body in that Toyota. Some state rep on Beacon Hill was agitating for public hearings on the incompetence—or maybe it was corruption—in the medical examiner's office.

When Ellen Stoddard heard about Albert, she held a press conference announcing that she was suspending her campaign to reconsider her situation.

Her Republican opponent, Lamarr Oakley, to his credit, did the same. Not that he had many options.

Two weeks went by, and then Ellen announced that she

had decided to continue with her candidacy. She owed it to the voters of the Commonwealth, she said. She did not mention Albert.

Bobby Gilman's story, with particular emphasis on Albert's role in it, was big news in all the papers, of course, but when they resumed politicking, both Ellen and Oakley refrained from mentioning it—which was probably a smart strategy for both of them. It was one of those no-win subjects.

Throughout the final month of the campaign, the political pundits kept trying to weigh what they called the "sympathy factor" against the "scandal factor." As election day drew near, they declared the race for senator between Ellen Stoddard and Lamarr Oakley "too close to call."

The pollsters kept asking voters whether Albert Stoddard's murder, and the events of thirty-odd years ago that led to it, made them "more likely" or "less likely" to vote for Ellen. "No difference" was consistently the most popular response.

Now, on election eve, they were calling it a "dead heat" and predicting it would "go down to the wire." Most of the other popular political clichés were being tossed around, too.

Evie and I had our stockinged feet up on the coffee table. I had my arm around her, and she was resting her cheek against my shoulder. Both of us balanced our wineglasses on our chests.

Henry had sneaked up on the sofa with us. He was curled in the corner with his back pressing against my hip.

"Did you vote for her?" Evie murmured.

"Sure."

"All along I thought I was going to," she said. "But when it came down to it, I couldn't."

"You voted for Oakley?"

"I left it blank." She hesitated. "She's cold, Brady. She's calculating and ambitious."

"Cold and calculating and ambitious aren't bad qualities for a senator to have," I said. "Anyway, I know Ellen. She's not really that way."

"Since when did it matter what a politician was really like?"

"You're right," I said. "It never did matter. It's all about perception."

Ellen waited until nearly midnight to make her appearance at her "victory party" in the Copley Plaza ballroom. Her supporters applauded long and loud when she stepped to the podium. The TV cameras panned over the crowd. Several people appeared to be crying.

Her concession speech was warm and gracious. She congratulated Lamarr Oakley and thanked him for focusing his campaign on the issues. She said she planned to return to her work for the D.A. prosecuting criminals, but she did not discount the possibility that she might run for public office again in the future. She thanked the people who had worked for her and the citizens who had voted for her.

She was smiling. She looked confident. Pretty. Sexy, even.

Nowhere in her speech did she mention Albert.

I figured Jimmy D'Ambrosio had written it.